MW01228042

Callatin

Academy

#4

Backroad

Reality

By Melissa Logan

Smashwords Edition

Published by Melissa Logan at Smashwords

Special thanks to Sarah Whipple of Sarah Whipple Photography for the amazing pictures she took for my cover (and back cover). She took my vision and made into reality. Also, I can't leave out my cover models either, they were absolutely amazing and good natured about everything; Thank you to Isaiah Guinzy and Jada Schultze for being my "perfect couple".

Chapter 1

Jordan

"Guess what?" I asked my boyfriend, Lance Bowman, excitedly during one of our eight p.m. phone dates. "I was voted Junior Homecoming attendant."

"Really? That's awesome. Congratulations."

"Zack Bentley is my escort." I added timidly. "But he's completely devoted to his girlfriend, so there's no need to worry."

"I trust you Jordan." He chuckled. "But oddly enough, Remy asked if I'd be her escort for our Homecoming court. She's one of the queen candidates. I already said yes, is that okay?"

"Of course." I giggled.

"So I *am* still looking for a date for the dance." Lance announced flirtatiously.

"Oh really? Who were you thinking about asking?"

"Well there is this incredibly hot Callatin Academy girl that I have my eye on. She's kind of been flirting with me, but I heard she has a boyfriend. Not to mention, she's *way* out of my league, so I'm a little nervous about asking her."

"Oh I know that girl and she *is really* out of your league. And her boyfriend is like the biggest loser I've ever met." I joked.

"I can't believe you'd bad mouth your brother like that." Lance laughed. I gasped. "So has Caleb asked Maddie yet or do I still have a chance?"

"What?!?" I shrieked.

"You know, your roommate Maddie? Does she have a date yet?"

"Lance Bowman *you* are an asshole and extremely lucky you're not standing in front of me right now, because I'd deck you."

"Fine, I'll take you if I *have* to." He whined playfully.

"No you won't. I refuse to be your second choice."

"Oh come on darlin', you know you'll always be my number one."

"Too little, too late."

"Ouch."

"You messed up Bowman, because you just lost the best thing in your life."

"Why? Did they stop selling beer?"

"Lance!" I scolded.

"Okay, I'll stop. It's more fun to aggravate you in person anyway." He laughed. "You're so hot when you're mad and I'm getting excited just thinking about it."

"Lance."

"And you're even hotter when I make you blush."

"Would you stop?"

"Not until you say you'll go to my homecoming dance with me."

"On one condition."

"Depends." He answered coyly.

"You'll be *my* date to *my* dance."

'Hell yeah!" He chuckled. "Maddie will be there right?"

"You are such a jerk!" I exclaimed.

"I know, but it's only because I'm imagining how frustrated you are and I'm getting turned on again."

"You *can't* get turned on when I'm not there."

"I do every night darlin', just thinking about your pretty face."

"Lance." I gasped.

"What?" He asked innocently. I rolled my eyes and smiled.

Lance and I attended two very different schools; I go to the prestigious Callatin Academy, where I am a Junior and he is a Senior at the nearby Mencino County High School, the difference is like Hollywood and Nashville but we're making it work, so far. I'd recently taken a big risk and told my boyfriend about my late mother killing herself and he's still here. To some people that may not be a big deal, in my past; I've only met jerks who like to use it against me.

I knew, without a doubt, that I was madly in love with him, but I was still hesitant to utter the words, I didn't want to scare him off. I was pretty certain he felt the same way, but the phrase would probably terrify any teenage guy.

I think after I told him about my mom and he told me about his brother, our relationship actually went to a completely new level. The two of us talked about everything, even how I knew his missing twin brother, Luke. We talked every night on the phone and there was rarely a dead spot in our conversations. I have never felt so comfortable and at ease around a boyfriend before.

Chapter 2

"Chopper do you carry moonshine with you everywhere?" I giggled as one of Lance's best friends winked at me. He nodded and grinned. We were sitting around a campfire by the lake a few towns over. The boys were staying here all weekend and I was visiting for the night.

"Yes ma'am, I do." He lit, as he passed his cup to me. "But only because I know how much you love it."

"She loves the moonshine, not you Chop." Cooper teased with a chuckle.

"A guy can dream, right?"

"Don't listen to him Chopper." I whispered loudly as I scooted closer to the dark headed boy. "I love you more than the moonshine." I put my head on his arm as he beamed back at the others. Chopper threw an arm across my shoulders and pulled me in close to him.

"More than Lance?" He whispered in my ear as my boyfriend made his way back to our campfire.

"Definitely, he ain't got nothing on you." I lit as I kissed him on the cheek.

"Hey now." Lance chuckled as he stood in front of us, arms crossed in front of his broad chest. "Why are you two snuggled together, is there something I should know?"

"I'm sorry Lance." I sighed. "I didn't want you to find out this way."

"You should watch your back dough boy." Lance hissed at his friend. Chopper slowly removed his arm from me, stood up and got in his friend's face.

"Let's go." He breathed. Lance chuckled, slid past him and plopped down in his vacant seat.

"You're too easy Chop." He lit as he pulled me onto his lap.

"Oh you thought I was kidding?" I asked with a pout. "I'm totally in love with your best friend." Lance's eyes narrowed as he pulled me in for a passionate kiss.

"Still in love with him darlin'?" He drawled breathlessly in my ear as he pulled away.

"No." I squeaked.

"My turn!" Chopper exclaimed as he tugged at my hand.

"That's where I draw the line." Lance stated as he held me tightly.

"Damn." Chopper cursed with a chuckle. "It's probably for the best beautiful, you would fall for me hard after we kissed."

"I know." I sighed. "Someday when I can cut him loose, I'm all yours."

"You two are hilarious." Lance laughed with a shake of his head. I leaned back into him and held his hands on my waist.

"How come you don't ever say you love me Jo?" Coop asked with a pretend pout.

"Because you don't have the same suave skills as Chopper does." I giggled. The tall, stocky blonde shook his head in shock.

"I...don't. I don't even know how to respond to that."

"I'm pretty sure that is the ultimate burn." Drew Bowman roared with laughter.

"Obviously it was a burn on all of us." Coop retorted. Drew stopped laughing and shook his head.

"That hurts Jo." He stated. I shrugged my shoulders and smiled sweetly. These boys were absolutely amazing. I hadn't known them very long but they treated me as if I had been a part of their group our whole lives.

Their weekend was supposed to be a guys only event, but they had no problem accepting that Lance had invited me to join them. Unfortunately, once it was out that I was allowed to go, it opened the door for others. Drew was dating a girl who threw a fit that she couldn't hang out with him, which then brought along Remy. Remy was a childhood friend of all the boys, they had all grown up together. She hated me and made it a point to exclude me as much as she could when we were all together.

I was less than thrilled to see her there and even less excited that Lance was her Homecoming escort, but I thought it would be childish to throw a fit about it. I just did my best to ignore her catty remarks and her, overall.

"Lance, are you coming to dinner Thursday night?" Remy asked sweetly, her eyes flitting to mine quickly.

"That's what my mom tells me." He shrugged. "Apparently, we're all going."

"Too bad you have school on Friday Jordan." She stated smugly. "Our get togethers are legendary." Drew shot her a funny look and rolled his eyes.

"Only because we're there." Chopper interjected drily.

"How are they legendary? We'll be gone by eight." Cooper added with a shake of his head. Lance shot him a dirty look, but Cooper wasn't saying it to be mean, that was obvious.

"You can't leave." Remy stated softly.

"How much trouble will you get in if you skip school?" Lance asked me with a raised eyebrow.

"Why? What are you guys doing on Friday?"

"Ball game."

"Ball game…you got tickets to one of the division games?"

"Yup, my dad has a box for the business."

"And you guys get to go?" I asked in awe. Drew nodded smugly. "I'm so jealous."

"You can come with us." Lance grinned.

"Is Lish going?" I asked, referring to my roommate who is also Drew's little sister.

"Possibly." Drew shrugged. "She is freaking out about some huge test and didn't want to risk skipping and getting caught."

"Daikman's class." I nodded. "If he found out we were going to the game he'd flunk us just for not inviting him."

"If you skipped school, then you could go to dinner with us Thursday night." Drew lit with a wink. He was goading Remy and it worked, her mouth dropped open to protest. I shook my head. Apparently, Drew had also noticed how rude Remy was to me, at least I wasn't imagining it.

"Uh, no thanks." I giggled as I rolled my eyes.

"Please go to the game with us." Lance breathed in my ear, my stomach fluttered as I grinned back at him.

"I would love to, I'll have to figure out how to finagle it though."

"You just made my night." Lance chuckled.

"It's a division game Lance, I would go with my mortal enemy just to see my Cardinals play." I lit.

"Gee thanks." He laughed as he tickled me. I shrugged my shoulders and pushed him away. I stood up and crossed over to the cooler for another beer.

"How many tickets do you have?" Remy asked Lance as I reached down into the cooler and pulled out two cans, one for me and one for Lance.

"Ask Drew."

"None, if Lish and Jo go."

"Why didn't you ask me to go?" Drew's date, Dena asked. His eyes flitted away quickly.

"Why didn't you ask me to go?" Remy questioned angrily. "I'm a huge Cardinal's fan."

"Name the first baseman." Drew retorted drily. Remy sputtered and Dena just shrugged.

"I bet Jo can give you the starting lineup." Sawyer Teems laughed. I rolled my shoulders nonchalantly and nodded my head. "Jordan and Alicia are diehard fans. They watch the games when they're on and listen to them on the radio when they're not around a television. They also know when there's a game on and not just because someone told them."

"So do I."

"But you can't name the first baseman?"

"They change."

"Name one of the pitchers." Remy glared at Sawyer. "How about the current manager. Name one person who has ever played for the Cardinals."

"I don't have to know the players to be a fan." She hissed at him.

"You're correct." Drew sighed. "But those are bandwagon fans and they don't get free tickets to a huge game." I stifled a laugh and watched as Remy shot daggers at Drew before turning to glare at me.

"Why is *she* here anyway?" Remy asked a minute later, looking directly at me, then Lance. "She can't let you have fun with your friends for one night?"

"I asked her to come." Lance replied, shooting a funny look at the dark headed girl.

"It's really pathetic that she doesn't trust you enough to let you hang out with us alone." I chuckled and snuggled back into my boyfriend.

18

"I would be worried, too." Sawyer interjected, shaking his red head. "I'm pretty certain Chopper is really trying to steal Lance from Jo, not trying to steal Jo from Lance."

"You've noticed that too?" I gasped playfully. Lance just shook his head and rolled his eyes. We went back to goofing off and every ten minutes, Remy would try to change the subject to exclude me from all conversation. I really disliked her.

Chapter 3

"You never told me what date your Homecoming dance is on." I mentioned into the phone a few days later. "I need to make sure we don't have any shows scheduled that night."

"It's the seventeenth."

"No, that's when mine is. I asked when yours is."

"It's on the seventeenth. The football game is on the sixteenth and the dance is the next day, on the seventeenth."

"Please tell me you're kidding."

"Why would I kid about that?"

"Lance." I whined. "That's the same weekend as our Homecoming."

"Shit." He cursed. "Well, it's not a big deal. We can do both. We'll just start mine and end at yours or vice versa."

"No, we can't Lance. I'm an attendant, I can't leave the dance and I can't come late because we do a ceremony at the beginning."

"I have the same problem." Lance admitted.

"Great, I have a boyfriend and I can't even go to a freaking dance with him."

"It's not the end of the world, Jordan. You can go with someone else if you want."

"I don't want another date." I whined.

"I just don't want your homecoming to be ruined because of me."

"Fine. I'll ask Keller." I harrumphed, referring to my loaded ex-boyfriend, who was trying desperately to win me back. I would never do it, but Lance didn't know that. The other end went silent.

"Anyone, but Keller James." He stated in a tight voice.

"Why? Because you hate him?"

"I don't hate him, I just am…"

"Jealous."

"A little. I pick you up, he's there. I drop you off, he's there. You two workout together. I know he can give you a lot more than I can. Honestly, Jordan, I have this fear that you're going to wake up one morning and realize Keller is a better match for you than me. I mean, people see us together and wonder why the Hell you're with me."

"First of all, you have nothing to be jealous of. Keller and I are friends. He just happens to be best friends with my brother and that's why he's always around. And you're silly, because you're the most perfect guy for me."

"You're just confused." He chuckled. "As soon as my farmer tan fades you'll move on."

"You're probably right." I teased. "But you'll be happy to know that Keller already has a date. Like ten girls asked and he made a big deal of narrowing it down to just one."

"Ten girls?"

"Yeah, he's kind of a hot commodity around here."

"I don't think I've had ten girls ask me out in my life, let alone for one date."

"If your father was one of the richest men in Kentucky, you'd have the same problem. It's not worth it though, I know for a fact that Keller would trade it all in a heartbeat to find a girl who genuinely liked him for him, but that's not gonna happen here at CA."

"What about you?"

"Uh, I'm taken." I answered uncomfortably.

"Yeah you are." He laughed as he realized he was being ridiculous. "You're skipping school on Friday, right?"

"If I skip school completely, I can't cheer Friday night." I sighed.

"You would choose cheering over a baseball game?" He asked sadly.

"I…it's not…" I stammered.

"You would choose cheering and school over hanging out with me all day?" He questioned roughly.

"School? I don't have school on Saturday." I giggled. "I'm teasing you Lance."

"Teasing how?"

"We have a football game on Saturday and as long as I put in a half day on Friday, I'm okay to cheer."

"So that means…?"

"I can leave at eleven, the game starts at two so that gives me and Alicia plenty of time to get to you."

"You don't want to ride with me?"

"I figured you guys had a whole day planned. I don't want to hold everyone back because I have to go half a day. Alicia and I…"

"We'll wait for you." He interjected. "We won't have near as much fun without you two there."

"Aww, are you sure? You really don't have to…"

"Jordan, I'm not a huge baseball fan and the only reason I wanted to go was because I knew you wouldn't turn down the offer. I am all about spending more time with you."

"If the next thing you tell me is that you are a Cubs fan, we can't date anymore."

"Ouch."

"Seriously Lance." I spit. He chuckled on the other end.

"I like baseball, I like the Cardinals. I'm just not as into it as you are."

"I really don't know if I can continue our relationship." I sighed. "I really think people who don't like baseball are not human."

"Is that right?" He chuckled.

"Yup, it's unnatural." I admitted. "I really think we should end this now."

"If you were in front of me right now, I would kiss you until you stopped talking such nonsense." Lance chuckled in a low voice.

"You can come over, maybe I can sneak out." I breathed. "The thought of you kissing me…"

"You'll have to wait until Friday darlin'." He laughed. "We don't want to jeopardize our date."

"You're right, you're totally not worth the risk of me missing the game."

"Ouch."

"That's what you get for teasing me with the thought of a kiss." I giggled.

"I can tease you a little more."

"Hush."

"So, I didn't want to say anything the other night for obvious reasons, but Drew wondered if Zack, Caleb and Maddie wanted to come along."

"Really?"

"There is room for all of us."

"Maddie will probably say no, but Zack and Cale will be all over it. Unfortunately, I might have to hurt Zack when he cheers for the other team though."

"He's a Yankees fan?"

"Yes, despite how many times I tell him that he needs his head examined." I answered drily. "Are you sure you want them to tag along, too? Cale probably won't be very nice to you."

"It'll give him a chance to get to know me, to see that I'm for real."

"I think you need your head examined as well." I teased. "But I'm absolutely grateful that you're trying."

"How grateful?" He flirted. I laughed out loud and shook my head.

"You know I need to go, right?" I sighed. "I need to get to bed and I'm keeping Maddie and Lish awake."

"I know, this is the part I hate the most."

"Me too." I whispered. "Good night Lance."

"Sweet dreams Jo." I hung up the phone sadly. I let out a sigh as I placed it on charge and then sunk under my covers. I loved our flirting and I especially loved hearing his low, deep southern drawl every night before bed. I was definitely

a lucky girl.

Chapter 4

"That was the longest three hours of my life." I whined as I fell into step with Alicia. My dark headed friend giggled and nodded her head.

"Agreed. I cannot believe Maddie wanted to go."

"I'm pretty sure it's only because we were leaving school early." I lit as our roommate met us at my locker.

"Like I'd miss skipping school with my boyfriend and best friends." Maddie harrumphed. "I'm borrowing one of your Cardinal shirts because I obviously don't own any."

"I'm aware." I laughed. "Cale and Zack are meeting us outside the dorms."

"They'll probably be waiting for us when we get there." Maddie stated as I pulled my messenger bag out of my locker, stuffed some things into it and the three of us started for the doors.

"Where are you ladies running off to?" Keller James asked as he met us in the hallway.

"Baseball game." I grinned.

"What game?" He questioned with a cocked eyebrow as he ran a hand through his perfectly spiked blonde hair.

"Cardinal game." Alicia answered as she shot me a weird look.

"What? Why wasn't I invited?"

"My dad didn't have very many tickets." Alicia stated awkwardly.

"I thought you had tickets to every game already." I shrugged innocently. My ex-boyfriend always bragged about his dad having season tickets, I'm sure he could've gone if he really wanted to. Keller's father was one of the richest men in the state of Kentucky, because they own a well know department store. Keller was hands down, the richest kid in our school and unfortunately, he reminded everyone of that often. He was hot and a nice guy, but I didn't like how he threw money in people's faces like it meant something.

"I can't believe you're going Maddie." Keller pointed at my dark headed, olive skinned friend. Maddie shrugged her shoulders and tucked a hair behind her ear.

"I'm just going to hang out with my friends."

"We should get going, we're supposed to meet Lance soon." I interjected as I started away.

"Lance is going?" He asked in a low growl.

"He is my boyfriend and Alicia's cousin."

"I didn't figure he knew what a baseball looked like."

"Don't be an ass." I hissed as I rolled my eyes and turned my back on him. My friends followed suit and we were out of the building in no time.

"Why didn't he know about the game? His roommates are going with us." I asked Maddie.

"They didn't want to tell him." She shrugged as she looked away quickly. "They figured he'd weasel his way into an invite or show up and brag about how his seats are so much better."

"Keller would never brag." I said sarcastically.

"He probably won't when he stops breathing." Maddie giggled. The three of us were at our dorm in no time and hurriedly went to our shared room to change. It was finally starting to cool off a little so I grabbed a pair of jeans and a fitted red Cardinals Tee before I grabbed a pink St. Louis shirt and tossed it at Maddie. I grabbed two hoodies just in case we needed them and placed them on the bed. I ran a brush through my auburn hair, found my worn out red St. Louis Cardinals baseball cap and placed it on my head. When I turned around the other two girls were ready to go, also dressed in jeans and St. Louis shirts. We were pretty darn adorable, if you ask me.

"Cale just texted to see what was taking us so long." Maddie giggled as she quickly typed a response on her iPhone.

"I'm glad you're coming Maddie." I admitted softly. "I'm really nervous about how Caleb is going to be towards Lance today."

"He'll behave." She smiled. "I threatened his life. Not to mention, he won't get too assholey when we're surrounded by Lance's buddies."

"True, but Cale can be pretty ridiculous sometimes." Maddie giggled as she nodded her head in agreement. My brother had an over protective streak a mile wide, especially when it came to someone he loved. Growing up, he made certain I was always safe and taken care of no matter what. That is not necessarily a bad thing, but when I moved here he tried to put bars on my windows and keep me locked away from the public.

"Just forget about it and have fun." We hurried down the hallway and towards the exit before anyone else caught up with us.

"Holy shit." I gasped when we opened the dorm doors and stepped onto the sidewalk. Zack and Caleb were sitting on a nearby bench waiting for us. "Zack Bentley is wearing a St. Louis Cardinals shirt and hat." And he looked damn good in them.

"Only because Caleb hid all my New York shirts yesterday." Zack grumbled.

"Nice." I giggled as I gave my brother a high five. "I would have hated to have to beat you up for wearing that crap to a Cardinal game." I told Zack with a sweet smile. He rolled his eyes and shook his head.

"Can't tell you two are related." He joked. "Pretty sure he said the same thing to me."

"Cardinals look so much better on you than the Yankees crap you normally wear." I flirted as I gave him a side armed hug.

"I think you'd look pretty hot in a Yankees shirt though." He teased with a wink. I giggled and pushed him away quickly.

"Where are we meeting Lance again?" Caleb asked.

"His house." I answered quickly. "That's where we're meeting everyone."

"Well, they'll be waiting on us so how about you girls put a little pep in your step."

"OMG." I giggled. "You really need to work on your impatience Caleb." He rolled his eyes and strode faster to the SUV in the parking lot. The rest of us practically ran to keep up with him.

It didn't take long for us to pull onto Lance's long gravel driveway. There were already a couple of extra vehicles parked in the front yard. We were apparently the last ones to arrive and Caleb let out a long, frustrated sigh when he realized that. He hated to be the last one to anything.

"Jordan!" Lance's nephew, Wyatt, yelled as he dropped what he was doing and raced towards me, before I even climbed out of the truck. He jumped into my arms immediately and wrapped his arms around my neck. I giggled and hugged the little boy back.

"Hey Wy, how are you?"

"Fine. I get to go to the game too." He grinned widely, as his brown eyes danced excitedly.

"You do? Are you sitting by me?"

"Yes ma'am."

"Sweet." I laughed as I set him back down on the ground.

"Hiya Miss Alicia." Wyatt said shyly as he hugged his cousin before taking off back to the house. He was absolutely adorable all decked out in Cardinal gear. Jenn waved from the front porch and started down the steps, just as Lance and the other boys came from the barn. My boyfriend's face lit up when he saw me. My heart beat quickened as he flashed a smile and a wink at me.

"It's really creepy to watch you go all gooey when my cousin is around." Alicia teased in a whisper. I rolled my eyes and smacked at her.

"Hey darlin'." He drawled as he kissed me on the cheek and squeezed my hand. He didn't get to linger long because his friends immediately shoved him out of the way to hug Alicia and me. I reintroduced everyone as Lance slid his fingers between mine and we walked towards the adults.

It seemed like the entire crew was going, except Lance's father. The adults were discussing who was riding where and I could tell my boyfriend wasn't thrilled with the fact that he wasn't driving us. I squeezed his hand and leaned into him.

"Alicia, do you mind riding with the boys?" Mrs. Bowman asked sweetly. "Wyatt really wants to ride with Jordan, that way we don't have to move around the car seat too."

"No problem." She shrugged nonchalantly as she walked towards her parents' SUV. Chopper and Coop loaded into the Cooper family minivan with the rest of the adults while Drew, Alicia, Sawyer, Jen and Rob climbed in with Alicia's parents.

"Please sit by me Jordan." Wyatt begged excitedly as he grabbed my hand and pulled me towards Mrs. Bowman's Dodge Journey.

"Well duh." I giggled as he practically drug me behind him. Zack, Caleb and Maddie climbed into the third row seats in the back. Wyatt climbed across to his booster seat and grinned back at me, when I slid next to him.

"I'm thinking I should sit in between you guys." Lance teased.

"Don't mess up our date Uncle Lance." Wyatt warned as he leaned forward and eyed his Uncle carefully. I giggled.

"Wyatt, please behave or you'll stay behind with your grandpa."

"Yes ma'am." He murmured softly as he ducked his head. The convoy of vehicles slowly started backing out and headed down the driveway.

"Did you get your test done this morning?" Lance asked. I nodded my head.

"Yes, Alicia and I went in early and caught him before homeroom."

"Good." He smiled as he squeezed my hand.

"Yea, I would have been stressing over it all weekend if I hadn't gotten it out of the way."

40

"You worry too much." Zack interjected from behind me. "You could pass without even studying."

"No, I couldn't."

"Yes, you could." He mimicked back at me.

"You really could." Maddie laughed. "You're taking college level classes Jo, you're going to have your associates degree before you even graduate high school."

"You're an overachiever."

"You're taking college level classes?" Lance asked in shock.

"I kind of had too." I shrugged embarrassedly. "The counselor made me."

"That's amazing." He grinned proudly. "What classes are you taking?"

"Everything." Maddie interjected with a giggle. "Don't let her fool you Lance, she is taking online college classes too. The counselor didn't make her do that."

"She is in honors everything, which is not an easy feat at Callatin." Caleb boasted as he flashed me a wink.

"Could we stop talking about me now?" I sighed. I was all about being the center of attention, but I didn't like my brother and friends bragging to my boyfriend about how smart I was. It made me feel uncomfortable.

"You two are probably taking the same online courses and didn't even know it." Mrs. Bowman stated from the driver's seat. My eyes flitted up to Lance. He shot his mom a dirty look from behind.

"What classes are you taking?"

"Science classes." He shrugged nonchalantly. "I want to go into the medical field and someone talked me into getting a jump on it, so I'm not killing myself in college like Jess is."

"Jess is doing a double degree, that's why she's putting in so many hours at school." Mrs. Bowman commented.

"What is she going for?" Maddie asked.

"Business and marketing. She figures she could get a job with one of the degrees." Lance shrugged. "I think she's doing sixteen credits a semester…whatever the max is, she's doing it."

"Yikes. Where is she going to school at?"

"SIUC. That way she's close enough to come home when she misses Wyatt too much."

"That must be tough." I murmured softly. Lance just nodded. Wyatt was in another world, watching the television screen that hung from the roof.

"She'll be done soon though."

"You know Jordan, she would be really good at helping your band get exposure." Mrs. Bowman interjected thoughtfully. "Jess really knows her stuff."

"We could definitely use all the help we can get." I smiled. We made small talk for the rest of the drive to St. Louis. I had been to the city a few times since I moved to Callatin Academy, but each time I was still in awe of the Arch on the riverfront and by Busch Stadium, the history here always touched me on a deeper level than most places.

The game was amazing, but being there with Lance, his friends and family, my brother and friends made it even better. Well, I guess it also helped that it was such a huge game. My heart was absolutely full. This weekend was starting out absolutely fantastic.

Chapter 5

"Hey." I breathed as Lance and Alicia showed up to the football game the next day. I walked into his open arms as he enveloped me in a strong hug.

"You look amazing." He whispered in my ear.

"So do you." I giggled as I kissed him on the cheek. He was wearing a black Hank Williams Jr. concert tee shirt, jeans and a baseball cap. He definitely looked out of place in a stadium filled with designer clothes and polo shirts, but he made my heart skip a beat. His fingers intertwined with mine and he squeezed my hand gently. "You sure about this?"

"I don't care what we do or where we're at as long as I get to hang out with you." He murmured in a low southern drawl. My heart melted.

"You don't know what you're walking into though."

"I have pretty thick skin darlin'." He chuckled as he squeezed my hand again. I nodded my head as I turned to see the game was getting ready to start. I let go of his hand and kissed him on the cheek quickly.

"I guess I should go with my squad." Lance threw me a wink just before he turned and followed Alicia into the bleachers It was almost like watching them walk into the lion's den. Zack and Keller were sitting at the top, right in the middle of everything. Zack nodded and waved them over. I was extremely nervous, I knew Zack and Keller would be nice. Of course, I wasn't stupid either, I knew Keller would throw him to the wolves if it would give him another chance with me.

Lance looked incredibly uncomfortable throughout the game and my heart clenched. I hated that my brother basically forced him into doing something he didn't really want to do. Of course, Lance was too honorable to tell him no. I felt horrible that he was even in this situation though, because it was easy for a girl to mold into his world but not for a guy to mold into mine, there were too many jealousy issues and jerks who felt threatened when one of their girls went looking for love in other places.

"Having fun?" I asked as I walked into Lance's arms as soon as our halftime routine was over. The boys were on the sidelines with, Alicia who handed me an ice cold bottle of water as soon as I approached.

"You are amazing, Lish." I breathed as I opened the bottle and took a long pull from it.

"It was my idea." Zack lit, shooting a disbelieving look at Alicia. I giggled, rolled my eyes and leaned into my boyfriend and gave him a quick kiss.

"You slummin' now Jordan?" Nathan Lousch asked as he and his friends walked by us.

"Only if I was dating you." I shot as I rolled my eyes and tried to ignore him, never moving away from my boyfriend.

"You'd be a lot better off with me than with a redneck townie." He retorted before setting his sights on Lance. "Why you drive that big ass truck anyway? Are you compensating for something?"

"That's funny coming from you, considering…" I interjected protectively as I wrapped my arms around Lance's waist.

"Considering what?" Nathan asked defensively.

"Oh you know…or don't you?" I laughed evilly.

"Enlighten me."

"Well, according to all of your exes you've been put on *the list*."

"What list?" His friend, Ben Seetar inquired.

"You know, the one that warns all the other girls that you're either under two inches or you only last two minutes, which means if you trick a girl into bed with you then it's not considered sex. According to some very reliable sources, you fall into *both* categories."

"You're a bitch." Nathan retorted as he stormed off.

"I try." I cut as I rose on my tiptoes and kissed Lance on the cheek. He chuckled, but I felt his body relax against mine.

"Does that list really exist?" Keller asked.

"No." I laughed. "People don't talk to me about sex because they think I'm a nun. Why, are you worried?"

"Uh no. I just…"

"Just stop Keller. You're making yourself look bad." Zack shook his head in disbelief. Half time was ending and I kissed Lance quickly as I went back to my squad to finish out the game.

When the game was over I was amped up over the win, something that happened often after the natural high I got from cheering. Lance and the others were making their way down the bleachers and to the field when Maddie slid beside me.

"You and Lance want to drive over to the house and we'll all load into the Tahoe to go to Pevey's lake house party."

"Pevey's? I thought we were staying at the house tonight." I responded, panic almost seeping through my voice. I watched as Lance's feet hit the pavement at the same time Nathan and his friends happened to walk by again.

"Change of plans." She shrugged as she looked down at her phone. "Cale says he's too hyped up from the game and needs to be around a lot of people. I think that will only benefit Lance, too." Nathan purposely bumped into Lance, shoving him down on the ground. My boyfriend lost his balance, recovered quickly and turned around with a laugh. Zack took a step forward.

"Watch it, Lousch." Nathan and his buddies just laughed.

"Are you his bodyguard?" Nathan chuckled, as he took a step closer.

"Grow up." Zack growled. "Getting into a pissing contest is only going to make you look like an idiot."

"I doubt that." Nathan barked with laughter.

"Run away Lousch." Keller chuckled as he stood behind Zack. "We both know I can make your life miserable without even lifting a finger." Nathan's eyes widened, narrowed and the guy quickly walked away, his friends in tow trying to figure out what just happened.

"I don't...I don't know if that's a good idea. Look at what just happened."

"Why not? What's wrong? Other than that Lousch is an idiot."

"I just...I worry about how people are going to treat Lance. He's not..."

"He's a big boy and if it bothers *you*, it's definitely going to bother other people."

"It doesn't bother me, people are such asses here and…"

"Like it or not, this is your world now J and if he can't fit into it then it's better you learn that now, rather than later." I nodded my head, knowing she was right.

"Hey." I breathed as I walked into Lance's arms again. There was really no place better than his strong arms.

"You were amazing out there." He whispered in my ear.

"Thank you." I sighed as I grinned back at him.

"Of course, I could watch you jump and shake all day long." I laughed out loud and pulled away from him. I slid my fingers in between his and leaned into him.

"I guess we're heading to a house party." I mumbled. "Cale wants us to meet him at the house and then we'll all ride over in the Tahoe."

"Sounds good." He grinned as he squeezed my hand and we started towards the parking lot. The others had all slipped away, so we walked alone. I was on high alert, paranoid that someone was going to jump us or, at the least, make a rude comment to Lance.

I could see his black Ford truck ahead of us, it definitely stood out with the oversized mud tires and lift kit, amongst the flashy SUV's and sports cars. I could see people pointing and talking about it.

"We don't have to go to the party if you don't want to." I mumbled nervously.

"What's wrong?" Lance asked, stopping to look at me. "You're acting weird."

"Nothing…I just…" I stammered, my eyes darting away quickly.

"You can't look me in the eye." He was right. I couldn't. I may be an excellent actress but I most definitely could not look my boyfriend in the eye. "Why don't you want to go to the party? Are you embarrassed by me?"

"Absolutely not." I responded without hesitation. "It's just," I inhaled, exhaled and then looked into his sad brown eyes finally. "The people I go to school with are condescending assholes, I don't…I'm worried about what they're going to say to you and…I'm afraid they're going to run you off, make you see that maybe I'm not worth the hassle."

"The only opinion that matters to me, right now, is yours." His hands went up to my cheeks as he gently cradled my face. "When I found out where you went to school, I knew then that this woudn't be easy, but it was too late and I don't care. You are most definitely worth any hassle I get from anyone."

"Lance." I sighed as my heart melted.

"You're out of my league Jo, I'm not an idiot. I just…I'm just holding on until you realize it, I guess."

"Out of your league?" I gasped. "Why would you think that?"

"The proof is all around us darlin'." He murmured softly. "But my heart can't see that."

"I'm only here because of my talent Lance, I am not out of your league."

"I want to be a part of your life, Joey, so not going to this party is out of the question. You fit into my world perfectly, I should fit into yours too."

"Thank you." I whispered as I pulled him towards me and kissed him gently. "We should head to the house then." Lance nodded, his hand finding mine again as we started back towards the truck. He opened the driver's side door and turned to help me inside.

"You are sexy as Hell tonight darlin'." He rumbled in a low growl as his mouth captured mine hungrily. I groaned, feeling his rough hands on the bare skin of my back drove me crazy. He pulled me into his hard body and I melted.

"We should go." He stated breathlessly as he pulled away. "Or we're going to do something that we're not ready to do." I closed my eyes and nodded my head as I tried to calm my racing heart. He was right, now was not the time or place to revisit our first sexual encounter. Lance Bowman already had my heart, he had every part of me, but I wasn't quite certain I was ready for that again.

Chapter 6

"Do you need a drink?" I asked Lance as soon as we climbed out of the Tahoe, a half hour later. He nodded and smiled, so I hurried to the back of the SUV where Zack and Caleb were already pulling coolers out of the back. I slid past Zack and leaned into the red Coleman he had halfway to the ground.

"Couldn't wait, or ask?" Zack lit. I shook my head no. Zack dipped his hand in the open cooler and flipped a piece of ice at me. I shrieked as it landed in my cleavage and immediately repaid the favor.

"You're wasting the ice!" Caleb yelled disapprovingly.

"He's right." Zack laughed, his green eyes twinkling as he put his hands up in surrender. He grabbed a can out of the ice and held it towards me as a peace offering. "I'll be good."

"I'm not falling for that." I giggled. Zack tilted his head, grinning mischievously as he reached into the cooler again and flung a handful of ice and water my way. I shrieked just as he rushed towards me and grabbed me in a bear hug. His hands were full of more ice. Cuss words and giggles flew out of my mouth as I tried to escape him.

"Nice to see you missed me, Zack." A female voice interjected angrily. Zack's girlfriend, Ellie Coelvin, was standing nearby, arms crossed in front of her chest as she glared.

"Hey El, I thought you couldn't come home this weekend." He mumbled as he put me down, making sure to shove the rest of the ice in his hands on me. I shrieked and jumped away with a giggle. "I'm glad you did though."

"Really? Doesn't look like it." She stated.

"I can't play around with my friends?" He asked with a roll of his eyes.

"Maybe you two should get a room."

"Shut up." He exhaled in exasperation. "Seriously."

"It's all right for the little bitch to hang all over you, but if I talk to one guy you get all pissed at me."

"Don't attack Jordan." He hissed, his voice going low and serious as he took a step towards her. "I don't care when you talk to other guys, we both know that jealousy is not my thing."

"Unless she's concerned. You sure as Hell get pissed when she's talking to someone."

"Ellie, why do you have to start drama every chance you get?" He sighed. I grabbed two cans out of the cooler and slid away, leaving Zack to deal with his angry girlfriend alone.

"Well that was awkward." I lit when I approached Lance, Caleb, Maddie and Alicia. I handed my boyfriend his drink and moved closer to him. Maybe I was flirting with Zack, but it was harmless. He was like a brother, just a really good friend, but I could see where it would look like more.

"Rumor has it she's been screwing around on him, she's just looking for someone to blame." Maddie shrugged. "Everyone knows you two are just friends." I nodded and looked over at my friend and his girlfriend, she was still throwing a fit and he eventually just walked off.

"And that's why I have more guy friends than girlfriends." I sighed. "You and Lish are the only girls I can handle for long periods of time."

"You suck at compliments." Alicia lit as she shook her head.

"Sorry J." Zack interjected embarrassedly as he cut into our little group.

"Don't be sorry Zack." I sighed. "It's not your fault."

"I know, I'm apologizing for her craziness. I don't know what her deal is."

"No big." I shrugged. For the next hour, Lance and I interacted with my brother and friends. Every once in a while, people would come up and introduce themselves to Lance or just hang out for a short period of time. I had forgotten my anxieties from earlier and focused on having fun. The only thing wrong with this picture was that Lance was not holding me as he normally did.

"I'm jealous." I pouted a little while later as I wrapped my arms around Lance's neck.

"Why's that?"

"Because I look freaking hot tonight and everyone else is getting your attention."

"I'm just talking. Trust me honey, *you* have all my attention. I haven't been able to keep my eyes off you. But then again, I never can." He drawled with a smile as he looked down at me. We were millimeters apart and just being so close caused me to grow flush.

"Well, I'm feeling neglected."

"I'll make it up to you when we're alone later." He promised suggestively.

"I can't wait that long." I whispered coyly as I kissed him.

"Could you two stop sucking face?" Alicia gagged. "It's really disturbing."

"Sorry Lish." I giggled. "I need to go to the bathroom anyway." She laughed and shook her head as Maddie interjected she had to go to, the three of us walked to find the nearest bathroom.

Chapter 7

"Seems like you're over your anxiety from earlier." Maddie stated, smiling at me. I nodded my head.

"As usual, Lance eased my fears. It's amazing how he can talk me down in a second."

"I never thought I'd hear anyone say that about Lance." Alicia laughed. "Seriously, he's usually the one trying to pump someone up to get into a fight or something."

"I could see that." I giggled. "Hey, did you notice Brennan hanging around earlier?"

"I think he was trying to ask you on a date LIsh." Maddie stated excitedly. "He's so sweet."

"He's not really my type." She shrugged. "But he is sweet."

"You should give it a try."

"Listen to Jordan." Maddie teased. "She tried it and strung the poor guy along her freshman year. Pretty sure he's still reeling from that one."

"Ouch. Thanks." I grumbled. "It's not like I did it on purpose."

"What about Will Cabrio?"

"Conceited ass." I answered quickly. Maddie just giggled and nodded in agreement.

"I do love to watch you girls walk away." A voice slurred behind us. "Can't even imagine how nice it would be to slam into those bare asses." My eyes grew wide as I looked at Maddie questioningly. Surely, I misunderstood the comment. It wasn't unusual for us to be subjected to catcalls and lots of unwanted attention, but it rarely went to this extreme.

"Jordan, why are you letting a townie hit it when you can have me?" Steve Collins asked as he moved in close behind me, his hands going around my waist.

"Because, *he's* not a cocky asshole." I grabbed his arms and tried to pull them away from me.

"Back off Collins." Maddie warned, with a roll of her eyes.

"Not cocky baby, just confident." He whispered into my ear. I rolled my eyes, I hated that comeback. "You don't need to slum anymore. I'm right here and I am so interested."

"And what makes you think *I* would be interested in you?" I laughed wickedly as I tried to wiggle out of his grip.

"Seriously, back off Collins." Maddie hissed as she tried to help me get away from him. Alicia tried tugging too, but the three of us together were nothing apparently.

"Because you're fooling yourself if you believe it'll ever work out between you and the country boy. You're here for a reason Jordan, because you're better than public school losers like that. You deserve the best and I'm right here in front of you." He growled as he spun and pinned me against the cabin.

"Back off." I warned as I gently pushed him. "I have a boyfriend and I'm not interested in some arrogant, roid raging asshole like you."

"Oh, but I think you are." He chuckled as he moved closer.

"COLLINS!" I heard Caleb scream.

"Cavalry's here." He laughed. "Just what I was hoping for. Maybe I should let you see what losers they *all* are. You come from shit Jordan, and always will, if you don't raise your standards."

Steve pretended like he didn't care that the boys were behind him as he moved his face so it was millimeters from mine. His eyes roamed my face, resting on my mouth.

"I bet…that mouth would feel amazing on my cock."

"What?" I gasped.

"Don't act so innocent J, we all know how dirty you really are. It's the only reason Bentley is always sniffing." He licked his lips as he moved in for a kiss, my arms were pinned behind me and no matter how much I struggled, I couldn't move. I went to headbutt him, for lack of a better option, but Lance had already grabbed him by his football jersey, yanked him off me and punched him in the face without hesitation.

Steve got up and charged, but my boyfriend held his own against a guy who was twice his size. Some of Steve's buddies tried to jump in, but Caleb and Zack intervened. After the fight had been broken up, Lance rushed to my side while the others tried to calm down. A few minutes later, Steve's buddies pulled him away and started to leave the party; their night was ruined.

Caleb and Zack had a newfound respect for my boyfriend though. Caleb was no longer the overprotective jerk of before; he knew Lance cared about me and would protect me, that much was obvious. Keller hung back, unusually quiet as he watched Lance gain approval and pats on the back. Lance barely noticed; he only cared about me. I could see his eyes dart towards me with worry anytime he was forced to focus on someone else. My heart melted. I was shaken up, but Lance's heroism washed it all away.

"I've got to find a bathroom." Lance whispered in my ear before he kissed my cheek and headed off towards the house an hour or more later.

"He's got my vote." Caleb announced once Lance was out of earshot. "How in the Hell he beat me to the three of you, I'll never know. But it doesn't matter. He looks out for the most important girls in my life and that's all I care about."

"Aww, Cale that's so sweet." Maddie teased as she kissed him on the cheek. "I told you he was a good guy. Jordan wouldn't care so much if he wasn't."

"He's been gone a while." I mumbled worriedly twenty minutes later. I looked around to see if he'd been sidetracked elsewhere, knowing Alicia was around somewhere. I didn't see him. "I'll be back." Caleb nodded an acknowledgement and I stumbled away to search for my boyfriend; dread filling my stomach.

I searched the sprawling, lavish house and when I couldn't find him I went outside.

"You know, I did see him go towards the clearing over there." Brennan Brookman said. "And come to think of it, Keller was talking to Collins and then his brew crew headed that way too, but that was at least ten minutes ago."

"I thought Collins left." I mumbled in shock.

"So did I." Brennan shrugged. "Want me to go with you to look for him?" I shook my head and forced a smile.

"No thanks B. But could you run and find Zack or Caleb; tell them exactly what you told me and then tell them where I went."

"I don't think you should follow in there. I'm sure he can handle himself. I don't trust those jerks."

"I'll be fine. It's probably just a coincidence." I lied hurriedly as I rushed towards the clearing in the woods. Something was wrong; I felt it in every inch of my body. My stomach clenched tight, I was nauseous and had started to sweat badly. Something was definitely wrong.

Just a little ways into the clearing, I heard rustling and laughter. I followed the sound to see Lance brawling with Nathan, Ben and another guy I didn't recognize at first. The three other guys were bigger than Lance but he was handling himself. I looked down quickly, searching the ground for a limb or rock; something to use as a weapon to help Lance out.

"What do you think you're doing sweetheart?" Steve drawled as one hand went over my mouth and the other locked my arms around my back. "Let the boys have their fun and we'll have ours." I struggled, but for a drunk guy, his grip was like iron handcuffs. I squirmed and squealed, but he overpowered me. "You going to be a good girl? All I want is a little taste of what no one else can have." Steve spun me around; his hand still covered my mouth as his hands groped roughly.

Tears rolled down my cheeks as I prepared for the worst; I knew

it was imminent as he forced me onto the ground underneath him.

No matter how hard I fought or struggled he was just too strong,

too quick for me. Damn steroids.

I turned my head and focused on Lance. I could barely

see him through the foliage and trees that surrounded us, but I

thought if I focused on him then I wouldn't notice anything that

was happening to me. I tried to force my mind away to better

things, to another time altogether. I prayed for an out of body

experience or someone to come rescue me. I knew it wouldn't be

Lance; he'd be lucky to walk away from tonight. I'd be lucky to

walk away from tonight. That much I knew.

Chapter 8

Keller

"Son of a bitch." I grumbled as I watched from a far. That asshole was supposed to rough up the redneck, not attack Jordan. I paid him and his goons to beat the tar out of Bowman; let Jordan see him for the weak loser he is. Collins was taking it too far. Although, from here I can see this may work to my advantage. I can see her staring off, watching her boyfriend get his ass beat and praying he'll come to her rescue any second. If I were to be the rescuer, well that could only benefit me right? Hmm, not bad Keller. We'll let Collins scare the shit out of her a little more...

"JORDAN!" Maddie's shrill scream cut through the night air like nails on a chalkboard. Fuck. I couldn't wait anymore. I have to rush in, make it look like I was searching too and then become her white knight.

"Jordan!" I hollered, feigning ignorance that she was mere feet away from me. Collins didn't notice. He was too doped up to pay attention to anything but his intended target. Too many steroids and hits to the head made this guy a little stupider every day; he had never been the brightest kid to begin with. I looked around a little longer, playing my part up as much as possible until I heard Maddie and the others get closer.

"JORDAN!" Lance's low voice ripped through me as he threw Ben, Nathan and Jack out of his way and raced to Jordan. Fuck, bastard is going to show me up again. I tried to intercept but was outdone by the hick. Lance charged again and beat me to the punch, literally.

Maddie rushed to Jordan's side, Alicia close behind and the two girls hugged her tightly; blocking her from the scene playing out. Lance grabbed Steve by the throat and had both hands wrapped around it, while Collins struggled to breathe and loosen Lance's grip.

73

"You worthless son of a bitch." Lance growled furiously. Steve gave a choking laugh and the hick tightened his grip as he stared back at him with empty eyes.

"If you ever come near her again I *will* kill you."

"I'm sorry." Steve choked out. But Lance didn't loosen his grip, Steve's eyes were bulging out of his head and his face was turning purple.

"Lance." Zack said loudly. "Let him go. He's not worth it." The hick didn't seem to register the words as he slammed Steve into a nearby tree.

"Zack get him." Alicia cried. "He won't stop. He can't." Zack looked back at her questioningly, but did as she asked. A tug on Lance's arm and the redneck came out of his fury, almost turning on Bentley. He threw Steve down to the ground and watched as he scurried away, gasping for air while everyone stared in disbelief. Lance turned around and looked at Jordan nervously.

"Are you okay?" He asked as he stepped towards her and reached out a hand. She noticeably flinched and I saw that as a good sign. Maybe she was freaked out by the psycho now. She nodded her head numbly, not looking at him or anyone else. "Are you sure? Did he…" Lance's voice cracked and I had to stifle a laugh to see that he was about ready to cry. "Do you need to go to the hospital?" She shook her head quickly and stared blankly back at him.

This was my chance.

"Jordan, baby, come here." I cooed, opening my arms up to her. "Brennan told me you were out here; I was going crazy looking for you." Jordan's face turned bright red as she pinned me with a death glare. If someone didn't know any better, they'd think I was the guy who'd just tried to rape her. "I'll make sure Collins and his hooligans pay for this."

"Back off Keller." Maddie said disgustedly. "Three people saw you talking to Collins before he followed Lance back here."

"You think I did this?" I asked in shock.

"I think you're behind it." She hissed. "And if I find out…"

"I'll kill you myself." Caleb growled as he stood in front of me. "Get out of here now."

"I would never do anything to hurt Jordan."

"But you could care less about Lance; especially since he stole Jordan." Zack interjected, stepping up beside Caleb.

"Get out of here Keller." Caleb repeated. "This is a family matter and you don't need to be around. We're going to get her out of here as quickly as possible and we don't need *you* making a scene."

"No one else is family." I stated flatly, trying not to let the whine show in my voice. "Lance is…"

"Get out of here." Caleb roared. "It's the last time I'm saying it."

76

I let out an exasperated sigh and looked back at Jordan quickly. I'd make sure whoever ratted me out paid dearly for it. I'd also make sure to clear my name as soon as possible. Lance Bowman may have won this round, but it would be the last time the hick beat me out.

Chapter 9

Jordan

"Could you say something Jordan? You're scaring me." Lance pleaded as he wrapped his arms around me and hugged me tightly. He continued to whisper sweet comments in my ear as I trembled.

"I'm sorry you saw that. I'm sorry that happened. I'm sorry I didn't protect you."

"I wanna go home." I slurred. "I wanna get outta here."

"Zack, go get her another beer." Caleb instructed. "Let's hang out here for a little bit and let things die down. Then we'll take off."

"I don't *want* to drink another beer. I just want to go home!" I exploded in a shrill voice, that wasn't my own.

"Jordan." Lance whispered as he pulled me closer. Caleb tried to protest but Maddie stopped him.

"She wants to go home, so let's go."

"She's in shock Maddie. Give her a beer, calm her down a little." Caleb instructed gruffly. "Besides, she doesn't want all those bastards out there," He made a gesture towards the house. "To see her like this."

"She'll be fine." She shrugged as she took my hand and led me to the SUV.

"Maddie. Just listen to me. She needs a hospital. She needs time. Look at her." Caleb begged in a tight voice. Maddie stopped at the urgency and pain in my brother's voice, we all did, and looked back at me. I did the same. Somehow, I was covered in dirt and grass, my cheerleading uniform was ripped and destroyed. I could see blood and bruises forming in different places and that's all it took for me to lose it.

"Don't touch me." I gasped quietly as I flung my arm out of Maddie's grip. She looked back at me in shock. "Don't touch me." I repeated as Alicia reached for me. "Nobody fucking touch me." I mumbled, my voice turning into a shrill gasp almost. Lance rushed towards me and I repeated myself again, this time louder.

"Joey, calm down." Caleb whispered as he placed himself behind me. "Don't cause a scene, okay? Just walk to the Tahoe and we'll get out of here. The asshole is gone."

"Don't touch me." I mumbled.

"Go to the car, sis. You're in shock." Caleb repeated as he stepped towards me. When he tried to grab me, I darted out of the way, screaming at him. I screamed at everyone. I screamed hysterically; things that made no sense to anyone but me. When Lance went for me again, I flipped out.

"This is all your fault. Don't touch me!" I screamed. His face fell and his brown eyes filled with pain. "If you weren't such a jealous, overbearing jerk this wouldn't have happened. Collins had to show you up for attacking him and I was the one who had to suffer for your actions!"

"This was not Lance's fault." Zack mumbled in his low, New York accent. "You can't blame him for protecting you, J. "

"No one asked for your input Bentley." I hissed. "You wouldn't have tried to kill the asshole like Lance did."

"He didn't..." Zack started. I narrowed my eyes at him.

"Don't you have a girlfriend somewhere? Why don't you put as much interest in her life as you put in mine?"

"No need to be a bitch to everyone J." He spit back at me. "Collins and his goons did this, not any of us."

"Oh yeah? He said he had a score to settle with you and Caleb, maybe you're wrong about that."

"Attacking us isn't going to make you feel better. You're just going to feel worse, you already do." Zack stated drily. I hated him for knowing me so well.

"I hate you." I hissed.

"It happens." He shrugged as he took a step towards me. "Now why don't you apologize and we can all be one happy family again."

"Screw you." Zack chuckled as he reached out to me. I was not ready to be touched. I shook my head and took a step back. "I'm ready to go home." I spun around on my heel and started for the SUV.

The ride home was absolutely silent and awkward. I curled up in the front seat, pressed myself against the door and hid from the rest of the world. The reality of my hateful words, what could have and should have happened to me slammed into my mind all at once and I began to cry and shake uncontrollably.

"Jo." Caleb mumbled in a broken voice. I could feel him reaching for me, but I pressed myself closer to the door.

"Don't touch me. Please." I begged. I could feel panic taking over my body and as soon as we pulled into the parking spot in front of my house, I fumbled for the door and took off at a dead sprint. I couldn't get away fast enough.

Chapter 10

Lance

"She's pissed at me." I muttered in disbelief as I ran my hands down my face.

"No, I think she's just freaked out. What would've happened had we not come up when we did? Collins is a roid freak. There's no way she could've taken him." Alicia explained. "She doesn't really blame you."

"Yes, she does. It's all my fault. She's right. I should've let her handle things in the beginning." I mumbled.

"Lance." Alicia gasped. "Shut up. Seriously, this is no more your fault than it is Jordan's. Neither one of you is at fault."

"Go after her Lance." Maddie interrupted softly, tears rolling down her olive cheeks. "She told me that you're the only one who can talk her down. You're the only one who can fix her. Just go, bring her back to us."

"I don't…"

"Yes you do. She loves you Lance, you're the only one who can help her." Maddie said reassuringly as she nudged me. I stumbled after my girlfriend. I was really in no shape to help her, I could barely stand, could barely see. I'd taken a beating from those jerks earlier, but all that was forgotten when I saw what was happening to Jordan. How could anyone try to hurt her? Granted the guy was plastered and probably won't remember it in the morning, but he still attacked her. It was a good thing he was drunk though, because had he been sober he would've done a lot more damage. As it was, he was too trashed to do much more than fall all over himself and try to keep her quiet. Thank God for that.

I found her a few minutes later; huddled beneath a large oak tree. Her knees pulled up to her chest as she sobbed uncontrollably. I watched in silence. I really didn't know what I could do to help her. I was terrified she'd blame me again; terrified she'd push me away or run off again. I couldn't handle losing her.

"Jo, darlin'?" I mumbled gruffly. She continued to sob, quieter now. I moved towards her slowly. "Come to the house baby." She shook her head quickly. "Can I carry you?" She didn't protest. "I'm going to pick you up, okay?" Again, she did nothing. "I won't hurt you darlin'." In one movement, I picked her off the ground and swept her into my arms. She clutched my neck and sobbed into my chest.

Everyone still stood around the front porch, ready to search for her if needed. Caleb and Zack both rushed forward, arms out to take her from me, but I wasn't letting her go. I couldn't. Maddie hurried to the house and held open the door for me.

"Can you carry her up the stairs to her bedroom?" Alicia asked worriedly. I nodded my head and followed my cousin up the wide staircase and into Jordan's bedroom. Maddie rushed to the bed and pulled the comforter back and I placed my girlfriend on the sheets softly.

"You know what?" Maddie started. "Alicia and I are gonna get her into the shower. She needs to get cleaned up and out of those clothes. Maybe it'll be easier to forget about tonight if she does that." I nodded my head as I helped the two girls pick her back up off the bed. Jordan flailed and fought saying she didn't want to leave me, but Maddie was adamant she'd be fine. My heart broke as I watched her go away from me; I just wanted to make her feel safe again.

While Jordan was in the shower, I went downstairs and called mom. I explained everything with just enough detail to make my point and mom said I didn't have to be home until morning. Dad was passed out already but I knew he wouldn't be happy. I didn't care. I couldn't leave her alone, not after the night she'd had. I didn't want to leave her ever, but I knew the morning would come too quickly. Mom was extremely sympathetic and tried to convince me to let her take a look at Jordan; since she has a nursing degree. I knew enough to know that would only embarrass and infuriate my girlfriend. More than anything, I wanted to get my hands on that jerk again and beat him to a pulp. I wanted to beat the Hell out of anything right now, to be honest. I paced the living room for a few minutes waiting for Maddie or Alicia to come back downstairs.

"How's Jordan doing?" Zack asked worriedly as he walked into the house without so much as a knock.

"The girls are upstairs in the bathroom with her now." I responded.

"Maddie thought it'd be good to get her cleaned up." Caleb mumbled.

"She's probably right." Zack agreed as he plopped down on the couch.

"I thought you were staying with Ellie tonight."

"Nope." Zack exhaled. "She's not exactly thrilled with me right now."

"Why not?"

"Um well, she's a little pissed I came back here. Super pissed actually. She thought I should let you all handle it. But I couldn't do that. I had to be here too, she doesn't understand that J is like my sister."

"Fuck her." Caleb growled. "I think you can do better anyway."

"Yeah. She seems to think she can do better than me." Zack shrugged. "More power to her."

"She dumped you?" I asked in shock. "For coming to check on Jordan?"

"So she says." He shrugged again. "I think she's been screwing around at college anyway, but she claims this was the last straw. She has been jealous of Jordan from day one. I told her to get over it, because it wouldn't change and she said she was done." Zack stood up and paced around the living room while Caleb and I sat there dumbfounded. "She probably thought I would beg her to stay. I didn't."

"I can't believe you got dumped." Caleb stated with a snort of laughter. "I didn't think that was possible." Zack rolled his eyes and chuckled too.

"Jordan freaked out and locked herself in her bedroom." Alicia explained breathlessly from the top of the stairs. "Maddie and I've been trying for five minutes to get her to come out, but she won't answer."

We bolted upstairs and took over Maddie's incessant pounding on the door. Nothing we did got her to reply and I started to panic.

"Move out of the way." Zack sighed as he went to the lock, he pulled a card out of his pocket and started messing with the door and knob.

"Um, how do you know how to do that?" Maddie almost gasped.

"What? My parents didn't send me here just because I was good at baseball." He shrugged nonchalantly with a wicked smile. The door knob turned and the wooden door swung open. Zack winked at Maddie before he looked in the room, his smile quickly dropped as he took in the sight of Jordan laying limp on the bed, blood streaks running down her arm.

Chapter 11

Jordan

When things get to be too much I slip my ear buds in and blast my iPod so loud that the rest of the world fades away. It usually works and people leave me alone. Not today. I stared at the door watching it reverberate under the incessant pounding, but I didn't move. I couldn't, nor did I want to. When I saw the doorknob turn, I flipped over so I was facing away from them all. I hoped my body language would give them a hint, but it didn't.

Lance removed my headphones and looked back at me sadly, contemplating what to say. I tried glaring and when that didn't work, I just focused on something else in the room, as if he'd just disappeared.

"Are you okay?" He asked quietly. "You're bleeding." I looked down at my arm, I had a large gash running from my elbow to halfway to my wrist, it looked pretty deep and was oozing blood. I rolled my eyes and glared back at my boyfriend. He looked down quickly and I knew he'd initially thought I'd tried slitting my wrist like my mother.

"Fuck you." I spit.

"Jordan, I…" He began. "Are you okay?"

"I'd be better if y'all would just leave me alone." I mumbled flatly through clenched teeth.

"I'm not leaving until you talk to me."

"You should know by now that I don't fucking talk."

"I know better than that. Do you want everyone else to leave?"

"No I want *you* to leave."

"Why?"

"Because I don't want to look at you." My southern drawl had become more pronounced, signaling to those who knew me best that I was more than pissed.

"Jordan." Zack scolded.

"Fuck you." I retorted as I turned around and narrowed my eyes at him. "It's your stupid friends who like to come after me. What do you do, tell them all I'm easy?"

"What?" Zack's eyes were wide with shock, before I could see the hurt I'd caused by my accusation.

I glared at everyone in the room. I began screaming for my friends and family to leave. Lance grabbed me in a bear hug and held me tightly until I stopped yelling and broke down in his arms and then, finally, everyone left us alone.

"What would've happened if...?" I sobbed. "Why couldn't I stop him?   He tried to take something so sacred and...I've only ever had sex with you and I'm in lo..."

"Hey." Lance interrupted. "All that matters is that you're okay and that nothing happened."

"But something did happen."

"What?!?" Lance exploded.

"He...he almost...You...you scared me."

"I scared you?" He asked sadly. "Jordan, I'm..."

"You could've killed him." I muttered. What was wrong with me? Had Lance not flown to my rescue Steve probably would have raped me. I should be grateful for Lance, but I was freaked out and couldn't focus on myself.

"I wouldn't have."

"But you *could* have. Maybe..."

"Don't finish that sentence Joey." Lance pleaded. "I thought he hurt you and I lost it. I get crazy when it comes to you."

"You should just walk away now. I make you crazy. This is the second fight you've gotten into because of me."

"And I'll get into a thousand more, just to protect you."

"I don't need you…"

"But I need you." Lance stated sadly. "I'll leave if you want because I don't wanna push you. I want to stay here and fix this; I just want to hold you."

"Just leave. It's better this way." I muttered. My boyfriend looked back at me sorrowfully. I could see the hurt in his eyes as he nodded and left the room. He immediately rushed back in and grabbed me in a bear hug.

"I can't leave when you need me." He announced. I wrapped my arms around his neck and held on for dear life.

"Please don't leave me ever."

"I don't plan on it." He whispered. I sobbed into his chest for most of the night. Once I was half-asleep I confronted Lance about my fears.

"I know you were just protecting me earlier, but have you ever…would you ever?"

"Is that what's wrong? Are you scared I'd black out with you?" He asked sadly. I nodded my head slowly and watched as tears filled his eyes. Lance put his hand up to my face and caressed my cheek gently. "I'd *never* hurt you. I may have my dad's temper, but I have restraint. No matter what, I'd never lay a hand on a woman. I've seen what my dad does to my mom. I couldn't…"

"He hits your mom?"

"Sometimes." He answered embarrassedly. "He hasn't…"

"Does he hit you?" Lance's eyes darted away as he answered without saying a word. "If he ever does, you can stay with me."

"I couldn't leave my mom and Wyatt alone with him."

"I know but I don't want…"

"Nothing's going to happen to me."

"Promise?"

"Yeah." He smiled as he kissed me sweetly.

"I'm all messed up Lance."

"No you're not. You're perfect." He protested as he kissed me lovingly. I finally fell asleep in his arms. Sometime around five in the morning Lance woke me up to let me know he was leaving.

"Will you come back early?"

"As soon as I can." He nodded his head and smiled.

"I finally got a whole night with you and I spent it crying, rather than kissing you."

"You went through a lot last night and I wasn't about to do anything but hold you."

"Thank you." I murmured. Lance nodded once, kissed my forehead and left my room. "I love you." I whispered after him, but he was already gone. It was for the best. I'm not sure if I'm ready for him to hear me say those words yet or ever; it would leave me too vulnerable.

Chapter 12

I slept in. My whole body ached whenever I moved, I had no desire to get out of my bed. I was grateful Keller didn't show up to go for a run, mostly because I couldn't move. Also because I was still trying to figure out his role in last night's events. He was shady and I had no doubt that he would do anything to get Lance out of the picture, even if it meant putting me in danger.

"Hey sleeping beauty." Lance drawled in a low voice as he walked into my room around noon. I smiled back at him. "How ya feeling?"

"It hurts to move." I mumbled.

"Did you take anything?" He asked as he moved closer to my bed. I shook my head. "Do you have any Tylenol in here?"

"In my purse." I responded. Lance went to the zebra print bag on my desk, found the Tylenol and brought me two little white pills. He handed me the water bottle sitting on the bedside table and helped me to sit up.

"Maybe that'll help." He murmured, watching me closely. "Do you want to have my mom look you over?"

"NO!" I exclaimed.

"Jo," He sighed, watching me worriedly. "She's a nurse and you need to be checked out. You have a lot of bruises and swelling."

"I'm fine Lance." I murmured. "Why would you even tell your mom about what happened? It's so stupid and embarrassing."

"Had I not told her then I wouldn't have been able to stay with you last night and come back today."

"I wish you would have lied."

"And been in worse trouble?" He asked in shock. "I'm not going to lie to my mom, she doesn't deserve that." I nodded my head, knowing he was right. "It doesn't change her opinion of you, if that's what you're worried about. I'm pretty sure you could kill someone and she'd still think you were perfect." I laughed and rolled my eyes.

"How long do you have today?"

"All day." He shrugged with a sad smile. "I got all my chores done before church and then came right here."

"You won't get in trouble?"

"It'll be worth it if I do." He teased, winking at me playfully. I chuckled and moved in my bed. Lance raised his eyebrows and looked at the door nervously.

"I'm not going to seduce you." I giggled. "I was hoping we could just watch movies in my bed all day."

"Sounds like Heaven."

"Wait, you might want to look through the DVD and BluRay collection first. Pretty sure it's Hunger Games or one of the Twilight movies in there." I giggled. "Or we can find something on Netflix." Lance chuckled and shook his head. He perused my DVD collection, before we went to the streaming website and found a newer movie with Mark Wahlberg in it. For the rest of the day, we watched movies. We talked, we snuggled, I napped and we just hung out. It was the perfect Sunday.

"Hey." Caleb interjected as he stepped inside my room. He didn't look happy to see Lance lying in bed with me. "We're working out the details of Homecoming. Are you two going in the limo with us?"

"I am, I guess." I mumbled as I looked down at my comforter.

"I don't..."

"His Homecoming is the same night. He already told someone he would be their escort, so he can't back out."

"Yes he can." Caleb responded, giving both of us a funny look.

"Don't worry J, I'll be your date." Zack offered with a flirtatious grin as he stood in my doorway, arms outstretched as he hung on the door frame, flexing his arms.

"Thanks Zack." I giggled. Lance shifted awkwardly.

"You're serious?" Caleb questioned, his eyes narrowing as he watched Lance carefully. "You're not taking my sister to her Homecoming?"

"It's not that I don't want to. I just…I had every intention of taking her until we realized it was the same day. I already promised Remy I would be her escort."

"Remy? Who in the Hell is that?"

"A family friend." Lance responded.

"A family friend." Caleb repeated, shaking his head as he looked back at Zack in disbelief.

"Let it go Cale." I hissed. Zack threw me a wink as he pushed my brother out of the room. "Sorry." I sighed, looking down at the comforter. "He means well, I think." Lance just nodded his head.

"So, I guess you're going with Zack then, now that he's single."

"I don't think he was serious with that offer." I laughed as I rolled my eyes.

"Pretty sure he was." He cleared his throat and started to climb out of the bed.

"Zack's never serious."

"I need to go darlin'." Lance murmured.

"No." I whined, pouting effectively. I leaned over and kissed him softly. "Please stay. I'm not ready…" I kissed him again.

"Jordan, it's hard enough to leave you. Please don't make it worse."

"Then don't walk away." I instructed as I tried to pull him back.

"I got my ass reamed this morning. I have to be careful or *he* won't allow me to see you anymore." He explained cupping my face in his hands. "I'll make it up to you, I promise." I nodded in resignation and let him help me out of my bed.

A few minutes later, I was standing on the front porch sadly waving goodbye to my boyfriend. When I went back inside, the wolves were waiting to pounce.

"Don't you think the two of you are moving a little fast?" Caleb asked. "Spending all day, in bed, together?"

"Mind your own business."

"You're fucking head over heels for this guy and he won't even take you to your homecoming dance!"

"There are reasons."

"Well, I know if Maddie and I were in *your* situation nothing would keep me from being at her dance when she's an attendant. It's a little fishy, that's all; he's willing to spend every free minute with you, until it's important."

"Maybe he's uncomfortable at CA, not everyone is that friendly to him."

"If he *really* likes you, then it wouldn't matter. I just think maybe he's trying to get laid." Keller accused.

"What would you know about a nice guy Keller? And who in the Hell said you could hang around me again?" I shot angrily before I went to my room to stew over my brother's jerkish comments.

Chapter 13

"I was serious about being your date for Homecoming." Zack announced later that night. "I don't have a date and I don't feel like looking for one either."

"I don't know if I should be flattered by the offer or offended."

"Flattered." He chuckled. "I know you're into Lance, so I…I just thought we'd go as friends."

"Thanks Zack." I grinned. "I appreciate that."

It didn't take long for word to get out that Zack was my date. Keller's homecoming date mysteriously fell through a few days before. Considering he'd had at least twelve girls ask him, he could've found back up. However, he was begging me to be his date so he didn't feel like a loser for going alone. I wasn't about to go with him, because I knew it would send the wrong message to him and the rest of the school. I would keep Zack as my date, but it didn't mean that I couldn't tell a little white lie to Lance.

"So, Zack was not serious about taking me to homecoming." I sighed into the phone Thursday night. "But, no worries, Keller offered to be my date. His ditched him at the last second."

"What?" Lance asked in a flat voice.

"Yeah, I didn't figure you'd mind so I didn't think to ask if it was okay."

"No, I…I'd hate to see you have to go alone." He mumbled.

"So, I guess that also means we're going an entire weekend without seeing each other."

"I thought we had plans for Sunday."

"Oh yeah, about that…Keller got tickets to watch the Lion King. I know I told you that. Anyway, I told him I'd go months ago and we get to meet the cast and…"

"Um, I'd remember that."

"I know I told you." I sighed. "Everyone else was supposed to be going, but they bailed. I can't do the same thing, you know?"

"Yeah, I guess you're right." He said in a low voice. "What time are you leaving?"

"First thing in the morning, which will suck, but I can sleep on the plane."

"Plane?"

"Well jet, actually. Keller's father has a private jet. The show is in Chicago so we are flying up first thing in the morning, hitting the stores, an early dinner and then the show. So I won't be able to make our phone call either."

"Yeah, sounds like you have a big weekend planned." He mumbled. So, the whole thing about Keller taking me to a show was an absolute lie, but I was really hoping to light a fire under Lance. Caleb had gotten into my head and I kept thinking that maybe he was right, maybe I was into Lance a lot more than he was into me. My heart hurt and tears rolled down my cheeks when we hung up that night, because not once, did Lance change his mind about taking me to Homecoming.

"Wow Jordan, you look beautiful." Zack breathed as he met me downstairs in a suave black tuxedo while everyone waited for us outside by the limousine.

"Thanks. You look pretty great too." I smiled, more than pleased with his reaction to my slinky silver dress. He handed me a corsage and helped me put it on.

"I have got to be the luckiest guy in the world. I can't wait to dance with you."

"Yeah?" I flirted. "I'm sure you won't get a chance, or rather I won't, because there'll be a line of girls waiting on you."

"Why would I want to dance with anyone else?" He asked coyly. I was caught up in flirting with Zack. I was thrown off guard by how good he looked and how bad my heart still hurt from Lance choosing Remy over me. Suddenly, Zack's arms were wrapped around my waist and our lips were millimeters apart. I closed my eyes and waited for the kiss without thinking of anything else.

"Jordan, what the Hell is taking so long?" Maddie hollered inside without looking. My eyes flew open and I realized what had almost happened.

"Oh my God." I gasped. "I'm so sorry. I don't know what…"

"Hey, that was…" Zack started. My face was bright red as I rushed out of the house. What in the heck was wrong with me? Zack Bentley was one of my really good friends and I just about screwed all that up because my ego needed a little boost. I could've just made things incredibly awkward between us, especially when he looked at me and said he wasn't

interested in me that way.

Chapter 14

"OH MY GOD!" I shrieked excitedly as I saw Lance standing in front of our limo waiting for me. He was decked out in a black tuxedo, a silver tie and vest to match my dress and holding a single white rose in his hand. He was grinning from ear to ear as I ran and jumped into his arms.

"What are you doing here?" I breathed.

"Taking my girl to her homecoming dance."

"But, what about…?"

"Being with you is all that matters to me." He whispered before I kissed him hungrily.

"You just made my night."

"That was my plan." He grinned. "Is it all right if we don't go in the limo? Mom wanted us to swing by the house to take pictures."

"I get to be alone with you?" I asked in awe. Lance chuckled and nodded. "Then it's absolutely all right." I kissed him on the cheek and looked back at my brother and friends. "We're going separate, we'll meet you at the restaurant."

"We can swing by Lance's house." Caleb announced. "It's not a big deal."

"Then we'll be late for reservations." I argued. "It'll be okay. We'll meet you at the restaurant."

"It's fine Cale." Maddie interrupted as my brother was about to dispute my reasoning. He nodded his head, but he didn't look happy at all. I waved and tugged Lance towards his truck. He helped me into the driver's side and kissed me again.

"You look absolutely breathtaking, darlin'." I couldn't stop smiling as I kissed him again, before scooting over and letting him climb into his truck.

"We don't *have* to go to the dance you know?" I said coyly as I traced designs on the inside of his palm. He started the truck and laughed before he looked down at me.

"Yes we do. You *have* to be there."

"You have no idea how much it means to me that you're here right now."

"Yeah, well Maddie kind of enlightened me. Not only did she point out how important this was, but she also explained that I was an idiot if I thought Keller or Zack couldn't steal you away from me in a heartbeat. She said Keller always gets what he wants, and he wants you, and he would take advantage of your disappointment of me not being here tonight."

"Whatever." I muttered rolling my eyes.

"Regardless, I wasn't about to take a chance and find out." He shrugged as he squeezed my hand. "I decided my homecoming didn't matter once you were voted on to your court. At least we don't have to worry about prom."

116

"Are you already asking me to prom?" I giggled.

"You're a busy girl; I just wanted to make sure you have the day free."

"That's a long time from now, are you sure we'll last that long?" I teased.

"I know I'm not letting go of you anytime soon."

"Good." I grinned. I didn't leave Lance's side at the dance very often. I danced with Maddie a few times but I mostly planted myself on his lap or by his side. We danced every slow song together and Lance held me as tight as he could while I rested my head on his shoulder.

"Hey, I owe Zack a dance." I mumbled as I watched him flirting with a senior. I grew a little jealous and prayed no one else noticed. I couldn't understand it really.

"I'm not gonna tell you no, but I don't want you to dance with him." Lance admitted.

"Uh I know. I wasn't asking." I shot. "Don't you trust me?"

"I don't trust *him*."

"Well you have nothing to worry about because I lo…"

"If he tries something I *will* lay him out." Lance interrupted before I could tell him I loved him. That was the second time he'd done that and I worried there was a reason for it, but I hoped I was reading too much into it.

"Behave." I warned with a playful smile before I made a beeline for Zack.

"Ready for that dance I owe you?" I asked my sexy blonde friend as I interrupted his flirting session.

"Hell yeah." He smiled as he blatantly ignored the girl and put his hand out to lead me to the dance floor. "So what's up?" He asked. I shot him a confused look and he elaborated. "You didn't owe me a dance. Wait, are you jealous?"

118

"No." I answered quickly. "I just think you can do better than her, she's a slut. Besides, I do owe you a dance because you went along with Lance and Maddie's plan. You asked me to the dance so I wouldn't look like a loser, even though you knew Lance was going to surprise me."

"Yeah, um, not a big deal." He stammered.

"Wait, you did know, didn't you?" Zack looked away nervously and I immediately felt like a horrible person. "Zack, I'm so sorry."

"Shut up. It's not a big deal."

"Yes it is, you blew off dates for me…"

"I just didn't want you to be lonely or miserable, that's all."

"Zack." I sighed again. He shrugged his shoulders and looked back at me with a goofy grin.

"Maybe we should pick up where we left off earlier." He suggested slyly as he leaned in to kiss me again. I almost faltered but turned to kiss his cheek instead.

"Thanks for being such a good friend." I whispered before I walked away. Lance was standing up, glaring at Zack.

"You ready to dance with me again?" I asked hoping I could defuse the situation as I wrapped my arms around his waist tightly.

"I'm ready to kick the shit out of *him*." He retorted.

"He has a reputation for being a relentless flirt, he was only doing it to save face for the whole situation. He was totally blindsided by you showing up today, that's not fair."

"I'm your boyfriend, he shouldn't have gotten his hopes up."

"Zack has no feelings for me whatsoever."

120

"You're wrong about that." He hissed in a low voice. I exhaled loudly, closed my eyes and shook my head.

"You have two choices Lance; forget about Zack, dance with me and kiss me all night long or be a fucking jealous jerk by getting into a pointless fight and lose me forever." I issued with a shrug. "If you don't realize you *have* me and he can't *get* me then you're an ass who doesn't deserve me." I spit angrily as I pulled away from him.

"Jordan stop." Lance protested as he grabbed my arm before I could walk away. "I can't help it. I don't know why you're with me and it makes me crazy to think I could lose you any minute."

"I can have any guy I want at this school Lance. I don't want them, I only want you."

"Trust me darlin', you already have me." He stated as he tipped my chin up and looked back at me sadly. "I'm sorry, let's go dance."

"No." I said shaking my head. Lance looked back at me nervously. "You really don't know why I'm with you?" I asked in a broken voice.

"No I don't. Have you seen a picture of us together? You're a supermodel and I'm like the dorky kid you feel sorry for."

"I *have* seen a picture of us and we look perfect together. I'm with you because you're amazing and I feel amazing when I'm with you. It doesn't hurt that you're incredibly hot either." Lance didn't reply instead he planted a sweet kiss on my unsuspecting mouth. I felt my knees go weak as I wrapped my arms around his neck.

"Mmm…" I breathed. "Let's get out of here."

"What?"

"Let's go. I wanna kiss you before my curfew." I stated as I grabbed his hand and yanked him to the door. I jerked him into the truck after me and began kissing him hungrily.

"Chill out Jordan, at least let me get out of the parking lot."

"Well you better hurry before I attack you right here."

"Attack? Wow!" He chuckled excitedly as he tore out of parking lot and headed for our spot, which was just a back road and empty field by his house. I was all over him as he drove. Before we had gotten off the main road, I had ventured out of my comfort zone.

"Jordan." He gasped. "Darlin', we've got all the time in the world."

The rest of the night, we didn't leave each other's arms but Lance was careful not to let it go too far. I was grateful; I still wasn't completely ready to take that leap again. But it would be soon.

Chapter 15

"There's pretty much nothing better than this." I sighed, leaning back into Lance as we lay in the back of his truck on a cool November night. Time had quickly passed, my whole existence revolved around our eight o clock nightly phone calls and the weekends where we were completely inseparable. We'd been to dinner and a movie, hung with his friends and now we were soaking up the last little bit of time before my curfew came. These were the moments that would always be etched in my memory, when we were ninety years old and I could remember nothing else, I would remember this.

"I'm certain you're right." He chuckled, the sound reverberating through my body just before he kissed me on the top of my head.

"I could stay like this forever."

"Me too." He murmured, his fingers playing with mine. "Thanksgiving break is next week, does that mean I get to spend more than the weekend with you?"

"Not really." I mumbled sadly. "We're going to Lakewood to spend Thanksgiving with my aunt. We haven't been there in a while."

"Oh." He commented awkwardly. "So you won't be home on Thankgiving?"

"No, we're flying out Wednesday and we'll be back on Sunday. Dad just kind of sprang it on us a few days ago. Didn't your mom tell you?" Lance shook his head. "She asked me the other day if I wanted to spend Wednesday night at Alicia's house with all the women while they prepped for Thursday. She asked if I wanted to go Black Friday shopping with them too, but I had to say no. Why?"

"She didn't tell me that. But I had hoped you'd hang out with me." He mumbled sadly. "We do Holidays big.

We'll all be at Alicia's for Thanksgiving, Chopper's for Christmas. My grandparents will be down."

"I wish I could go." I sighed as I turned to look at him. "I would rather be with you. Kyler can't come home for break, so it won't even be like a real family thing. I would have been more thrilled if my dad said we were going to Maryland for break."

"Will he be home for Christmas?"

"Possibly." I shrugged. "I miss him so much." Lance hugged me tighter . "I'm extremely proud of him, grateful for our troops, but I hate that the military took him away from us."

"It was his choice." Lance muttered quickly. "It didn't really take him away, he's trying to make a better life for himself."

"Away from us, is not a better life."

"I'm sure he won't be away from you forever, the beginning is always rough." I nodded my head, swallowing my arguments. "Your break started already?"

"Yup, I have cheer practice on Monday and Tuesday, but that's it."

"I don't get out until Tuesday at noon. Can I pick you up afterwards for a date?"

"Absofriekinglutely." I giggled. Lance chuckled as he leaned down and kissed me softly.

"You know I have to take you home now, right?"

"Noooooooooo." I pouted. He chuckled and kissed me again. "Pretty sure if you keep doing that, we're both going to get grounded."

"It'd be worth it."

"We'd never survive being away from each other so long."

"True." He sighed as he kissed me again and moved to get out of the truck bed. He helped me down and the two of us grabbed the blankets and threw them in the backseat of his truck. We got in the front seats and he steered us towards Callatin Academy. I snuggled as close as I could to him. I hated when he had to drop me off, but I also knew he would get in worse trouble than I would for missing curfew. So I said goodbye when he pulled up in front of my house and floated inside. I'm pretty certain that life couldn't get any better than this, how many girls actually find their perfect match while they're still in high school?

Chapter 16

"Sorry I'm late." Lance murmured as I met him at the front door. "Something came up at the farm."

"No worries, I knew you'd be here sooner or later." I giggled as I kissed him quickly.

"I hate to keep you waiting though." I smiled and hugged him tightly. "Did you eat already?" I shook my head. "Good, because I packed us a picnic."

"Really?" I asked in shock. "That's amazing."

"I'd hoped you'd say that." He chuckled. "Mom made everything, of course."

"I would think you were too perfect if you told me you made it all and then I'd have to break up with you immediately."

"Why's that?"

"Because you'd be too good to be true. Seriously you're hot, thoughtful, sweet and you can cook? Way too good to be true." I teased. He chuckled, slid his fingers through mine and led me to the truck. I hated the fact that I would be away from him for the next five days. It was something we were definitely used to since I wasn't allowed to see him during the school week, but the fact that we were both out of school would make it hard to swallow.

We climbed into his truck and just as he started it, pain shot through my stomach. I doubled over in reaction, but covered it by pretending to drop my purse. Panic shot through me. Poop pains? Seriously, I was getting poop pains and we were about to be out in the middle of nowhere eating?

"I forgot my phone." I lied quickly as I sat up, opened the passenger side door and rushed inside. Luckily, I had taken my purse with me so he couldn't see that it was inside of it. I sprinted to the bathroom as another pain rocked me. I tried to go to the bathroom, but nothing was happening. After a few minutes, the spasms were gone. I drank some water and hurried back outside, running into Lance.

"I was getting worried about you." He lit.

"I'm fine. Sorry, I found it."

"Are you sure? I've never seen you that worried about not having it before."

"Yeah, I just...I...it's a safety thing, I guess. Sorry." Lance nodded his head, but he eyed me carefully sensing something was wrong. How could I tell my boyfriend that I thought I had to poop and that's why I ran inside? Yeah, that wouldn't happen, ever.

As we climbed back into his truck and drove out of the Academy gates, I pushed the incident out of my head. Lance's hand was intertwined with mine and that's all that mattered.

"We can eat and then go hang with the guys for a bit, if you want. They're riding on some trails today and asked if we wanted to join. Well, I should rephrase that, they asked if you wanted to join, I wasn't invited."

"Yes you were." I giggled. "Shut up."

"Pretty sure my friends would rather hang out with you, than with me."

"They do love me." I grinned.

"How could they not?" He chuckled as he kissed the back of my hand. I couldn't stop smiling, a natural thing with Lance. He drove us to the pond behind his house. He pulled up near the dock, but pulled everything out by a nearby tree. The trees were almost all bare, but it was still a beautiful spot.

We ate lunch and talked about random things. An hour later, we loaded up and headed to Lance's house to get his four wheeler.

"I hear the cavalry coming." Mrs. Bowman smiled as she walked outside and gave me a warm hug. "Will you be out all day?"

"Yes ma'am. I finished my chores this morning before school, so I could spend time with Jo before she heads to Texas tomorrow."

"I know bud." She mumbled with a sad smile, she looked out towards the barn.

"Where's Wyatt?"

"Jess took him to Jenn's for a bit so I could get some meal prep done for Thanksgiving dinner."

"Aww, I was hoping to see him."

"I'm sure he won't be happy when he finds out he missed you sugar." She grinned as she gave me another hug. "You two should get going before your dad gets back from town Lance." My boyfriend's face turned serious as he nodded his head. He looked at his mom for a moment and that's when I noticed the red rimmed eyes and the hitch in her voice.

"Are you headed to Jenn's later?" He asked, his words were almost a statement rather than a question.

"Depends how much I get done." She shrugged, looking away quickly.

"Do you need help with anything?" I asked, not wanting to leave her alone. She looked so sad, so scared that Lance's words came sliding back into my head. Sometimes Mr. Bowman had a little too much to drink and would slap her around. Was it really a good idea to leave her absolutely alone when he'd be back at any time? "I mean, I really don't know much when it comes to the kitchen, but I follow directions well."

"No thanks sweetie." She laughed. "Baking and cooking is where I clear my head. Sometimes I start making peach cobbler and just know that Luke will smell it and walk into the kitchen again." My heart broke. I didn't know what to say so I just hugged my boyfriend's mom again. Her emotions had nothing to do with her husband and everything to do with the fact that it was a holiday and one of her children was missing. I was complaining about not being with Kyler and Lance was basically going through the same thing, except I can talk to my brother at any time and Lance cannot. No one knew where Luke Bowman was or even if he was still alive or okay out there. Because of his father's drinking and temper, he'd walked away from his family and friends one day and never looked back.

"We'll be around if you need anything." Lance murmured as he hugged his mom too. She nodded her head and wiped at her eyes.

"Look at me." She laughed as she shook her head. "I'm a blubbering mess. I'm so sorry."

"Don't apologize." I murmured. "Holidays are hard, it's when I miss my mom the most." Mrs. Bowman smiled softly at me before she wrapped me in a tighter hug.

"This Thanksgiving I'm pretty grateful to God for bringing you into our lives." She whispered in my ear. "The changes you've brought out in Lance, and Wyatt for that matter, are astounding."

"I feel the same way about you guys." I murmured as I hugged her back.

"I hope you'll be able to spend Christmas with us."

"Me too." I pulled away and looked back at Lance, he smiled and hugged his mom quickly before we headed to the four wheeler parked in the nearby pole barn.

"I don't feel right leaving your mom." I whispered, looking down at the ground when we stood next to the four wheeler.

"Holidays are hard." He mumbled. "Dad always gets on edge around this time and it rubs off on mom. She also has this crazy idea that Luke is just going to show back up one day, but it only hurts her worse when he doesn't."

"You don't think he will?" Lance shook his head and looked over at the second four wheeler sitting in the corner of the barn.

"No, I don't. I can't get my hopes up anyway." I moved closer and wrapped my arms around his waist.

"I'm sorry I was whining about being away from Kyler for Thanksgiving, I didn't even think about Luke."

"As long as we've been together, he's been out of the picture. Why would you think about him?"

"I'm your girlfriend, I *should* think of that. He will always be a huge part of your life."

"No, he won't." He stated in a low voice. "He chose to leave, he's just a part of my past."

"Lance." I began. He shook his head and pulled away, signaling he was done with the conversation.

"The guys will be here any second. Dad will pull me away if I'm still here when he gets back." I nodded my head and climbed on the back of the ATV. Lance straddled the machine, started it and backed us out of the barn just as his friends approached.

"What?" Chopper gasped when he saw us. "You're not riding with me?"

"Too late, I guess." I teased with a shrug.

"You'll regret that. Lance is not a very safe driver."

"I'll take my chances." I giggled. Chopper shook his head before shooting off ahead of us. We all followed. I wrapped my arms around Lance's waist and held on tight, mostly because I loved the feel of him. I watched the guys ahead of us, whooping and hollering and releasing all their emotions into the wind. I was the only girl with them and they didn't act like that was awkward for them. They had accepted me into their little group without hesitation and I was only recently realizing how amazing of a thing that was.

Chapter 17

"We're just going to stay back and hang out here for a little while." Lance told Drew. His cousin's eyebrow popped up in question and he shook his head.

"Why?"

"Because we want to be alone for a bit before curfew." He shrugged nonchalantly. Drew eyed us both carefully, Chopper pushed him forward knowing that he wouldn't move on his own.

"Have a safe trip to Texas." Chopper grinned, winking at me before he climbed off the four wheeler and hurried over to give me a hug. The other boys followed suit.

"I love your friends." I giggled as they took off on the ATV's.

"So you've mentioned." He chuckled as he leaned back on the four wheeler. "They absolutely adore you." I grinned and nodded. "I won't lie, I sometimes get jealous of your relationship with them."

"What?" I gasped. "Why?"

"It's stupid, I wasn't serious."

"Yes you were." I sighed as I walked over to him. "You wouldn't have said it if you weren't."

"I'm pretty sure they would choose you over me in a heartbeat."

"No they wouldn't." I laughed. "You're being silly."

"Hopefully, we'll never have to find out."

"Agreed." I giggled as I touched his arm softly. "I had fun today."

"Me too." He pulled himself up and leaned forward on the handlebars. "But I always have fun with you."

"I'm going to miss you this week."

"Me too. What are the odds of this happening again at Christmas?"

"Hopefully it won't. I'm kind of surprised we're even going as a family, he usually doesn't like to leave the campus in case there's someone who wasn't able to go home."

"Maybe I can pay someone to stay at Christmas so I can have you for a few weeks." He teased.

"Might get expensive, are you sure I'm worth it?"

"Definitely." He reached out, pulled me towards him and moved his hands to my waist.

"Can I ask you something?" He nodded his head. "Do you really believe that Luke won't come home?" He shrugged his shoulders and pulled away. "When my mom died, I kept praying I would wake up and it would've all been a nightmare. I think I was ten when I finally stopped sitting up in my bed and staring at my door, willing her to walk in."

"It's different for me. I wasn't four when…"

"But they both chose to leave." I shrugged. "They both felt like it was the only choice, right? Caleb used to tell me I was stupid for thinking she'd come back, but I felt like he hoped the same thing. You have to, don't you?"

"No." He mumbled flatly. "He walked away on his own, because he was tired of dealing with my dad. We made a pact to protect our family, to never let him win and he backed out of that."

"I get that you're mad at him."

"Weren't you mad at your mom?"

"Still am." I chuckled drily. "There are some days that I want to hate her, other days that I miss her so bad my stomach hurts. I just...I don't understand why she chose to take her own life and I pray that I'm never that low to know why she did it."

"I could never have done what Luke did. I couldn't just up and leave my mom and Wyatt alone in that house. How can we be brothers, raised exactly the same and not have that same thing that makes me stay and him go?"

"I don't know." I sighed as I leaned against the four wheeler. "I used to get so angry at my dad around holidays and birthdays because he never even made an effort. He'd disappear and just abandon us. If it weren't for my Aunt Becky I might have never learned what a birthday party even was. Normally our Thanksgiving dinner was tombstone pizzas or grill cheese."

"I couldn't even imagine." He murmured. "But then, you probably couldn't imagine what it would be like to hear someone scream, cuss and throw things just because the steak touched his mashed potatoes."

"You're right."

"Your dad becomes absent and mine becomes withdrawn, but then he finds a bottle of liquor and makes his issues, everyone else's issues."

"Is it bad?"

"Not all the time." He shrugged. "Now though? Around the holidays mom is more emotional and so he drinks to shut it out and it's pretty bad. The tiniest thing sets him off."

"I'm sorry you have to go through that."

"Some days I think of running away, that it would be so much easier. Then I think of Wyatt growing up without someone to run interference and I...I stop being selfish."

"You could never be considered selfish." Lance laughed and shook his head.

"You don't even know Jo." He mumbled as he climbed off the four wheeler and started digging through the bag that rode on the back rack. He pulled out a blanket and two bottles of water. "I'm a selfish bastard. I'm too proud, too stubborn and most of the time, I put my needs before others."

"No, you don't. At least, you don't do that with me." Lance started to shake out the blanket and placed it on the ground. He handed me a bottle and then plopped down on the blanket.

"You make me want to be different." He stated softly. I inhaled deeply and closed my eyes.

"I don't need you to be different, I'm pretty smitten by you just the way you are." I lit as I sat down next to him.

"I really don't know how we ended up together." He chuckled as he looked back at me. "But I'm glad it happened."

"Me too."

"I just…I can't even remember life before you."

"Good." I breathed, leaning closer to him before our lips met. All the emotions of the day collided when our bodies touched. Every feeling, every thought, bad or good, we had about things in our life exploded and we explored and examined our feelings through touching and discovering.

It didn't matter that we were laying on an old blanket in the middle of a field in November. I didn't notice that the temperature had dropped to forty degrees, nor that the moon was high and nature around us was coming to life again. We were a million miles from reality and sanity right now, because together and in each other, we could forget about all the bad things that happened in our lives. We could take our heartbreak, give it to the other and mend it into oblivion. This time, when things escalated Lance didn't slow down and neither did I. We jumped in with both feet and made love again, because we could show so much better than we could say, right?

Chapter 18

"I love you Lance." I breathed in his ear as we lay in the darkness, trying to calm our racing thoughts and hearts.

"Jordan." He began as he stared back at me timidly. "I…I need some air."

"What?" I gasped, dumbfounded as Lance scurried to put his clothes on. "We're outside." I mumbled stupidly. He was dressed in seconds and off the blanket and hurrying away as if the world were on fire.

My hand covered my mouth as I fought back the tears and watched him run away from me. I didn't even know what just happened. I didn't…I couldn't breathe as the sharp pains in my stomach started again. I clutched at my midsection and let the tears fall. I was completely naked and vulnerable as I tried to figure out what had just happened.

Lance was nowhere in sight as I finally started grabbing my clothes and dressing myself. The more clothes I put on, the angrier I got. So, not only was I hurt and confused, but now I was enraged and ready to beat the Hell out of someone I loved very much. I grabbed my phone out of the four wheeler bag and dialed Maddie's phone number.

"Hey J, what's up?"

"Can you…can you come pick me up?" I stammered.

"Are you crying? Are you okay? What's wrong?"

"I don't know." I sighed. "Can I just…can you come get me and I'll explain in the car."

"Yeah. Where are you at?"

"I don't know." I sobbed.

"Cale, something's wrong. J needs me." Maddie explained urgently to my brother.

"What's wrong?" I heard Zack ask before Caleb.

"Do NOT bring them Maddie, please, I'm begging you."

"She needs *me*." Maddie murmured.

"If something is wrong, I'm going."

"Caleb please." My friend begged. "Let me handle this, okay?" I could hear words between the three of them, but finally Maddie was back.

"I'm on my way."

"Do you remember how to get to Lance's farm?"

"Yes."

"Just go that way and I'll figure out where I'm at and I'll text you."

"Okay. Are you sure you're fine J?"

"No, but…I…" I took a deep breath and tried to shove the pain and confusion into an unknown, never to be found place. The keys were still in the four wheeler so I grabbed them out and started walking. I didn't know where the Hell I was, but I could surely find a road and Maddie could use her GPS to find that road. At least, I hoped that's how it would go.

"Please hurry Maddie."

"I'm walking out the door now." I hung up the phone and looked around. Lance was nowhere to be found. I stuck the four wheeler key in my pocket and started walking the way we had originally came, hours ago. If the bastard could just walk away from me when I was naked in the middle of nowhere, than I certainly had no qualms about leaving him stranded either. Why didn't I just take the four wheeler? Knowing my luck, he'd report me for stealing it.

How could I be so ignorant? Shouldn't I have figured his game out when he completely blew me off after we screwed the first time? I mean, it only took him three months to ask me on a freaking date! What kind of sick asshole does this kind of thing to someone? He made me fall head over heels for him just for sex? I hope it was worth it for him.

I continued to grow even angrier as I stormed through the weeds and logs. I heard a noise, when I looked up, I saw Lance walking towards me. His head was down so he didn't see me when I darted behind a tree in the nearby woods.

"FUCK! I'm an idiot!" Lance yelled into the darkness as he picked up a large stick and slammed it into a tree near me. "What the fuck is wrong with me?"

Lance passed me by without realizing it. Once he was far enough away I started walking again. I continuously looked over my shoulder to make sure he hadn't spotted me yet. I never wanted to speak to Lance Bowman again in my life and I prayed Maddie would find me before he did. I kept close to the trees, hiding in their darkness so Lance wouldn't spot me easily.

"Jordan? Jordan? Joey, where are you?" He screamed fearfully into the night about ten minutes later. I kept walking, not looking back. He continued to call my name frantically. Ten minutes or so later I heard the four wheeler start. Damn it, apparently there was a spare. Against my better judgment I moved into the trees and Lance came barreling through the field, looking for me.

"Mom, I'm gonna be late." I heard him explain into his phone as he stopped the ATV and looked around. "We got into a fight and she took off. I can't find her. I messed up bad, I'm an idiot and a jerk…No, no, no I'll call as soon as she turns up." I stayed where I was, trying to calm my rapid breathing so he wouldn't hear me. He hung up the phone, looked around and then buried his face in his hands.

"What in the Hell is wrong with me?" He asked out loud. I had a lot of answers come to mind, but I bit my tongue and started walking again. It's not easy to be quiet while walking in the dark of the woods.

Lance's phone rang and he reluctantly answered it.

"I'm not leaving without her!" Lance yelled heatedly into his phone seconds after he answered. "You're wrong dad, you're wrong. I'll be home as soon as I take *her* home."

Lance slammed his phone off in frustration. At the same moment I felt something rub against the back of my leg, I looked down to see a field mouse running by. I screamed and raced out of the woods.

"Jordan! Are you okay? I was worried about you." Lance stammered as we locked eyes and he hurried to me.

"Yeah, I bet you were." I shot coldly as I started away. Lance grabbed for me, but I shook him off.

"Please get on the four wheeler and let me take you home."

"Fuck you." I hissed over my shoulder.

"What are you gonna do, *walk* home?" He laughed as he started towards me.

"Stay away." I warned. He didn't listen, so I sprinted towards the road. I prayed Maddie was nearby.

Somehow, Lance caught up with me, grabbed me and in the same movement knocked me to the ground. I screamed in shock and pain as I felt my ankle roll.

"GET THE FUCK OFF ME!"

"I didn't mean to…Jordan I'm sorry. I'm sorry." He mumbled. "I didn't mean to knock you down. I was just trying to get you to stop and listen to me. I'm sorry."

"Stay away from me. Just go home and leave me alone." I hissed as I bit down on the tears and pain that were quickly boiling to the surface.

"I'm *not* leaving you." He began as he tried to help me up. I slapped away his hand and struggled to get up. I tried to put weight on my right foot, but pain shot throughout my leg, causing me to wince and allow a small groan to escape my mouth.

"You already did." I grumbled as I felt myself teeter.

"What's wrong?"

"Like you care." I hissed as I limped away.

"Did I hurt you? Oh God, Jordan I hurt you. I'm sorry. I'm sorry. I'm sorry." He rambled in a broken voice.

"I called Maddie; she'll be here any minute to get me. You're off the hook, you can leave."

"You called Maddie? Did you tell her what happened?"

"How can I when *I* don't even know?" I asked in exasperation as I stopped and turned around to glare at him.

"I'm not letting anyone else take you home."

"You don't have a choice." I snapped.

"Wanna bet?" He asked as he grabbed me and threw me over his shoulder. "You're the biggest jerk in the world Lance. Just let me go! Put me down and let me go. I don't want to talk to you. I don't want to touch you. I don't want to fucking look at you!" I screamed as I flailed and tried to wriggle out of his tight grip. He continued to carry me like a sack of potatoes as if I weren't putting up a fight at all.

"Stop being difficult. I'll take you to Maddie, if that's what you want. But I'm not letting you walk by yourself out here. It's too dangerous."

"You're the one who's dangerous. You left me *naked* in the middle of a FIELD an hour ago. You didn't care then, so why are you pretending to care now?" I spit.

"I *do* care Jordan. I just freaked out. I care about you more than…and I don't want anything to happen to you. I know you're extremely pissed and you don't mean what you're saying."

"Yes I do. I fucking hate you."

"No you don't. You *love* me." He teased inappropriately as he stood in front of the four wheeler. He was making fun of me and I was livid. I punched him in the back as hard as I could and he fell to the ground still holding me.

"Fuck you asshole!" I shrieked through clenched teeth.

"Dammit, Jordan! Did you have to hit me?" He howled. I tried to get away but he scrambled to his feet again and grabbed me tightly as he pinned me against a tree.

"Please don't do this. Please don't freak out and be stubborn. Just calm down, get on the four wheeler, and let me take you home." He begged sadly.

"Why should I? I bared my soul to you and you took off. You left me naked, confused and humiliated in the middle of nowhere Lance. Why should I do anything you ask?"

"Because I'm begging." He stated in a broken voice as he got down on his knees in front of me. "I'm down on my knees *pleading* you to just get onto the four wheeler with me. I'm an idiot. I messed up. Please Jordan."

"I don't want to talk to you." I breathed tearfully.

"Then you don't have to. Just please let me take you home."

"Lance." I sighed.

"Jordan please. I'm dying here."

"I don't care. You really hurt me." I sobbed as I reluctantly climbed onto the four wheeler. "In more ways than one."

"I know. I'm so sorry, so incredibly sorry. I just wanted you to stop and I wasn't thinking. I just acted. God Jordan, I'm so sorry, I didn't want to hurt you in *any* way."

"What'd you think would happen when you were running away from me?"

"I *wasn't* thinking. I was scared. I freaked out."

"*You* were scared?" I retorted. "Is my body that hideous?"

"No, you're beautiful and you know that." He hissed. "We're just going so fast."

"You weren't complaining when I was sucking your dick." I growled.

"Jordan." He sighed in exasperation. "That's not…"

"What the fuck Lance? It's too fast? We've been together for four months and *now* you're saying it's too fast? You couldn't have thought of this on our first date when I was meeting your parents, or you asked me on a date for the next day? Or how about on our second date when you asked me to be your girlfriend, was it too fast then? *I* am not the one who calls *you* every night at the same time. I'm not the one who initiates dates every single Saturday and Sunday, all day. *You* are the one who has moved so fast and *now* you have a problem with it, when I've fucking fallen for you?"

"You have a problem with all that?" He asked obviously hurt by my comments.

"No. I loved it all Lance. I just don't understand…"

"Me neither. I don't know what's wrong with me. I'm crazy about you but…"

"You don't love me?" I cried. "That's just fucking great."

"It's not *that*. I…I'm just nervous about being…never mind I'm sorry Jordan. I'll take you home."

"Take me to Maddie. She will meet me as soon as I can tell her a road name."

"Tell her to go to County Highway 16, it's a crossroads about five miles up." I nodded and pulled my phone back out to text her the information. I slid it back into my pocket and clutched the back rack, I would not hold on to him. It was hard enough being this close to him, feeling how badly my body wanted to mold against him and the absolute shattering of my heart.

160

Maddie's little yellow convertible sat on the side of the road. Tears streamed down my face knowing this was the end. I had no clue what had happened, other than my heart was broken, and Lance would probably never know how badly he'd hurt me.

As soon as he stopped the four wheeler, he scurried off and turned to help me, offering me his hand as he did. I slapped it away.

"I don't need you…"

"Yes you do, you're hurt."

"Thanks to you." I cut. I bee lined for Maddie's car but Lance grabbed me and pulled me to him.

"I told you I'd never let you leave without kissing you."

"It doesn't matter now…" Lance didn't let me finish before he planted an amazing kiss on my lips.

"I do. You know?" He mumbled and I looked back at him in confusion.

"Jordan, we gotta go, Caleb is freaking out and said if I'm not there in ten minutes he's calling your dad." Maddie informed me from the car.

"I gotta go too. I'm already in a lot of trouble." He admitted. "Are we okay?"

"What?" I shrieked.

"Just promise we'll talk when you get back from Lakewood. It'll give you time to calm down and me time to figure out how to explain what's going through my fucked up head."

"What's the point? Why prolong the inevitable? I can't ever trust you again."

"Please."

"Whatever Lance, you can call me whenever you think of a fucking lie for why you're an asshole."

"It won't be a lie. I told you I'd never lie to you."

"You also said you'd never hurt me."

"Cheap shot, but I deserved it." He muttered. He kissed me on the cheek as he opened the door and helped me into Maddie's car. "I'm sorry Jo." He shut the door, got on the four wheeler and was gone before I could comprehend where I was.

Chapter 19

"What happened? Why are you limping?" My best friend asked before she put the car in drive.

"I don't even know what happened other than I think I sprained my ankle.

"What do you mean you don't know what happened?"

"We had this amazing day. AMAZING. We made love and I told him that I loved him and he acted like I told him I used to be a man. He seriously took off like I had four heads. I don't even...how can he not love me too, Maddie?" I sobbed. The pains in my stomach were getting worse and all I could do was grip my midsection and pray I didn't vomit or crap all over Maddie's perfect car.

"He freaked out when you told him that you loved him?" She asked on a long breath. "I don't understand that. It's obvious he loves you J, I don't see why he would be shocked by you saying that. Unless, do you think he was upset he didn't say it first?"

"If it were that simple, why wouldn't he just tell me that? Why would he sprint away?"

"Guys are weird." She shrugged. "Caleb wants everything a certain way. He thinks he can only hold the door for me and not the other way around. Maybe it's kind of the same thing with Lance."

"Why are you sticking up for him?"

"I'm not, I'm just trying to rationalize the situation maybe. You're not...you're not thinking clearly because he obviously hurt you. I just don't want you to act on impulse and do or say something that you'll ultimately regret. As far as I can see, you and Lance are amazing together. I'm just flabbergasted by all this."

"You and me both." I murmured with a sniffle.

"Do you want to call Alicia and ask her if he's bi polar or something?" She lit. I giggled, rolled my eyes and shook my head. It was almost one in the morning, way past both our curfews. I wasn't going to wake her up over something ridiculous that she probably couldn't explain either.

When we finally arrived at the house Caleb and Zack were waiting on the front porch. They pounced on me and both nearly lost their minds when they saw me limping. I ignored them, pushed past them and hobbled up the stairs and into my bedroom. I didn't want to see another male for a long time. Unfortunately, that wasn't possible.

Chapter 20

Lance

"Fuck, I'm such an idiot." I growled into the night air as I punched the seat underneath me. I watched as Maddie's expensive car disappeared into the night and then I turned around, gripped the throttle and tore off towards home. Maybe the speed would help clear my head before I got home and walked into Hell.

I was just about to say I love you to her, it was on the tip of tongue and she said it first. It's not how I imagined it happening and maybe that's what caused me to freak out. My heart stopped when I heard the words roll over her tongue and my stomach dropped, because in a matter of seconds, our relationship had completely changed.

In a way, I knew the second I saw her for the first time that I was in love with her, but I'd never admitted it to myself. Our relationship had been at a different level from the beginning because of that, as well, so I don't know why the thought and her words had terrified me so. I'm a Junior in High School, destined for Army boot camp directly after high school graduation, I didn't need to be putting myself in this relationship right now, right? I mean, Jordan deserved a Hell of a lot better than some farm boy from the sticks. I would never be able to give her all that she ever dreamed of and if her music ever took off, I don't think I could handle that either. All these thoughts rolled around in my head, but my heart was screaming to shut up and forget about the details, because everything would work itself out.

When my house came into view I slowed the four wheeler, pulled out my phone and looked down at it. I should call her and apologize, tell her all the fears that were floating through my head and we would fix this. I could send her a text message doing the same, but those were both the coward's way out. I should hop into my truck the second I get home and go to her, I should tell her all of this in person, because that would be the right thing to do. However, I knew my father would be waiting for me the second I pulled into the barn and chances are, I wouldn't be physically capable of leaving the house once he got a hold of me. I could hear him in the background screaming at my mother and I could not leave my mother alone with him any longer than I already had. I would never forgive myself if he laid a hand on her.

The porch lights blazed on, lighting the darkness of our country surroundings. As I steered down the long gravel lane, I could see the front door open. My father stood in the doorway blocking the light from inside and looking bigger, angrier and drunker than he ever had before. He stood there and waited for me to park the four wheeler and come out of the barn.

"What the fuck did I tell you about that little bitch?" My father growled as he flew down the steps and stood in front of me, looming like a grizzly bear.

"We got into a fight dad; she ran off, I couldn't leave her in the middle of nowhere."

"It would've served her right." He chuckled. His face clouded over again and he pointed a callused finger in my face. "I told you if you were late again there'd be Hell to pay."

"It's not like I didn't call." I mumbled. Immediately, I felt the sting of my sarcastic remark as dad backhanded me.

"You will *not* disrespect me, you ungrateful son of a bitch." He screamed, that's when I noticed the half-empty Jack Daniels bottle in his right hand and the smell of whiskey battered my senses.

"I'm sorry, I didn't mean to." I grumbled, trying my best to get out of the situation. It was days like these, when he was drinking liquor that he was at his most dangerous. Beer made him sloppy and a jerk but liquor; no matter what it was, made him worse than a caged, starving and tortured lion.

"You're done with that little bitch. You and the Callatin whore are through. Do you hear me? You will not see her, talk to her or even think about that little tramp for the rest of your life."

"Dad."

"Don't sass me!" He yelled, hitting me again. I stumbled backwards, tears pricked at my eyes, a natural reaction to the sting of his fist, but I wouldn't let him see. If he did, there would be even more Hell to pay.

"William, that's enough." Mom murmured warily from the front porch. "He called and explained everything, way before curfew. They had a fight, honey, he's had a bad enough day as it is."

"Shut the fuck up, Sara." He bellowed. My fists clenched and my jaw tightened in response. If the old man went after mom, I'd have to fight back.

"You'll get up in the morning and help me with the cattle, you've been slacking off around here and that's over with." He instructed. "You're done with the nonsense of that tramp, this farm is the only life you have and will ever need. Besides that Lance, you need to think about your future. That bitch will not settle for being a lowly housewife and you can't have anything else."

"Yes sir." I mumbled. My dad moved out of the way, he seemed to be happy with my easy submission and let me go in. I cringed when I heard him laugh to himself.

"I mean it Lance, there will be Hell to pay if I catch you with that little whore. She's nothing but trouble. You're seventeen, you should be screwing every pretty little thing in the county not being whipped by one."

I ignored him and stalked into my room. I slammed my fists into the punching bag Luke and I had hung in the corner of the room for such moments. It didn't help squelch my anger at all. Ten minutes later, I could hear dad and mom talking loudly in the living room.

"I will not have another bastard child running around here Sara. Those two are entirely too involved and they'll think a baby wouldn't be a bad thing."

"Lance is a smart boy, Jordan's a smart girl. They're not headed that way, they're…"

"Do you honestly think that little bastard tells you everything? You're an idiot; he wouldn't tell you if he was fucking that little bitch."

I turned on the television and tried to drown out the voices. I prayed Wyatt was sound asleep and hadn't heard anything. All I could focus on right now was the anger at myself for my reaction to Jordan's words.

Why couldn't I just tell her the truth? Why couldn't I tell her that I love her too?

I should leave; she told me I could stay with her if he ever hit me again. I wonder if she still feels that way after what I did. Then again, why would I introduce her to this world? I had hurt her tonight, physically and emotionally, who is to say that I'm not headed in the same direction as my father? I'm certain he wasn't always the angry, alcoholic bastard he was now.

I do love her and I can't imagine my life without her, but what if me staying away is really the best thing for her?

Chapter 21

Jordan

We were leaving for the airport at eight a.m., but I hadn't slept more than five minutes. I rolled over and looked at the clock through water filled eyes. The red numbers told me it was five a.m., Lance would be awake and in about twenty minutes he would be starting his work on the farm. He always got up at five a.m., I knew that he rarely deterred from that schedule. I loved him far too much to just let our relationship end like this. I pulled on a tee shirt, jeans, a hoodie and my favorite pair of cowboy boots before I crept outside and climbed in the car. I started the engine, backed up and headed towards the Bowman's farm. I had to know where we stood before I left. I had to know what was going on with him.

Just before their driveway, a few cows were standing in the road. As I got closer, I saw Lance on a four wheeler trying to corral them back into the fence. He was wearing a brown Carhart jacket, a brown hat and a pair of muddy coveralls. My heart swooned at first glimpse but as I stopped, put the car in park in the middle of the road I felt tears sting my eyes. He didn't look thrilled to see me, he looked pretty angry actually.

"What are you doing here Jo?" He asked quickly as he looked around nervously.

"I had to know...I..."

"You should go darlin', I've got too much to do. I'll call you tonight." He reassured me as he fought the urge to come closer to me.

"Lance, tell me what happened last night. Tell me, that you feel the same way. I'm going crazy; I'm freaking out and thinking that I'm the biggest idiot."

"Jordan, not here. Not now. I can't." He sighed, the look on his face was a cross between anger and sadness.

"We'll talk darlin', I promise. I just can't right now. Dad's been on me... I've got a lot to do today and…"

"What happened to your face?" I asked, as I moved closer and tried to touch his face.

"Nothing. One of the Mustangs got me, that's all."

"And it's already…?" I started, realizing he was lying to me. His father bellowed angrily at him from the barn and as we both looked back at him, I knew what happened.

"Lance did he…" I asked in a broken voice. "Oh my God, baby, I'm so sorry. It's all my fault."

"None of this is your fault, Jo. You need to go, he's already pissed that I came home late."

"Lance, come with me. Go to Lakewood with me, don't stay here. And don't lie to me."

"I'm not…I'm not leaving my mom and Wyatt to fend for themselves when he's in one of his moods. I can't and I won't." He stated. "You need to go, now."

"Okay." I sighed reluctantly. I wrapped my arms around him tightly and tried to kiss him goodbye, but he was stiff as a board.

"It's gonna be okay Jo, I promise." He mumbled, as I pulled away. "I'll explain everything when you get back."

I nodded my head and left. Dread filled my stomach as I murmured goodbye, because he couldn't look me in the eye and I knew he was lying.

Chapter 22

Lance

Thanksgiving day started out just like any other day. I got up before my alarm, headed out to the barn and started my chores. I fed the horses, cleaned out the stalls, fed the dogs and cats, started milking the cows and I was halfway through everything when mom came out with breakfast.

"You need to eat Lance." She sighed when she pulled up a stool and put the food down on it.

"I know. I will." I mumbled, focusing on my work.

"Were you not able to talk to Jordan last night?"

"No." I lied. I could've called her, but I didn't. I could blame my father and fear of consequences, but it was me. "They're flight probably got in late."

"I know how much you care about her bud, don't let your father take that away from you. Standing up to him, for her, will speak volumes." I nodded my head. "Lance, look at me." I didn't want to, because I knew I couldn't look my mother in the eye. "I'm sorry about this life, about the way your father treats you and your sisters, how he treated Luke. If I could change it all, I would, I wish every day that I stood up for myself and you guys a long time ago."

"Don't apologize for our life mom, it's a pretty good one."

"Most of the time, you're right, it is." She smiled. "When you let someone bully you into submission Lance, you forget how really amazing life can be though. People, a lot of people, usually get hurt along the way because you're too scared to tell them the truth and they leave, thinking they're the issue."

"Then those people don't belong in your life."

"Not necessarily. I'm lucky to have a very tight knit group of friends, if it weren't for you boys all being so close though, I probably wouldn't have those friends anymore." I shook my head as I stood up and went over to the sink nearby. I cleaned up and went over to the food she had set down. I picked up the plate and plopped down on the stool.

"Where's dad at anyway?"

"He didn't come home last night." She shrugged. My eyes flew up to hers and she looked down quickly. "I told him to leave after you went to bed, it's the first time he's ever listened."

"He hasn't called?" She shook her head and started messing with the hem of her apron. I inhaled deeply as I watched her closely. She'd been crying, probably all night and all the makeup in the world couldn't hide the bruise on her cheek. "He hit you?" My heart shattered as guilt swaddled me.

"Don't do that." She warned firmly. "None of this is your fault."

"It is mom, I…"

"Lance, he's an angry, angry man with an addiction to alcohol and power. None of this is your fault and you should not saddle yourself with the burden of it all." I shook my head and closed my eyes.

"Will you let him come back?"

"I…no, no I won't." She responded firmly. I nodded and inhaled, I prayed she was this certain when he came begging her to take him back, because he would. "Eat your breakfast bud, finish your chores and then get cleaned up. We're supposed to be at lunch at noon." I nodded my head.

"Are you sure you want to go mom? I mean…"

"It's not the first time I've gone somewhere without your father."

"I know, it's just…"

"Your sisters will be here soon, too. I asked them to come here first." She started to walk away, then turned around to look at me. "If you need to talk about what happened between you and Jo, I'm always here. I can only pray that you won't let your father bully you into staying away from her though."

"She told me she loved me and I freaked out."

"Why?" She gasped. "You love her, too."

"I do, I just…I don't know. She terrifies me mom, it's all so scary."

"That's the funny thing about love." She murmured. "Don't let your fear of getting hurt hold you back though, because she is a very special girl. The relationship you guys have is…it's something rare and amazing, I hope you realize that."

"Maybe I do." I responded. "Maybe that's what is so scary." She nodded, hugged me quickly and left me with my thoughts. Not talking to Jordan last night was incredibly hard. I went to call her at least ten different times, but I can't help but think she's better off with someone who doesn't have issues at home. Of course, if my father stays gone for good this time, I may completely change my mind.

Chapter 23

I finished my chores and by the time I was coming out of the shower, both my sisters were already in the kitchen helping my mother load everything up before heading over to my Aunt and Uncle's house. Everyone was in excellent spirits despite Luke's absence. Jenn was finally starting to show her pregnancy with a little bit of a waddle to add to the baby bump; she was beautiful and glowing.

We all loaded into mom's vehicle and headed to Drew's house. I was in another world, thinking about Jordan. I couldn't get her out of my head, all I could do was stare down at her picture on my phone.

"You okay Lance?" Jess asked, as she leaned forward. I nodded my head. "You and dad get into it?" I shook my head "Then where did the black eye come from?" I shrugged my shoulders.

"He and Jordan had a fight." Mom informed her from the front seat.

"Is that her?" Jess asked, grabbing for my phone. "She's gorgeous." I nodded. "A fight can easily be remedied, you know? You just go to her, tell her you're an idiot and beg forgiveness." I snorted and rolled my eyes. My older sister was always very blunt and always certain the man was to blame for any issues in a relationship. In this case, she was absolutely right.

"Your father grounded him from seeing her, for the time being." Mom murmured. Jenn made a sound of disgust and shook her head.

"Did you tell him to go to Hell and that's why he hit you?" I shook my head.

"Did he knock your voice box out or what?"

"He's in love with her Jess." Jenn interrupted in exasperation. "Romeo is a little thrown off by that, can't you

186

tell?" I rolled my eyes and mentally cursed Luke for leaving me in a house of women.

"And the plot thickens." She mused. "I'm interested to see how this one plays out."

"We all are." Mom admitted. "She's a good girl Jess, you will fall in love with her too."

"What does the goof crew think about her?" She asked, referring to my friends.

"They think she hung the moon." Mom giggled. "She keeps those boys on their toes."

"There has to be something wrong with her."

"Ask Wyatt what he thinks of her." Mom grinned.

"I'm going to marry her someday." He stated proudly. "Since I can't marry you mommy." Jess laughed and gave her son a side armed hug.

"Well, I guess she's got to be something if Wyatt approves. He's usually too shy and terrified to get to know anyone."

"She definitely has a way with him." Jenn admitted. "She has infinite patience, too."

"And this is the wedding singer, the girl from the lake?"

"One in the same." Jess nodded her head slowly as she continued to watch me carefully.

"If you love her bud, you should stand up for your relationship." I nodded. They were right, they were all right, but I couldn't focus on anything except for the fact that it had been over twenty four hours since I had talked to Jordan last and that it was the first time it had happened in a very long time.

Chapter 24

"It's really not the same without Jo around."

Chopper sighed loudly, after lunch. He was right, I'd been

thinking it the whole time. None of my friends knew about our

fight. As far as they knew, we were still a perfect couple. No

one had mentioned my black eye and wasn't that something?

What did it say about our friendship, or my life, if my own

friends didn't question a new bruise on my face? It was

incredibly sad that they didn't draw attention to my dad's temper.

"She is definitely the life of the party." Coop

chuckled.

"Hopefully she won't leave for Christmas." Alicia

stated. "I'm going pretty crazy without her and Maddie. I didn't

realize how much I relied on those two girls." I nodded my head.

My phone vibrated in my pocket and I looked down to see a new

text message.

Happy Thanksgiving! I miss you! Jordan had typed. I cleared it, typed back the same thing and hit send. The front door of the house flew open and my father stumbled inside. He was filthy and, probably, still intoxicated from the night before.

The entire house grew quiet as my Uncle jumped up to greet his brother. "Will, what on earth happened to you?" He asked as he helped him stand upright. My father looked back at his brother as if he didn't even recognize him. "Are you hungry? The ladies are starting to clean up the kitchen, let me have them make you a plate." My Uncle started for the kitchen and my dad followed, his eyes scanned the living room before they landed on me with such disgust that my breath hitched. I did not miss the giant, greasy hickey on his neck.

"William?" I heard my mother gasp. "What...where?" He chuckled before he threw out some hateful words. Mrs. Choupeau scurried to fill a plate with food, she was a firm believer that if you were eating then you didn't have time to cause trouble.

A skanky looking blonde with tattoos, piercings and too tight clothing stumbled into the house. "Um, can I help you?" Drew asked awkwardly as he stood up and started towards the door.

"William?" The woman called in a raspy voice, her eyes were bloodshot as she looked around the room. "William baby, where are you?"

"You need to leave now." I growled as I shot off the couch. The woman laughed as she called for my father again.

"Will baby, I thought you were taking me to dinner." She pouted, as she tried to find him. My father stumbled into the living room and laughed.

"This is it, Reta." He stated as he spread his arms wide. "Family dinner. Come on in."

"She is *not* staying." I hissed.

"You better watch your tone boy." He spit, taking one long stride and getting in my face in no time.

"I will not let you disrespect my mother." I growled back at him, I would not back down on this.

"Get out of my face."

"No, she will leave now." I demanded. "You are still married to my mother, and until that changes, she won't be anywhere around."

"Who are you...?"

"William, that's enough." My Uncle began. "Lance is right, she needs to go." My father spun around on his heel, his dark eyes piercing through his older brother.

"Go home Reta." My father spit. "Apparently, my family isn't feeling hospitable today." The woman harrumphed, but left without much of a fight. Dad shook his head and glared at the roomful of people. He didn't say a word as he grabbed a beer out of the refrigerator and went back to the table to shovel food in his face.

The entire house was awkwardly silent as we tried to figure out what just happened. The women went back to cleaning up the kitchen while everyone else piled into the family room to watch football. It only took about ten minutes before my father was joining us. He climbed into an open chair and stretched out, a beer in both hands.

"You're getting fat, Jen. You need to go on a diet, lose that ass of yours."

"William." Mom gasped.

"It's okay, mom." Jen whispered, feigning a smile. "I'm pregnant dad, that's what happens." She stated with a little laugh.

"Stay out of it Sara. Stop fucking sticking up for your bratty children." He cut. His eyes grazed over me roughly.

"I thought *you* were the good kid. I thought you were going to be the smart one, take over the farm and grow up into a son I could be proud of. Then you meet that stupid little bitch and started acting like a pussy, just like your brother." He growled. "She's just using you, dumbass. She's just another rich little tramp, trying to piss her daddy off, she's a tease just like your momma. That dumb cunt..."

"Stop it dad." I grumbled under my breath.

"Then the whore shows up yesterday morning, unbelievable. I told you that you two were done, I told you that you weren't seeing her ever again. That whore is out of your life for good. She's too fucking stupid and easy to be serious about."

"Dad."

"What would have happened had you got the little tramp pregnant, Lance? Huh? Her parents wouldn't have let her keep it, nope, it would've been dumped on us *again*. I'm not raising another bastard child, do you hear me? "

"That's enough dad." I growled as I stood up quickly and glared down at my father. I could hear the entire room gasp collectively, prepared for the worst.

194

"What are you going to do, you little pussy?" He laughed before he turned his attention to the others and began verbally assaulting Wyatt and Jess next, spouting every derogatory thing he could think of. Wyatt was in tears, which only fueled his hateful words more. He started in on Jen and her husband too, but they stood up and left.

"William, you've said enough. I think you should leave."

"Don't tell me what to do in my brother's house, woman." He hollered as he jumped up and lunged for his wife. In one swift movement, I'd gotten a good shot in on dad. Within minutes, Thanksgiving was ruined as everyone watched in shock as my father and me began beating the Hell out of each other. It was like déjà vu, like Luke and dad were beating each other senseless again; only me in my twin brother's place. No one could break us up, no matter how hard they tried.

Chapter 25

Chopper

I had never seen anything like this before in my life. How could a man beat the Hell out of his son, without blinking an eye? Lance was a beast, he'd blacked out and was focused on his father, and no one else. I'm certain he didn't hear his mother and sister pleading for him to stop. I know he didn't even feel Drew's dad or my father trying to break it up. Not a lot of people knew the Hell William Bowman had put his family through over the years, but I did, and I couldn't have been more proud of my best friend than I was at this moment.

When the cops arrived, they took one look at Lance's bloody face and handcuffed Mr. Bowman without another thought. They'd been to the Bowman farm on more than one occasion when Luke was still at home, they knew what a worthless jerk the man was. Lance didn't walk away, didn't

196

show his wounds until the cop car blazed off with his father inside.

As an officer took his statement, Lance stumbled backwards and drooped into a chair, unconscious. He was done and hurt worse than any of us could have even known. The county fire department had already been dispatched because of the domestic call, luckily they were still on scene. They rushed him to the hospital.

"Someone should call Jo." I mumbled as we were headed to the truck to follow the ambulance.

"I don't think that's a good idea." Alicia stated with a shake of her dark head. "She's in Texas and can't do anything, it'll drive her crazy."

"You know Lance better than anyone Chop," Drew began with a sigh. "He won't want her knowing about this."

"I hate to say this, but he's absolutely right."
Cooper agreed. "He needs to tell her this, not us. She may not
even know the history and…"

"Then I won't call her. I'm just saying, she needs
to know and not telling her, isn't right." Everyone nodded in a
mumbled agreement and climbed into the vehicles.

We all filed into the emergency room and quietly waited
for some sort of update on how Lance was. When Mrs. Bowman
came out sometime later, she explained that Lance would
undergo surgery to repair a tear in his lung from a cracked rib.
They would also set his broken arm and cast it while he was
under. Unfortunately, we all knew the surgery couldn't repair the
massive amount of emotional damage my best friend was
suffering.

Jordan needed to be here. Lance needed her now. He
would need her by his side to keep him sane or he would
probably disappear into the world just as Luke had. However, he

had specifically asked his mom not to call her. He begged her to make certain no one let her know what happened, he wanted to be the one to tell her about his hospital stay and surgery. I was certain he would never tell her, if possible.

Chapter 26

Lance

It took until Monday morning for them to release me from the hospital, no matter how much I begged to get out of there. I couldn't stand being laid up, mostly because I didn't know if my family was safe.

On Tuesday, dad was back in the house as if nothing had happened. I was so mad at my mother that I couldn't see straight. It didn't help matters that my Uncle spoke to the hospital staff so they wouldn't involve child and family services, like they were required too. My mother wouldn't press charges, so dad barely saw jail time or any consequences for his actions. Sometimes, living in a small town sucked. I would hope that if we were in a bigger town, where people couldn't be convinced to turn the other cheek, Luke would still be here and my father would be in a prison cell somewhere.

"Uncle Lance?" Wyatt asked later that night. "Are you ever going to see Jordan again?"

"I hope so buddy."

"Why doesn't Grandpa like her?" He questioned incredulously as he climbed up and sat next to me on my bed.

"I don't know."

"Me neither." He sighed as he put a chubby little hand up to his face and rested his head there. "I love her."

"Me too buddy." I smiled sadly. Wyatt sat there quietly for a few minutes, which was an eternity for the little guy, I'm sure. Then he looked back up at me with sad, cobalt eyes. Sometimes, it was as if I was transported back in time and I was looking at my twin brother ten years ago.

"Uncle Lance? Will you promise me that you won't fight with Grandpa anymore? It was just like it was with Uncle Luke and I don't want Grandpa to kill you too."

"Grandpa didn't…"

201

"Promise me?"

"I promise bud." I murmured. Wyatt hugged me before he snuggled down into my bed and closed his eyes.

I fell back against the headboard and swiped my hands over my face. We were all walking on eggshells, hoping not to irritate dad again. I was certainly in no shape to defend myself, or anyone else, for that matter. Now I'd just promised Wyatt I wouldn't fight anymore and I don't know if I can keep that promise. If he goes after mom, Wyatt or Jess I'll go for his throat. I hate that I can't protect my family from that monster. Unfortunately, I have no choice but to abide by my father's rules until I figure out something else. Until then, life was going to be Hell and I can only pray that Jordan will understand and wait for me.

Chapter 27

Jordan

"Hey Lance." I breathed nervously into the phone on Sunday afternoon. "I'm home from Texas. I was hoping we could talk today before I have to go back to the dorms. I just…I don't like how we left things and…I'll be around, I hope to hear from you soon." I ended the call and threw my phone onto my bed. I busied myself with unpacking my suitcase and getting a load of laundry ready.

My stomach was still acting up, I'd get sporadic sharp shooting pains that would have me doubled over in pain. I'd been fine all day, working on anything to keep my mind off Lance, when I howled from the shock.

"Did you miss me?" Zack lit as he sauntered into my bedroom. "What the…are you okay?" He asked as he rushed to my side. "What's wrong?"

"I don't know." I whispered breathlessly. "My stomach." I was gripping my belly, squeezing my eyes shut in hopes that it would stop the pain, but no such luck. Zack grabbed my arm and led me to the bed. He helped me down and then knelt in front of me.

"Where does it hurt?" I made a generic gesture to include my entire mid-section.

"Did it just start?" I nodded my head. "Do you still have your appendix?" I nodded my head again. Zack looked at me as he absentmindedly laced his fingers through mine and let me squeeze his hand to redirect the pain. "Did you eat something bad?"

"No, I don't think so." I took a breath as the pain eased. "Maybe I have to poop." Zack burst out laughing.

"I'm so glad you feel comfortable enough around me to say that."

"Sorry." I giggled as I buried my face in my hands. "Momentary lapse of sanity." Zack chuckled and shook his head.

"You okay now?" I nodded my head. "You should probably get checked out if it was that bad."

"I'm fine Zack, if it happens again I'll get it checked out." He looked at me warily but nodded his head.

"What are your plans for the day?"

"Getting all my crap together to go back to the dorms tonight." I shrugged. "Nothing big."

"Jets are playing in about twenty minutes, do you want to watch with me?"

"Absolutely." I giggled. "Like I turn down anything sports related."

"Good." He chuckled. "I think Caleb and Maddie are making a food run into town. Do you have a preference?"

"Steak." I grinned. "I'm starving."

"That's seriously sexy J." He admitted flirtatiously. "I love a girl who eats."

"You love all females Zack, you're not fooling me." He made a funny face before he shrugged and nodded.

"I'll put in your food order, but there's no guarantee of its safety if you're not down there when it gets here." I rolled my eyes and nodded. Zack strutted out of my room and I couldn't help but laugh. I was seriously lucky to have that goofball in my life.

I grabbed my phone off the bed to see that I had missed a call from Lance. Dang it. I pushed the voicemail notification and put it on speaker.

"Hey Jo, I uh, sorry I didn't call you sooner. One of the farmhands got hurt so things have been pretty hectic and

I've had to pick up a lot of the slack. I, um, I'm headed to bed now because I've got to get up an hour earlier to get everything done before school. I guess I'll talk to you tomorrow, maybe." He exhaled a long breath. 'Don't worry about us, okay? I'm sorry about that night, I was an idiot. We're okay, darlin', please believe that."

I tried calling him back, but he didn't answer. It was awfully nice of him to tell me that we were fine, thinking his apology was enough to explain how he just abandoned me in the middle of nowhere like I meant nothing to him. I was livid.

For the rest of the week we played phone tag and he wasn't even bothering with leaving me a voicemail or texting me.

Are we doing anything this weekend? I texted him on Friday. He immediately responded.

I'm going deer hunting with the guys.

I know. Chopper invited me.

Oh, he didn't tell me. I'm sorry Jo, I'm swamped with the farm responsibilities and keeping up with my schoolwork. I just...I can't afford to waste my weekend.

Waste? Thanks.

I didn't mean it like that.

Sure. I didn't send anything else and he didn't respond.

For the next three weeks, I only talked to him via text message and even those were scarce. He was rolling out one excuse after the next. If I called, it went directly to voicemail. My stomach pains were still coming and going, but I attributed them to my stress over my relationship with Lance. It also didn't help that my period was late. We had been so caught up in our emotions that night, we were stupid and didn't think about using protection.

I felt like a blessed idiot. I was heartbroken. The more I thought about everything though, the more pissed off I got. So, without hesitation, I dialed his number and when it was dismissed to voicemail, it only fueled my anger.

"You know what Lance? When you decide you have time for me and grow the fuck up then you can give me a call, but it'll only be so that I can laugh in your face!" I stated in a low, precise southern drawl before I hung up on his voicemail. I wanted to punch him in the face for hurting me so badly. And honestly, I wish I had thought of something a little more clever to say.

Chapter 28

The following evening at seven p.m. my phone rang and Lance's gorgeous face popped onto the screen. My heart soared at the thought of him coming to his senses. My threat had worked, he was realizing he was about to lose me. I calmed myself down as I answered.

"Hey." I breathed.

"Miss Jordan?" Wyatt asked softly on the other end.

"Wyatt? Are you okay?"

"Yes ma'am. I miss you." He took a deep breath and his voice became muffled.

"I miss you too, bud."

"When are you gonna come see me again?" He asked sadly. "I miss you and so does Uncle Lance."

"I don't think Uncle Lance misses me buddy."

"Yes he does. He's sad because he can't see or talk to you anymore because Grandpa..."

"Wyatt? Who are you talking to?" I heard Mr. Bowman yell in the background. "Get off the phone NOW!"

Within seconds, I heard Wyatt squeal and cry before the line went dead. I tried to call back, but I was shaking too much. Finally, when I called back it rang four times before someone answered.

"Do not call this number again." Mr. Bowman hissed on the other end. "Lance got a piece of ass and that's all he wanted. Stop calling here and torturing Wyatt." The phone went silent. My whole body shook as tears rolled down my face. There was so much venom in his voice that I couldn't focus on anything but that. I could only pray Wyatt was okay, because I certainly wasn't calling back. I thought about calling Alicia, but that would probably make the situation worse, right?

211

I lay awake in my dorm room later that night, staring up at the ceiling and thinking about everything. Mr. Bowman said Lance had gotten a piece and was done, if that were the case and I was truly pregnant, what in the Hell would I do then? Would he come back to be with me, just because of that or would I see his true colors?

My text message indicator went off at almost midnight, startling me out of my haze. I looked down at the phone and swiped the screen to see a message from Lance.

I saw you called a few times today, everything okay?

Wyatt called me.

He shouldn't have done that.

Your dad caught him and there was a lot of screaming, is he okay?

He's already asleep. I would know if there was something wrong though. I'm sorry he called you, he really misses you.

Do you?

Of course I do. He replied.

Your dad said I was just a piece of ass to you and that I shouldn't ever call you again. Is that true?

Why would you believe that?

You've screwed me twice and disappeared afterwards. I told you that I loved you and you ran off like your cock was on fire, that's why I would believe that. Not to mention, you won't even have a real conversation with me.

I've been swamped, I thought you understood that. I can't talk.

You're talking now.

I'm texting now. I'm not supposed to be on the phone after eight, if I get caught I'll get grounded.

Yup, I bet that's it. Lance didn't respond and I just left it hanging there. I put the phone back on my dresser, rolled over and stared at the wall. Tears rolled down my cheeks, I closed my eyes and just let them fall.

I had given Lance my virginity a long time ago, but more recently, I had given him the last four months of my life. Every weekend was his, every night was his. I handed over my heart and soul to him and he tossed them in a dumpster as if none of it mattered. As if I didn't matter at all to him. His father said I was just a piece of ass, which made my stomach start hurting again. I hugged my midsection and tried to quiet my crying so my roommates didn't wake up. I had fallen so hard for Lance Bowman, head over heels, in such a short amount of time that he had been able to play me like a fiddle. I was so naïve, so stupid and so incredibly devastated.

My first love, my first real heartbreak. I didn't know how I'd ever heal from such a horrible blow. After everything I'd been through in the last year with guys, I was unsure that I could ever trust anyone else again in my life.

He wasn't even man enough to end it himself either. Unfortunately, that meant my head could convince my heart that there was still something between us, that there was possibly hope for our relationship and my shattered heart.

Chapter 29

Lance

"No Jordan tonight?" Chopper asked as he followed the rest of the guys up to the front porch. I shook my head and looked down at the ground.

"I told you guys I wasn't doing anything tonight. I can't. I'm technically still grounded, but I have way too much crap to do here."

"According to your momma, you're cleared to hang out with us tonight. No one said we were leaving." Chopper shrugged with an ear splitting grin. I rolled my eyes. It would be nice to hang with my friends again, but it wasn't right that Jordan wasn't here. I'm also certain the guys won't stop reminding me that she's not here either.

"I'm really just not in the mood." I sighed, scrubbing my face with my good hand as I leaned back against the porch post.

"We know." Coop responded. "We're here to fix that."

"You've been talking to that little bitch, haven't you?" Dad growled as he stalked to the house and got up in my face.

"No." I responded. He reeled back and punched me square in the jaw.

"Do not lie to me." He spit as he held my phone up in the air. Crap, apparently I'd dropped it without realizing it. "You've got that little brat nephew of yours calling her for you, too. You thought you'd get out of it that way right?"

"No sir."

"I told you to stay away from her. I made it clear that you two were through. That little bitch is turning you into a disrespectful, lazy punk and it goes no further."

"I have tried…" I began.

"You're a pussy." He spit as he shoved me backwards and strode into the house. My friends just stood there, looking around in shock.

"You okay?" Chopper asked. I nodded my head. "Let's get out of here before he comes back."

"William!" Mom screamed before there was a crashing sound inside. Wyatt began screaming hysterically just as my father raced out the door with his rifle and a nine millimeter in hand. I smacked straight into his chest as I tried to race inside. He shoved me out of the way.

"If you won't stay away from her, I'll make certain she can't come near you."

"Mr. Bowman." Chopper began as he yanked me off the ground and scurried after my father.

"I'll show that little whore what it's like to be with a real man and then I'll teach her to stay the fuck away from you and this family."

"It's a closed campus Bo, he won't get passed security."

"Security?" Dad roared with laughter. "Alicia texted you earlier to say that Jordan was playing at a bar in town, no security there." He was at his truck, opening the door.

"You're not going near her." I hissed.

"No, *you're* not going near her. I'm going to find your little girlfriend, fuck her brains out and then as she's sucking my dick, I'm going to put an end to the bitch." I charged towards him and tackled him to the ground.

Chapter 30

Chopper

My best friend was straddling his father, fists flying and there was no doubt that he didn't know what he was doing. Once Mr. Bowman threatened Jordan's life, Lance lost all sense of sanity and attacked.

"Coop, call 9-1-1." I spit as I started towards the fight.

"Already did."

"Aunt Sarah needs an ambulance." Drew announced breathlessly as he raced outside. "My phone is in the car and the house phone won't work. He cut the line."

"They're on their way." Coop advised as he looked back at me in disbelief. Drew went back inside to be with his Aunt while Sawyer, Coop and I approached Lance from behind. I grabbed his arms and pulled him back and up with the help of the others. He was struggling to go back at his dad, but I held tight and Sawyer stood in front of him.

Mr. Bowman was moving slowly on the ground, trying to get his bearings. It didn't look like he would be getting up any time soon.

"Chill out Lance, you got him. He's not going anywhere."

"I won't let him go near her."

"Cops are on their way. He's not going anywhere." Sawyer stated.

"I will kill him if he goes near her." Mr. Bowman chuckled before he pulled himself off the ground.

"You're too much of a pussy to stop me. That little bitch will beg me…" Lance fought loose and charged again. Mr. Bowman grabbed his rifle off the ground and slammed the butt of it into Lance's head, before he could land a punch. My best friend stopped suddenly and fell backwards. Sawyer caught his limp body before it hit the ground. "Dumb ass." Mr. Bowman spit as he tried to climb into the truck.

"You're not going anywhere." I stated flatly. "The cops are coming down the lane now."

"Fuck you fat ass." He hissed as he grabbed the back of my head and slammed it into the truck.

Chapter 31

Sawyer

Self-preservation. I was not being a pussy if I was protecting myself and the others from getting murdered by the psychotic, piss drunk bastard that had just taken out two of my best friends. The cops would stop him before he got too far anyway, I would just make sure he didn't attack Coop or I and that was good enough, right?

Chopper was unconscious near the truck tires and as Mr. Bowman slammed the door and started the old Ford, Coop did everything he could to move Chopper out of the way. By the time Mr. Bowman was peeling out of the gravel, Cooper had gotten our friend away from the tire tread.

The truck tore past us and went straight past the barns, through the barbed wire fence that kept the cattle in and was gone before the cops even realized what happened.

"What in the Hell?" Connor Cooper questioned when he slid to a stop and jumped out of his police car.

"Mr. Bowman strikes again." Coop answered drily. "He attacked Lance, went inside and apparently attacked Mrs. B, then came back out with a pistol and rifle. He threatened to rape and kill Jordan and Lance flipped out."

"That's him in the truck?" Coop nodded. His brother grabbed his radio on his shirt and talked into it. "We've got a runner, if we're lucky he'll bottom out in the creek out there."

"I think he's headed into town to one of the bars, wherever Jordan's band is playing tonight." I stated just as the first responders and fire department arrived, they immediately split up to figure out who needed what. They helped me out from under Lance and got him to wake up.

"I'll call Alicia and find out where." Drew interjected as he came up behind us.

"You need to call your parents and tell them what happened, he may show up there." Connor instructed. "Chop's mom needs to be called too, have your mom do it." Drew nodded and called Alicia first, he got the name of the bar and then asked to talk to his mom.

"Isn't anyone going to go after him?" I asked in shock, realizing none of the police cars had left.

"He'll come out at another jurisdiction, they'll be waiting for him at every possible spot. We've got a squad headed to Callatin and four more headed to the bar to wait him out." Connor informed us.

This was the most ridiculous thing I'd ever witnessed in my life. I couldn't believe that Lance was a product of that man, nor that he was even still allowed near his own family. I looked around, taking it all in as the paramedics arrived and the fire department helped them bring Mrs. Bowman and Wyatt out of the house. Four people were loaded up on stretchers and taken to the hospital, all because of one drunk asshole of a man.

Chapter 32

Jordan

"So our show is cancelled." Izzy Dramen stated matter of factly on the other end of my phone. "The bar called to say there is a man hunt through town for some crazy drunk, they've shut every bar and business down in town until they capture him."

"Is that a joke?" I gasped.

"That's what I asked too." She chuckled. "But I turned on the television and it's all over the place. They're not releasing names yet or anything, but they are on the lookout for a 1970's style red Ford truck. Supposedly the guy is a bad drunk, he attacked four different people and then took off running."

"Oh my God." I gasped, a picture of one of Lance's farm trucks popped into my head. Could it be Lances dad? Surely I would've heard something from someone. Alicia would have called me, right? Because chances are, Lance was one of the people he had attacked.

"What channel?"

"Five, four and two. Whoever thought this Podunk town would take over the St. Louis stations."

"No doubt." I murmured as I hurried to find the television remote. I turned it on, but I couldn't see or hear much. I stared at the television hoping to catch a glimpse of Lance, only because it had been so long since I'd last seen him. "I'll talk to you later."

I looked down at my phone, searching the message and call list, just in case I'd missed something. I hadn't. I texted Lance, against my better judgment, but my stomach was hurting so bad that I just knew he was involved in this whole thing somehow.

Something on the television made me think of you.
I hope you're okay.

I stared at the screen willing him to respond, but of course, he didn't.

Please tell me this truck I'm seeing on the television doesn't belong to Lance's dad. I texted to Alicia, she didn't respond either. I just plopped down on the bed and glued myself to the television. Surely, they would give me some type of information and I would know for sure if Lance was safe.

Chapter 33

Alicia

How was I sitting in the ICU waiting room with my family and friends again, just weeks after we were all hanging out downstairs impatiently waiting to hear how Lance was doing? It was like déjà vu. This time Lance, Chopper and Aunt Sarah were all in ICU until they got them stable from their head trauma. Wyatt was fine, terrified, but fine.

"Jordan texted me. The manhunt is all over the St. Louis news channels." I mumbled to my brother as I stretched out and leaned my head against the wall behind me.

"Did she know it was Uncle Will?"

"I think she has an idea." I showed him my screen. "I'm not responding. I should. She needs to be here, but I also don't want to put her in danger. If he was threatening to go after her, he may be waiting outside thinking she'll show up here and the cops don't even know it yet."

"You're right." He nodded as he inhaled and exhaled slowly. "Lance wouldn't want her here anyway, you know that, right?"

"I don't care what he wants. She needs to be here. He needs her."

"Maybe so, but he'll never admit it." Drew shrugged. He was absolutely right and I hated that. I wouldn't respond to her message, I would just play dumb because it was too dangerous and if Jordan learns Lance was protecting her then she would blame herself for the situation before us. It could also scare the daylights out of her and she'd bail on Lance, and me, for that matter, forever. I was certainly torn.

Aunt Sara was released from ICU after two days, but remained in the hospital because she was having dizzy spells.

Chopper had a slight concussion and once his memory returned

he was released to his parents. Lance was still in ICU,

unconscious because of the medication. They were trying to get

his pain under control since he'd suffered a concussion, whiplash,

broken ribs and nose, and he had also had his arm rebroke. He

was an absolute mess.

Uncle Will had been caught outside of the bar Jordan was

supposed to perform at. He was arrested and being held, but the

charges were pending. We were hopeful that Aunt Sara would

keep the order of protection this time, but we'd all been through

this before. Too many times.

A week later, when Lance was finally released from the

hospital, no one had enlightened Jordan to the situation and I

wasn't about to be the person who did. Uncle Will was still in

jail and his entire family had moved into my house until they got

the farm security system updated. How was this the life my

cousins and Aunt lived? It was something out of a bad Lifetime movie, it shouldn't be there actual reality. They were too good. I wanted to scream at my Aunt for allowing him back in the house, for letting it continue for so long, but I also had no clue how scary it was to be on my own after being with someone for so many years. Love was a scary thing.

Chopper's family wasn't pressing charges, even though they should. The State was prosecuting this time, because of Uncle Will's violent history. The fact that had taken so long to happen was pretty sad, we're absolutely lucky he hadn't killed anyone yet.

I was too terrified to tell Jordan any of this, though. Who would really want to be a part of this life? My friend had lived a pretty sheltered life and to throw her in the middle of this, to let her know her life could be in danger if she stayed with Lance or was near me when my Uncle came around, could make her totally abandon me and my cousin. I couldn't accept that. Jordan was like a sister to me, but she was so much more to Lance. He needed her, but the thought of her running terrified, like any sane girl would, kept me from telling her everything. Losing Jordan would do more damage to Lance Bowman than all the physical

and emotional trauma Uncle Will had unleashed on him.

Chapter 34

Zack

"Hey Kaya," I greeted the short blonde with a sweet smile. She grinned back, her face going flush instantly.

"Hey Zack, what are you doing in the girl's dorm on a Friday night?"

"Better question would be, who is the lucky girl?" Sage Qualls purred as she came up behind me and wrapped her arms around my waist.

"No hot date tonight, Sage?" I asked drily as I took her hands off me.

"You asking?"

"Nope, I have plans already." I stated. She put out her bottom lip in a pout, I rolled my eyes and looked over at

Kaya. "You seen J? I was told she was in her room, but I can't find her."

"About an hour ago." Kaya shrugged. "We were hanging out for a bit, then she said she had to get ready for a date with Lance." My eyes narrowed in confusion, before I shook my head and shrugged my shoulders. According to Alicia, Jordan and Lance hadn't talked in weeks. That could always change I guess, but something didn't feel right.

"I thought she was hanging with us tonight." I sighed. "Guess we're not as good as Bowman."

"Whatever." Sage cackled, rolling her eyes as she pushed Kaya out of my view and stood in front of me. "A common hobo is better than that redneck townie."

"Sage." I began.

"Especially if Jordan is standing *you* up for him."

"Trust me, if J had plans with me Sage, she wouldn't even contemplate skipping out on them." I drawled with a wink as I turned on my heel and walked off. "Thanks Kaya, see you around."

"Bye Zack!" She called after me. I knocked on Jordan's dorm room door again, but there wasn't an answer. The doors in this place were not made very well at all, a couple quick jerks of the knob and the wood slid apart and I was inside the room.

No one was there, but I went inside anyway. All the dorm rooms were considered suites. Three students to each room, connected by a bathroom and a living room type of room, and another dorm room on the other side. There was no one around and a quick look through Jordan's side of the room, showed me that she wasn't around.

I left the room, closing the door behind me as I typed out a quick text to Caleb.

J's not here. Kaya said she had a date with Bowman.

BS She's not home. Where in the Hell is she?

I'll find her

I didn't know the whole story of what happened between Jordan and Lance, I'm not sure Jordan even knows it all. And no matter how high I turned up the Bentley charm, Alicia wasn't saying anything more than Lance was having a lot of issues at home, but he was still devoted to Jordan. That had to be a load of crap, but I couldn't understand why Alicia wasn't telling the truth.

I left the female dormitory and headed to the athletic building. Normally Jordan would run, lift weights, hit the punching bag or go to the batting cages to hit balls and I was really hoping that's where her confusion had taken her this time.

I broke into a jog as I crossed the sidewalks and grass. Crazy thoughts whirled through my head about the direction Jordan could be headed in. It was no secret that she was really into Lance Bowman. Although he wasn't her first boyfriend, he was definitely her first love. Her mother was manic depressive, which meant Jordan could very well inherit those traits.

I used my key card to get into the fitness center and heard the beautiful sound of metal hitting leather. I closed my eyes and inhaled deeply. Thank goodness she was using this to relieve her frustrations. I jogged the rest of the way to where the indoor batting cages were set up. Old school rock n roll blared from her phone as she was dressed in black yoga pants and a purple tank top, helmet on her head as she sang along and swung at the balls being shot her way. I heard her grunt and scream as her bat connected with the ball.

"You're going to hurt yourself." I announced drily. She ignored me. I walked over to where her phone sat and turned the music off.

"Go away Zack."

"What'cha doing?"

"What does it look like I'm doing?"

"Hitting practice on a Friday night, even I'm not that dedicated."

"Can't be the best if you're not." She muttered.

"We're headed towards St. Louis in a few, you're going with us."

"I am busy."

"Maddie wants to go see the lights at Our Lady of Snows, or whatever it is, and Caleb doesn't want to go alone. I refuse to be a third wheel by myself."

"There are a hundred girls in the dorms right now who would chew their arm off to be your date tonight Zack."

"Only a hundred?" I scoffed. "I must be losing my touch." She rolled her eyes and looked back at me.

"I'm not really in the Christmas mood Zack. I'm not going."

"There will be Krispy Kreme donuts involved." I sing songed. She stopped what she was doing and shook her head with a laugh. "Please J?"

"I am really not in the mood to be around anyone right now."

"Don't do this. Do NOT let some asshole ruin a minute of your life because he's too stupid to see how fantastic you are."

"Zack." She sighed as she lifted her bat to hit another ball.

"Stop feeling sorry for yourself. You're letting that bastard win and you are better than that."

"I'm not."

"You are. You lied about where you were, for one. You're in here by yourself on a Friday night when you should be hanging out with your friends. Get over it."

"I can't just get over it. I'm so pissed at myself and at Lance that I just want to beat the Hell out of everyone right now."

"I get that." I shrugged as I walked over to the pitching machine and shut it off. I grabbed a five gallon bucket and started picking up the balls while she stood there staring at me in disbelief. "You gonna help me?" She rolled her eyes, took off her helmet and began picking up balls as well.

"Do you get that I don't want to be around you right now Zack?" She asked, her voice full of pain and anger.

"What did I do?"

"You and Lance are just alike. You do shit like this all the time without any repercussions. You have sex with a girl and then high tail it right after, you don't care who you hurt as long as your cock gets what it wants."

"I am nothing like Lance Bowman." I mumbled evenly, feeling like she had just slapped me across the face. "If I had a good girl in front of me, I sure as Hell wouldn't ditch her without so much as a text message."

"How do you know if you have a good girl when you're too busy trying to get into their pants, rather than getting to know them?"

"Jordan." I sighed as I put down the bucket and walked over to her. "I found a girl who I thought was a good one, I really cared about Ellie and she turned out to be a different person than she portrayed. She hurt me, but you never saw me lash out at you, did you?" She looked down and shook her head. "If Lance used you for sex, he wouldn't have put as much work into it as he did. There has to be something that we don't know about. I'm not sticking up for him, because he's an idiot for treating you like this."

"How can you…how can you do that without having any feelings whatsoever."

"Oh there's plenty of feelings." I drawled flirtatiously, she looked away quickly so I moved closer to her.

"These girls use me for a million different reasons and not one of them know the real me, despite what they think. I may have a bad reputation because I go along with it, I'll be the scapegoat, but ninety percent of those girls find me J."

"Because you have a reputation." She snapped.

"Maybe." I shrugged as I took her hand in mine. "I don't completely ignore the girls though, I'm not a complete asshole to them J. I'm not saying I'm perfect, I just…I'm not as bad as you believe me to be."

"I know you're not bad Zack." She murmured as she looked down at our entwined fingers. "I just…I'm sorry. I feel like such an idiot, like I'm so naïve for being blindsided by this."

"You're not an idiot. It's part of life, everyone goes through it at some time. What is important is how you react to it, how you dust yourself off and get back up from it."

"What if I don't want to get back up from it?" She sighed.

"I don't see Jordan Donaldson letting someone beat her." I chuckled. "You're a tough girl, but you're too competitive to let anyone think they beat you."

"True." She admitted with a little giggle.

"Come on J, there's so much we can do to keep your mind off things. Please go with us tonight."

"Fine." She sighed. I wrapped her in a quick, excited hug and smiled down at her.

"It gets better, I promise." She nodded her head and hugged me back. "Let's go before Caleb calls security to find us."

She broke our hug and headed to grab her stuff. I followed and as she was pulling on a Cardinal hoodie, I grabbed her things up. I kind of enjoyed holding her hand and carrying everything would keep my mind off it, right?

"Thanks Zack." She murmured as she leaned into me. "And I really do know you're not bad." I laughed only because I didn't know how else to respond. "I just…I wish you didn't…" My phone rang, Caleb's ringtone blared through the night.

"We're headed towards the house." I sighed into the phone.

"You found her?"

"Yes sir." I lit.

"Good, she's going with us tonight then?"

"Yup."

"Good, maybe she'll see you'd treat her better than Bowman ever could or would."

"Caleb." I hissed.

"You don't have me on speaker, do you?" He chuckled.

"No, but…"

"If she knew, Bowman wouldn't even be an option." Caleb stated quickly. "I'll tell Maddie you guys are on your way." He hung up the phone without saying goodbye, something he did often to anyone that wasn't Maddie.

"I don't understand what I did wrong." She mumbled, hugging herself tightly as her house came into view. I looked back at her quickly, wondering what she was talking about. The look on her sad face was a dead giveaway.

"You did nothing wrong, I'm certain."

"Well I wish Lance would tell me that."

"You can't let one guy do this to you, J."

"He's not just any guy."

"C'mon, let's go to the house and you can change before we head out."

"I don't want to go."

"You don't have a choice." I stated evenly.

"You're going." I shrugged. I wasn't letting her out of this. She would go and she would have fun.

And she did. We went to see the lights, hung out at the mall for a bit before we went to the movie theater. We swung through the donut place on our way home. I'm certain that not one time she thought about Lance Bowman or her heartbreak. I made sure I spoiled her rotten, that I made her laugh and have a blast. Now, if only she could see that as something she wants on a regular basis, we would both be happy.

Chapter 35

Alicia

I sat on my bed and watched Jordan closely. She was lost in her thoughts, staring at her computer screen as if she was studying hard. I knew better. She was supposed to be writing a term paper, but she wasn't getting anything done. And I knew why. It was completely obvious that Lance's situation was killing her; the worst part being she knew nothing about it. She was devastated, depressed, heartbroken, angry and beside herself. She won't admit it though. Hell, half the time she tells people he's busy with the farm and they see each other when he has time, other times she breaks down and says he's blown her off.

I wish I could tell her the truth. I wish she knew even a little of the Hell that Lance had been through since they last talked. I wish she knew more people in town, could hear the gossip Lance's father was out on bond but there was a no contact order out where he couldn't come near any member of his immediate family, because then she would know the truth and it wouldn't have come from me.

I wish I could tell her everything, but I promised Lance. I swore his secret would stay within the family and that Jordan would never know. He said he was just trying to protect her. Unfortunately, it was alienating her in the meantime.

I thought about dropping hints to Jordan, telling her that Aunt Sara, Wyatt and Lance are all staying at the house with us, because Aunt Sara is in no condition to take care of Lance. He can't do much, even though he tries. I really want to accidentally invite her over so that she can see Lance for herself and he'd have to explain then, but I can't be that devious.

It's not fair for her to think she did something wrong. It's not fair for Jordan to suffer like this and believe that Lance doesn't care about her. I know he loves her; that much is painfully obvious. But he won't listen to reason and therefore my roommate is left in the dark and absolutely miserable.

Chapter 36

Jordan

"The devil went down to Georgia, he was looking for a soul to steal." Lane Holloway sang the Charlie Daniels classic into the microphone one Saturday night as I let loose on the fiddle nearby. Everyone went wild as I showed my hidden talent to the crowd at The Tubes, a college bar close to the academy.

"Ladies and gentleman, give it up for the one and only, Miss Jordan Donaldson!" Lane introduced me to the crowd with his thick Australian accent once we'd finished the song. I grinned and giggled to myself, it never ceased to amaze me how that accent wasn't ever noticeable when he was singing.

We took a quick break and I joined my underage friends and brother at the bar for a quick drink.

"That was freaking awesome!" Caleb exclaimed as he hugged me tightly.

"Yeah, and I hate country music." Zack drawled in his thick New York accent as he enveloped me in a bear hug as well.

"Then why'd you come?"

"Don't listen to him, Jordan. He's a closet redneck." Alicia giggled. "You were amazing up there."

"Thanks." I shrugged nonchalantly. I couldn't stop grinning; I was on top of the world and had temporarily forgotten my heartache.

I turned around to survey the crowd, it was standing room only and they all loved my band. It was hard to see anyone I knew in the craziness of it all but, suddenly; I recognized a face at the back of the bar. He was standing against a wall, drink in hand and wearing dark, worn out blue jeans, a hunter green ribbed sweater, and a broke in baseball cap pulled down low over his eyes. His cousin, Drew, was standing next to him as they skimmed the crowd too. My eyes locked with those sad brown ones and I felt my confidence recede quickly.

"You got a boyfriend sexy?" A tall, dark headed college boy whispered into my ear as he handed me a bottle of beer and snapped me back to reality.

"Not at the moment." I drawled with a wink.

"Well you can tell everyone that you do now." He whispered confidently as he gently touched my bare arm.

"I'm not that easy sweetie." I cut flirtatiously as I walked quickly to the exit, where I had last seen Lance and Drew. They were gone; I raced outside and didn't see them anywhere. I shivered as the cold, December air hit me. I was only wearing a hot pink, shirred tank top that was dangerously low and a dark pair of super tight jeans, I knew I looked hot, I had been getting hit on all night long by college boys, even though I was only sixteen, they were clueless. I wondered if he'd seen all the attention I was getting, if he'd been jealous and that's why he left so quickly. I didn't understand why he was there in the first place or why he left without acknowledging me. I looked down at my watch and realized it was close to curfew.

I was devastated, again. With a flip of my long, auburn hair, I ducked back into the bar and headed to the stage.

My band, Down Under, started our last set for the night and I quickly went back to being a confident vixen who could have anything she wanted. My music always transformed me and was extremely therapeutic, as well.

It was last call and the bar was still packed, begging us to continue, but we couldn't. We broke everything down and thirty minutes later, we joined my friends outside.

"I'm not ready to call it a night." Lane said as he looked around and eyed the various drunk girls hanging around the parking lot, searching for a good time.

"You can so do better." I groaned, shaking my head in disbelief.

253

"I know, but they're good enough for tonight." He grinned as he sauntered over to an oriental girl, who was incredibly overdressed for the bar. Two minutes later, his arm was around her waist and he was headed to our band's van with her.

"I guess we're going for breakfast." Collin chuckled.

"Oh, I am so in. I am starving." I gushed, realizing my stomach was growling.

"What a surprise, Jordan's hungry." Maddie lit.

"You and Izzy can ride with us, Collin." Caleb advised as he jerked his head towards Kyler's Chevy Tahoe.

"You rock." Izzy giggled as she headed towards the silver SUV.

"Jordan, ride with me?" Keller asked as he held out his hand towards me.

"Keller." I sighed hesitantly.

"The Tahoe's full." He grinned smugly as he opened the door to his yellow Porsche boxster.

"Did you plan that?" I asked with a playful glare.

"You'll never know." He flirted as he walked to the driver's side. I shook my head and rolled my eyes as I watched him closely. I was crazy for not jumping on this chance, for keeping him wanting me. Keller was gorgeous in his black argyle sweater and dark stonewashed, snug fitting jeans. His sun streaked, shaggy blonde hair hung in his eyes, but there was no hiding that gorgeous, boy next door look.

"I love watching you perform. You're like a completely different person up there."

"Thanks, I think." I responded with a quiet giggle. I stared out the passenger window as Keller pulled onto the road and headed to the nearby Denny's. As we did, I noticed the black Ford truck with giant mud tires still in the parking lot. Keller didn't see it, or him, but I did. I saw as he and Drew watched the Boxster speed away with me in the passenger seat.

"Is that Lance?" I mumbled, contorting in the seat to get a closer look. Keller ignored me and began talking about his most recent debate for school. I was in another world. I wanted to go back to the bar, to corner Lance and scream at him. Mostly, I wanted to go back, wrap my arms around him and kiss him for the rest of my life.

At the restaurant, I was considerably withdrawn and back to the depressed state I'd been in for the last three weeks. So much for getting over him.

"Was Drew at the bar Lish?" I asked in a hushed voice when our food arrived. She looked at me sadly and nodded her head. "And Lance?" She nodded again.

"They had to get back for curfew." She mumbled, keeping her eyes far away from mine.

"Why does Drew have a curfew and you don't?"

"It's Lance's curfew." She stated. "Uncle Will's pretty strict." I nodded and fell back against the seat. I knew

Alicia was avoiding any real answers and trying to smooth things over for Lance. I watched her closely. I hadn't known her long, but I could tell she was lying, hiding something from me. I wish I knew what. Had Lance moved on and she was scared to tell me, for fear of me hating her or something?

My school friends had been doing their best to cheer me up, telling me that it was doomed from the start since we were from two different worlds. They'd say, he's a farm boy and you're an athlete, an actress, you're on to great things and he's not. But my close friends just told me he was an idiot for letting me go, because he'd never find anyone better. Maddie and Zack repeatedly referred to him as the dumbass and just tried to tell me I'd get over him soon. They were the only ones who really knew how bad he'd hurt me and was still hurting me.

Keller, on the other hand, saw my heartbreak as his opportunity to move in on me again. He was using my vulnerability to his advantage, trying to pretend to be a good friend to me and use every minute to hit on me.

Keller forced me to go Christmas shopping with him on the first day of our Christmas break, he wasn't taking no for an answer. I reluctantly agreed, but it was only because I hadn't done any shopping at all. I'd been hiding out in a depressed funk since mine and Lance's initial fight, no matter how many times Zack harassed me and made me do something with him. Even if we went to the batting cages or worked out together, he wouldn't let me wallow in my self-pity alone. If nothing else, my breakup had definitely made Zack and me a lot closer.

The only time I emerged from the sanctity of the house or dorm was when I had a performance, school, cheerleading or workouts. Maddie tried to fix me up with guys, but I wasn't ready. They were the only times I had a temporary reprieve from my heartbreak, the only time I could momentarily forget Lance.

Keller and I were at one of the big mall's a few towns over and I was actually having a good time. I wasn't interested in

Keller anymore, but I definitely liked having him around. He was good for my ego, at least. The two of us were talking animatedly, laughing about everything, as we carried numerous shopping bags to a nearby restaurant where Keller bought me dinner. He was getting cozy and I was tolerating him, but I was careful not to send the wrong message. I didn't want to put a damper on the fun time we were having.

As we walked out of the restaurant, I spotted Lance's nephew Wyatt. The brown haired little boy was holding a girl's hand, talking excitedly, as he used to do with me. My heart sank, tears filled my eyes and jealousy took over. Lance was walking with them and to my horror, I watched him laugh and playfully put his arm around the caramel headed girl's shoulders and pull her in for a hug.

"Are you kidding me?" I gasped tearfully.

"What? What's wrong?" Keller asked as he looked back at me before following my gaze and landing on Lance.

"It was all a game? He just uses Wyatt to get girls?"

"I'm sure it's not what it looks like." Keller reassured, as he grabbed my wrist and tried to guide me in the other direction.

Lance would've put his hand on the small of my back and led me away, I missed that. Fuck. Not the time to think about that.

"Miss Jordan!" Wyatt exclaimed as he raced to jump into my arms. Supposedly, the four year old little boy was normally shy and rarely opened up to anyone, according to Lance. The minute I met him he was attached to me, an hour later he was calling me his girlfriend, and ever since, he was trying to boot Lance out of the picture. Now I realized it was all just a lie.

"Hey Wyatt." I murmured forcing a smile as I hugged him. I started to tear up as Lance and his date approached us. I tried to quickly exit the awkward situation before anyone realized I was crying. "I need to get going buddy. Have a Merry Christmas, okay?"

"Jordan." Lance murmured softly as he took a step towards me. He shot Keller a dirty look as he greeted him icily. For a second, I thought he started to hug me or kiss me on the cheek as he always did. At the same time, I noticed his arm was in a sling and his face showed signs of a recent battle.

"What happened to your arm?" I asked worriedly, as I took a step towards him. "It was you." Immediately, I wanted to kick myself for allowing him to see I still cared and quickly backpedaled. "Never mind, I don't care. You're a jerk, Lance Bowman."

I slapped him across the face as hard as I possibly could and scurried away before he could see I was crying. Keller shot Lance a dirty look and hung back a second as he said;

"Thanks plowboy. You just made this a very Merry Christmas for me."

Keller raced after me and led me out to his car. I sobbed

uncontrollably the entire way home. I couldn't believe I was

such an idiot falling for his stupid, pathetic game. Seeing Lance

with someone else hurt like Hell and made me realize that maybe

we weren't hanging in the balance like I'd thought.

Chapter 37

Lance

"What did you do to my Jordan?" Wyatt gasped in shock, just before he kicked me in the shins. I barely noticed as I fought every urge I had to pounce on Keller James.

"Lance, don't even think about it." Jess interjected as she grabbed my arm and held me back. My fists were clenched tight. I wanted to pound Keller James' face in and it was taking everything in me to refrain. I was still in no shape for a fight. I should've known that jerk would move in on Jordan in my absence.

"What the Hell?" I asked in bewilderment.

"You totally deserved that." Jess chuckled. "I told you to call her, to tell her what happened. It's your own stupidity."

"I wrote her a letter."

"A letter? Are you kidding me?"

"Drew was supposed to have given it to her." I mumbled, as I touched my face, feeling the sting from the slap.

"*You* should've done it, dumbass." She stated as she slapped me upside the back of the head.

"Apparently." I mumbled. "Damn it." I cursed as I grabbed my head in my hands and paced.

"Who *was* that guy?"

"Supposedly just a friend, it's nice to see she ran to him. I guess she really didn't care about me like she said."

"After the way you reacted? I don't blame her." Jess stated. "Seriously Lance, if you weren't such an idiot, you could still have her. I know you love her, why didn't you run after her? You can still catch her, Lance, go after her."

"It's too late; I can't compete with Keller James."

"Lance, a girl doesn't slap her ex across the face because she's over him." She informed me with a roll of her eyes. "I think you should go after her."

"It's better this way." I mumbled as I looked out the doors she had just raced out of. I should go after her. I know Jess is right; she always is. But Keller's family won't hurt her like my father could. She's safer with him. She's better off without me. He can give her a Hell of a lot more than I can, I know that much.

"I guess I don't have to look for her Christmas present anymore." I sighed with a self-deprecating chuckle. "I thought she'd wait for me."

"Well, I'm still getting her a present." Wyatt harrumphed as he shot me a dirty look. "She will always love me, even if she hates you." I nodded my head and looked down at the ground. I should've known Drew wouldn't give her the letter, considering he's had a crush on her since way before I even met her.

265

What was she doing with Keller again? I thought she loved me, if that were true then why did she run back to that jerk?

Being away from her was not easy. I went to call or text her at least ten times a day, but I always stopped myself. I couldn't be with her because of my father and as long as he was still in the picture, Jordan couldn't be. It wasn't safe for her and I couldn't endanger her life for my selfish needs or wants.

Seeing her now, with Keller, however made me want to forget my father's warnings and rush to her. I wanted to kiss her and feel her in my arms so badly that my whole body ached with the thought. My jealousy though, my envy had my blood pressure sky rocketing as I thought of all the ways Keller James was much better for her than I was.

God, she looked absolutely beautiful. I can't even…I can't even begin to picture my life without her in it. I needed her like I needed air.

"It doesn't have to be this way Lance." Jess stated under her breath. "Dad won't go after her. I really don't see him

266

risking it anytime soon." I nodded my head. She was right. My father had violated his bond and was locked in a jail cell for an unknown amount of time. My mother was pressing charges for real this time, she was keeping the order of protection intact and we would become a normal family soon. My father and his temper would be an absolute thing of the past.

It was time I shoved Keller James smarmy look down his throat and won my girl back.

Chapter 38

Jordan

On Christmas day, I sat in my room wallowing in my own self-pity. Zack was at home with his family in New York. Alicia was with her family, even though she invited me to the big dinner that Lance had invited me to last month. I couldn't do it, I couldn't be around his family and friends, couldn't be around him as if he hadn't shattered my heart into a kazillion tiny pieces. Maddie and Caleb were with the DeMarina's until they came to celebrate with us later in the afternoon. So, in short, I was pretty depressed and miserable.

The house phone rang and I jumped up from my bed to answer the cordless that stayed in my father's bedroom. The house phone rarely rang unless someone couldn't get a hold of my father.

"Miss Donaldson?" A voice asked on the other end. "This is Hank at the Security station. You have a package up here."

"A package? From who?"

"I'm not at liberty to tell you that ma'am."

"Not at liberty, what the heck does that even mean?"

"I swore I wouldn't ruin the surprise." He stated evenly. "I can tell you that it was a nice young man in a very large truck though, he didn't say I couldn't give you hints."

"Thank you." I replied. "I'll try to get up there before you leave." I hung up the phone and looked around the room.

Why would Lance leave me a present at the front gate? Why wouldn't he bring it to me himself? Why was he messing with my head?

How's your Christmas now? Zack had texted. He had already called at six a.m. to wish me a Merry Christmas. Sometimes it was like he knew when I needed to smile.

Just got weird lol

Why?

The security guard called to say Lance left me a gift

Why didn't he bring it to you?

My thoughts exactly.

I'm sure there's a reason.

Yeah, that reason is he's a bastard who's playing with my head

Did you go get it yet?

No and I don't plan to. Ever.

I understand. Did you open the gift I left under your tree?

You didn't leave me anything.

Check the tree dude lol

I walked downstairs and into the living room where our massive tree was crowding a corner of the room. There were gifts underneath it, of course. And sure enough, there was one from Zack. I opened the perfectly wrapped gift quickly and stared back at a leather bound journal.

I thought you could use a new place to write your lyrics. I know how close you are to filling up your other one. I know things have been rough lately, but they will get better. You're an amazing girl J and there are HUGE things in store for your future. -Zack

Tears rolled down my cheeks, how did he know me so well? I hated him for making me cry though.

Thank you.

Just thank you? Lol

You're pretty freaking amazing, but you know that already lol

It's nice to hear it from you though ☺ *Wish I could be there with you to cheer you up*

You're doing a good job from there

☺

Zack and I texted back and forth the rest of the holiday. He was definitely making me feel better and for that, I was absolutely grateful for having him as a friend. It wasn't until almost eight o clock that night that the doorbell rang.

"Joey!" Caleb yelled. "You have a visitor." I went downstairs, half hoping Lance was here, even though I knew it wouldn't happen. Hank, the security guard, stood awkwardly in the foyer in his brown security uniform.

"Sorry ma'am, the young man paid me to insure you received this package. I wouldn't feel right about taking his money if I didn't give it to you personally."

"Thanks Hank. I appreciate you bringing it by."
He dipped his head in response before starting out of the house.

"Merry Christmas Miss Jordan."

"Merry Christmas." I mumbled as I stared down at
the silver wrapping paper.

"What's that?" Caleb asked as I stumbled into the
living room and towards the steps. "Zack send you something
else?" I shook my head.

"It's from Lance." I whispered. I heard Caleb
mutter a curse word, but I didn't turn around, I just went upstairs
and dropped the package on my bed. I didn't want to open it,
ever, because I was terrified it would be the end of our
relationship. Maybe I was more scared that it would also be
something to keep me hanging on to him.

Two hours later, I finally ended my torture and opened
the large box. Inside were newspaper clippings and a compiled
DVD of home movies of my late mother. The clippings were

reviews of her productions or concerts that she had locally performed, all raving about her talent.

Thank you. I texted Lance a few hours later. I knew it was late and I was hoping he wouldn't reply.

For what?

The gift.

What gift?

Again with the lies. I only know one guy in a 'monster' truck Lance. Why do you have to confuse me so much? How can you do something so sweet and amazing, like you used to, after being such an ass lately?

I have my moments. He replied.

Where'd you get them from?

I have my ways. I wanted to get you something memorable.

Me too. I typed as I looked at his wrapped packages I had stacked in the corner.

Merry Christmas Jordan.

Merry Christmas Lance. Please tell your family that too.

I will. They missed you today. I missed you today.

Did Wyatt have a good Christmas? Did he get the gift I sent?

He did. He loved it. Thank you.

I'm glad. Bye Lance. He didn't respond. There was so much I wanted to say, so much I needed to get off my chest, but I restrained myself and figured he wasn't worth it anymore. It was hard to tell my heart that though.

Chapter 39

Down Under was performing at Maddie's annual New Year's Eve Party. It was always elaborate and a black tie event. I dressed in a key lime, French twill, strapless, vionette dress that went to mid-thigh. It looked great against my tanned skin. Maddie and I were the hottest girls at the party, by far, and I made sure to take dozens of pictures to post on my Facebook page, in hopes that Lance would see them. Pathetic, I know.

I channeled my anger, confusion and hurt into my music and gave another blowout performance.

At midnight, Keller met me onstage and grabbed me in a hungry kiss. I was in shock, so I pulled back and slapped him across the face as I glared angrily at him.

"You're two years too late Keller!" I spit with a roll of my eyes as I walked away from him. When I first moved here, Keller and I had an instant attraction to each other. At the time, we'd only been making out because I was still wary of trusting him. I told him if he found me at midnight, proved to me that he was seriously interested in me, then I was all his. Instead of kissing me at the strike of the New Year, he was making out with someone else. I should have steered clear of him from that moment on, but I'm a glutton.

I wanted nothing to do with Keller James or any other guy on the planet. I only wanted Lance Bowman. I missed the way he was always kissing and hugging me, his hand on the small of my back, his arm constantly on my shoulders, his hands caressing my face and just being with him. Everyone else was coupled off and I wasn't, I was miserable.

Not to mention, as the clock struck midnight my brother was down on one knee proposing to my best friend. It was incredibly romantic and I was proud of my brother for it. I was thrilled that Maddie would be my sister in law soon as well, but I'd be lying if I said I wasn't jealous. Why does everyone else get the happily ever after and I get the frogs?

277

Excuse me while I go drink a bottle of whiskey to numb the reality of my pathetic life.

Chapter 40

"Please tell me that you haven't wallowed in your self-pity the whole time I was gone." Zack sighed as I met him at the baggage claim of the St. Louis airport.

"Go to Hell." I mumbled as I looked down at the ground.

"You look like shit J." He shook his head and let out an exasperated breath. "Any guy who could ditch you like this, is not worth your pain. Please know that."

"It's easier said than done." I mumbled as I looked up at my friend. He nodded his head and wrapped his arms around me in a hug.

"I know. I'm back now, so I won't let you feel sorry for yourself any longer."

"Whatever." I rolled my eyes and pulled away from his embrace. "You have to catch up with all the girls who missed you while you were gone."

"Did you miss me?" As he dipped his head in an attempt to get me to look him in the eye.

"I talked to you every day." I mumbled uneasily. I did miss him, but I wouldn't tell him that. I was still trying to figure out why I missed seeing his smile daily. Of course, I shouldn't have missed his face since he was repeatedly sending me selfies of said face.

"True, Maddie is the only other girl who can say that though." He shrugged indifferently as he turned to grab his bags from the baggage carousel. I nodded my head as I thought about that. Caleb and Zack were best friends, because of that he'd gotten pretty close with Maddie and me as well, we were one big happy family.

"I guess you know they're engaged."

"I knew before it happened." He chuckled as he started for the exit.

"Not fair."

"Caleb didn't want to add insult to injury." He rolled his shoulders and looked down at me. "But could you have really kept that secret from Maddie?"

"Ugh yeah. That's like a secret you don't want to spill." I rolled my eyes at him as I pushed through the doors that led us to the parking lot.

"Hard to believe they haven't even graduated high school yet and are planning a wedding."

"I know." I chuckled. "I don't think waiting would matter though. They are pretty much made for each other. There's no doubt in my mind that they will last forever."

"Very true." He nodded. "We watching basketball when we get home?"

"Planned on it, until I have to head back to the dorms."

"My kind of girl." He flirted as he winked at me playfully. I hit the key fob and unlocked my powder blue Mustang and popped the trunk for Zack to throw his stuff into. We climbed in the car and headed out of the airport.

"You hungry?" I asked hopefully. I'd overslept and skipped breakfast. That was three hours ago and I was starving.

"Always." He chuckled. "I'm buying since you came to get me."

"You don't have to do that."

"I do." He argued. "Logan's Roadhouse when we get into Fairview?"

"You don't have twist my arm." I giggled. "I could always go for a steak."

282

"Well aware." He chuckled. He leaned forward and scanned through the radio stations, he was probably the only person that I ever let touch my radio. However, he always found good music so I would let him until he messed it up. We sang and talked until we made it into Fairview where I pulled off the interstate and into the restaurant. We were seated fairly quickly and Zack didn't even look at the menu before he ordered an appetizer of nachos. He ordered his meal as well, as did I. Pretty sad that we'd been here so much that we didn't need to look.

"Besides my sisters, you're probably the only girl I know who eats like me."

"Is that a compliment or are you telling me I'm a fat ass?" I lit.

"Compliment, what fun is a picky eater?" He chuckled.

"How many sisters do you have?"

"Two older sisters. They're quite a bit older than me."

"So you're the baby of the family, too?"

"Yup, they didn't stop till they got it right." I giggled and shook my head.

"You going to plan a big bachelor party for Cale?"

"Hell yeah!" He laughed. "It'll be epic, well as epic as it can be since we're not twenty one."

"That does put a damper on things." I smiled. "Basketball practice starts back up tomorrow, doesn't it?"

"Unfortunately. I'll be thrilled when the season is over and baseball starts up."

"Yeah, I bet it sucks being so good at something you hate." I retorted drily.

"It does." He chuckled. "You going to force me to workout with you when we get home?"

"Hell yeah, I'm exceeding my daily calories in one meal. Can't exactly throw a lard ass up in the air."

"Why do you talk so bad about yourself?" He questioned seriously, his head tilting to the side. I shrugged my shoulders. "Did Lance say stuff like that to you?"

"Absolutely not." I mumbled. Keller did, Keller was all the time telling me I was too heavy or that I needed to work out more.

"You're not fat and you're far from it J. You shouldn't be so hard on yourself." I shrugged my shoulders and played around with the food on my plate. "But I'll still do Insanity with you when we get home."

"Good, I wouldn't give you a choice." I giggled.

"Only because you're sexy as Hell when you're all sweaty."

"OMG." I threw my head back and laughed. "It's pointless to flirt with me Zack, I know you better than that."

285

"Do you?" He asked, narrowing his eyes at me. "I'm pretty certain you don't know me as well as you think."

"Whatever." I rolled my eyes and was absolutely grateful when the waitress brought our food to the table. I tried to pretend like his flirting went unnoticed, that it didn't affect me. It was all a lie though. Zack Bentley was an amazing guy, too bad he would never, ever see me as more than a sister-like figure in his life.

Chapter 41

I was the first one back to the dorms that night. Maddie would be in later, once she pulled herself away from my brother. Lately, Alicia would come back at the last minute, almost as if she were afraid to be alone with me. I only took that as a bad sign. I wanted to ask her a million questions, wanted to force her to tell me what the Hell was wrong with Lance and who his new girlfriend was. But I didn't.

"You should've gotten this a lot sooner." Alicia murmured as she plopped her things down on her bed and handed me an envelope. "Apparently Drew *forgot* to give it to me for you." I nodded my head and looked down at the letter. Lance had scrawled my name on the front; I closed my eyes and exhaled before I tossed the envelope into my nightstand.

"Jordan." Alicia sighed. "He *does* love you. It just…I think he tells you in the letter that he is dealing with family issues, which is a version of the truth. His dad won't let him see you. He's banned from you."

"And he couldn't tell me that himself?" I asked drily. Alicia just shook her head sadly.

"I wish I could tell you everything, but I can't. It's not my place and I don't know it all either. He still tells people you're together though. He hoped you'd wait it out for him."

"Maybe he should've told me that." I grumbled. Alicia just nodded and got ready for bed. She mumbled an apology before she climbed into bed.

"Alicia honey," I sighed. "Please don't think I'll hate you because of Lance. You're my friend. A very good friend and Lance has nothing to do with that."

"Thanks." She smiled before she climbed into bed and went to sleep.

I stared at my nightstand. I got up, put on my pajamas and climbed into my bed, all the time watching my nightstand as if it were going to dance for me. My heart was screaming to burn the letter and my head was telling me to read it. My stomach was telling me to run for the bathroom, because I was going to puke from all the emotions streaking through my body. I closed my eyes and took a deep breath, attempting to calm the wave of nausea washing over me.

I went to the nightstand, grabbed the letter out and tore it into a million different pieces. I didn't care what it said, well maybe I did, but I needed to forget about it. Zack was right, if Lance didn't think I was important enough to explain things to, then he wasn't worthy of me. I could do better. I could find someone who would treat me like a princess. I didn't need to be someone's second choice or person in the shadows, I deserved to be front and center in a relationship and Lance Bowman was not giving me that opportunity at all. We were done. The sooner all parts of my body realized that, the better off I would be.

Chapter 42

"You know we play Mencino tonight, right?" Zack asked me as he sidled up next to me.

"You're only the fifteenth person to mention it, but thanks." I answered drily.

"I just didn't want you to be blindsided." He shrugged nonchalantly.

"Chopper and Coop both texted me this morning to make sure I'd be at the game." I sighed.

"Will Lance be there?"

"According to Drew, yes." I mumbled. "He texted me last night to say he was playing for some record. He was pretty excited there would be scouts there tonight and even more thrilled that I'd be there to see it. And then he asked me on a date."

"Alicia's brother?" Zack roared with laughter.

"Lance's cousin. Alicia's brother. Yes. He's asked me on about ten. Don't get me wrong he's pretty cute, but he's totally not my type. The fact that he's my roommate's brother doesn't help matters either."

"Your other roommate is engaged to your brother."

"True, but different somehow. I think it has everything to do with my prior relationship with Lance." I shrugged.

"I can understand that." Zack stated with a nod as he walked me to my locker. "I wish I could stick close to run interference for you."

"I know." I smiled softly. "I'm a big girl though, I'll be okay." Zack nodded again and looked around. He moved closer to me, pulling me into him as he looked down at me.

"I am available to piss Bowman off though." His hand went up to my face. "I wouldn't be opposed to showing him what he lost."

"And risk alienating all of your dates for tonight?" I scoffed as I stood completely still. "Every girl in this school would despise me."

"So?" He chuckled. "It'd be worth it and you know it."

"I won't argue with that." I breathed. "I just...I don't know that I could pretend..."

"Who says it would be pretending?"

"J!" Maddie hollered as she came around the corner. Her eyes went wide before a grin spread across her face. "Sorry to interrupt, go back to what you were doing."

"You weren't interrupting anything." I mumbled as I pulled away, grabbed my bag out of my locker and started to walk away.

"Don't run away J." Zack whispered in my ear.

"I cannot be that girl for you Zack. I won't be someone you screw and throw to the side. I can't do it. Our friendship would never be the same and..."

"Who says it has to be that way? I'm not...I'm capable of a relationship and..."

"It's not nice to make fun of me Zack." I mumbled tearfully as I scurried away. He hollered after me, but I didn't turn around.

"What the heck was that?"

"He thought it would be funny to pretend..." I started.

"First of all, Zack would never do anything to hurt you." Maddie interjected loudly. "I think you should go back and let him finish his sentence."

"I can't do it. I am physically and emotionally nowhere near ready to hear whatever else he has to say."

"J."

"No Maddie." I retorted evenly. "I won't." I veered off and went to the music building. I didn't know what Maddie even originally wanted. I just knew that I had to get the Hell away from everyone else. I needed to bury myself in my songs and a guitar, I needed to go where no one could bother or interrupt me. I would not last through tonight, knowing Lance would be there possibly with his new girlfriend, if I didn't get my head into a good place right now.

Chapter 43

I was not ready to see Lance Bowman. I poured my heart and soul into my music prep and my stomach was still killing me from anxiety. I just wanted to puke. I went home, changed into my cheerleading uniform and did everything I could to avoid getting a moment alone with Zack. Luckily, he had to leave for the gym before I did.

"Hey girlie." Alicia greeted me with a grin as she entered my bedroom.

"Hey, did you just get here?"

"Yes ma'am." She giggled. "You ready to go? Caleb left and Maddie is on her way up." I shook my head.

"I'm nowhere near read to go." I sighed. "But I'll go, because that's what I do."

"That's right. You are a bad ass bitch who won't let a guy get her down." Maddie stated as she came into my room. I laughed and rolled my eyes.

"Maybe showing him how bad he hurt me would make him think twice before he did it to someone else." I murmured.

"Doubt it." She stated with a shake of her dark head.

"For what it's worth, he really misses you." Alicia interjected softly as we walked out of my bedroom and down the stairs. "Did you read his letter?"

"Absolutely not. I tore it into pieces."

"What?" She and Maddie gasped simultaneously.

"One of two things was in that letter and frankly, I'm not strong enough to handle either of them."

"What do you think he said?" Maddie asked as she grabbed our jackets out of the living room, handed them to Alicia and I before starting out of the house.

"He either told me it's absolutely over or that he wants me back and it's all a big misunderstanding."

"It kind of is a big misunderstanding." Alicia admitted. I closed my eyes and shook my head as we loaded into Alicia's car together.

"It doesn't freaking matter Lish." I sighed. "I...I feel like if he loved me as much as I love, loved him, then he wouldn't have pushed me away without even a tiny bit of an explanation. He just cut me off, stopped talking to me and completely blew me off. Who does that?"

"He...he wouldn't have done it if he had a choice."

"You tell me that, why couldn't he?"

"Because he's an idiot." Maddie responded. "You deserve someone who puts you on a pedestal." I nodded my head, so did Alicia. She started the car, put it in reverse and drove the short way to the gymnasium.

The game was set to start in thirty minutes when we walked into the gymnasium. I wish we'd walked in with only seconds to spare, but I wasn't so lucky.

"Will you talk to him? I know he really wants to talk to you. He does miss you Jo."

"*He blew me off.* Besides if he really missed me, I wouldn't have seen him at the mall with some other girl."

"Some other girl?" Alicia repeated in disbelief. Suddenly her eyes lit up and she started to speak.

"J!" Zack yelled. "Heads up!" A ball was flying towards my head, I reached out and caught it quickly. "Damn girl, nice catch." He chuckled as he jogged over. I tossed the basketball back to him.

"Were you trying to knock me out?" I lit.

"I just saved your life." He moved the basketball to the side as he took a step towards me. "Why are you so sure I'm an asshole?"

"I never said you were an asshole."

"You don't have to say the exact words. Today alone, you've showed it at least five times."

"I…" I couldn't finish the sentence, because I didn't know what to say. I haven't been very nice to Zack at all, when he's been fabulous towards me. I looked away and hugged myself tightly, hoping it would stop the pains in my stomach from growing worse.

"J, why won't you let me in?" He was standing in front of me, looking down at me and I wouldn't look at him. I searched the gym for a way out. I spotted Lance immediately, his smile grew wide and then fell as he saw Zack.

"What are you talking about?"

"I think you know."

"Zack." I sighed.

"I could kiss you right now and you'd forget about Bowman." He murmured as his hand went to my face. "Added bonus being he would see how stupid he is for letting you go." His mouth was mere millimeters away from mine, my whole body hummed in anticipation.

"Bentley!" Tate Donovan yelled. "Layups!" He was chuckling as he shook his head. "Do you really have to kiss a girl before every game?" I shook myself out of the stupor and pushed away from him.

"Damn it J. Quit pushing me away, please." Zack begged. I shook my head, trying to shake Tate's words out of my head. Zack was playing with me, he always kissed a girl before a big game. When I didn't turn around he went to his team and I went to my squad, willing away any tears that were about to fall.

"Miss Jordan!" Wyatt yelled as he bound towards me. I turned around and caught him in my arms just as he jumped into them. "I've missed you so much. What are you doing here? Did you know Mr. Drew is going to be a professional basketball player? Do you still hate Uncle Lance? If you hit him again, can I help you?"

"I'm sorry sweetie. He saw you and took off before I could grab him." Mrs. Bowman explained as she tried to pull her grandson away and then hugged me sweetly. "How have you been dear? We've really missed you at the house."

"I'm good." I lied with a smile. "How about you?"

"We're good. I've got two sad boys moping around the house without you in their lives, though. Wyatt asks Lance every night if he's going to call you."

"Aww...I miss you too buddy." I mumbled in a broken voice as I hugged Wyatt again. "*You* can call me anytime you want sweetie."

"I was sad to hear that you two broke up. You mean a lot to him, but he said you've already moved on."

"Not as fast as he did." I retorted without thinking.

"I don't know what you're talking about honey. Lance rarely leaves the house anymore. He's usually holed up in his bedroom writing. It's going to be a long time before he gets over you."

"Then why did he break up with me?" I asked rudely, I covered my mouth with my hand quickly. "Sorry, I didn't mean to sound so rude."

"He says *you* broke up with him." She answered in surprise, right before Mencino and Callatin started their entrances into the gymnasium.

"Sorry, I gotta go." I stated regretfully. Mrs. Bowman nodded her head and smiled before her and Wyatt went to their seats. I took a deep breath and shot Maddie a funny look.

We cheered, danced and flipped for our guys as they made their entrance after Mencino. While the two teams warmed up, we went up into the bleachers with all the students and got them all wound up. Some girls may have lost their focus and performed like crap, but not me. I used Lance's stares as motivation to look as hot and perfect as possible so he could see what he gave up.

"Hey." Keller smiled a few minutes before the game started. "I wouldn't be opposed to an amazing kiss if you wanted to make some jerk, who can't take his eyes off you, jealous.

"Keller." I giggled as I shook my head. I decided it might not be such a bad idea since Lance has always been extremely jealous of him. Even if Lance didn't have feelings for me anymore, I knew it would get under his skin and that was motivation enough for me. I grabbed Keller's hand, pulled him towards me and turned just enough to make it look like we were in a scorching lip lock.

"Thanks." I whispered in his ear a few minutes later.

"No prob." He chuckled nonchalantly. "It was really for my benefit anyway. I do love to piss that redneck off."

I looked towards the MHS stands and saw Lance starting to leave. The girl from the mall chased after him, grabbed his hand and pulled him back to the bleachers. From my vantage point, I could see the two of them were arguing while they watched me and I suddenly grew uncomfortable. My own immature plan, had just backfired on me, because now I was feeling like crap.

My squad and I headed across the floor to our perch in the corner, waiting for team introductions. As we passed the Mencino team, Drew and Sawyer hollered at me.

"Hey gorgeous." Drew greeted me as he gave me an enormous hug before the game started.

"Damn Jordan, I never thought I'd be turned on by a girl in a Callatin uniform."

"Oh whatever Sawyer, you know you're checking us all out." I lit.

"Maybe you're right." He laughed with a low whistle as a few of the upper classmen walked by. I made it a point to flirt with both of them in hopes that it would bother Lance again. He didn't look happy at least.

Chapter 44

At half time, we finished our dance routine and started back for the sidelines just as Lance and his buddies started towards me. Chopper was the first to grab me in an enormous bear hug.

"God, I have missed your gorgeous face." He breathed as he squeezed me tight. "You look amazing, as always."

"Aw Chop, you sure know to make a girl blush." I giggled as I hugged him back just before he set me on the ground and Coop grabbed me in a hug as well.

"Hey darlin'." Lance mumbled as he started towards me to hug me as all his friends had done. I moved out of his way and began talking to Chopper as though Lance didn't exist.

"I sure have missed having you around." Chopper admitted. "It just isn't a party without your crazy ass. Just because you're not with my dumbass friend doesn't mean you can't come around."

"I never got an invite before." I flirted. "Besides, don't you think it would be a little awkward if your dumbass friend was there too, with someone?"

"Lance with someone else?" Chopper and the others roared with laughter. "That's hilarious. We're lucky to get him to hang out with *us* anymore!"

"He's been grounded for over a month." Coop advised me with a shake of his head.

"What happened to his arm?" Coop and Chop both looked from me to their friend with wide eyes.

"You don't know?" Chop asked me, then his eyes flitted to Lance's. "You lied to me?"

"C'mon guys she needs to go, the game's about to start again." Lance interjected as his eyes darted away nervously.

"He said he told you." Coop informed me. "He should be the one to tell you." My face was flaming with anger. "Wait, you really don't know?"

"No, I am clueless. I just know that he flipped out on me one night and it was the last time I really talked to him, because he's been blowing me off ever since." I mumbled as I stared questioningly back at Lance.

"Jordan!" Maddie hollered. I turned to look at her as she motioned for me to get back to the sidelines. I nodded my head and looked back at Lance who was trying to sneak away.

"Why do they know and I don't?"

"*Now* you want to talk to me?" He asked rudely.

"Oh fuck you!" I hissed. "*You* blew me off first asshole or don't you remember that? So, you'll have to excuse me if I don't pretend to be your best fucking friend."

"I didn't blow you off."

"Really?" I laughed sarcastically. "Ya could've fooled me."

"I guess maybe it seemed that way, but it's not what I meant to happen." He mumbled regretfully as he tried to touch me. I quickly moved out of the way and he became a little frustrated. "What does it matter anyway? You and Keller are obviously an item. Or is it you and Bentley, you looked pretty chummy with both of those fuckers."

"Don't concern yourself with my private life. Especially when you moved on long before I ever did." I accused angrily.

"*No,* I didn't." He protested as he reached out to me, trying to take my hand in his.

"Don't." I warned furiously. "All I wanted was an explanation Lance and you couldn't give me that then, so I'm not going to give you the time of day now." I spit in a harsh whisper.

"Please." He begged. "I'll get down on my knees in front of everyone if I have to."

"Save your shit for your *new* girlfriend Lance, because *I'm* over it." I lied as I stormed away.

"You okay?" Maddie asked worriedly when I returned to the squad.

"No. Next time I'm going to pretend to be dead so I don't have to put myself through this torture."

"It'll be easier next time; it won't be so soon after the break up."

"I doubt it." I rolled my eyes and forced my tears to go away. I couldn't cry over Lance Bowman anymore, especially not when I was surrounded by him, his friends and family. I put all my energy into cheering, knowing I'd be able to drown my pain in alcohol shortly. The sooner this game was over, the better off I'd be.

Chapter 45

Drew got his record and helped his team win by five. Overall, it was an awesome game and Drew definitely had everyone buzzing about his skills. I gave him a congratulatory hug and escaped giving him a reply when he asked me on a date before he was rushed by his teammates, family and friends. I was walking away when a dark headed girl with tight curls stopped me.

"So you're the girl who broke my baby's heart?" She smiled as she touched my arm gently.

"Excuse me?" I asked rudely. "I think you have me confused with someone else."

"You're Jordan right?" She asked. I nodded my head warily before I realized she was the girl from the mall and I recognized her from Lance's sister's wedding. She smiled back at me and extended her hand as she introduced herself as Wyatt's mom, Lance's sister.

"*You're* Wyatt's mom?" I asked confused as I began to feel like a jerk for my psycho reaction at the mall.

"Yeah." She giggled. "If you feel bad for slapping Lance, don't, he totally deserved that and more for the way he treated you."

"I'm pathetic." I mumbled as I closed my eyes and prayed I could melt into the floor.

"You really did a number on Wyatt *and* Lance, ya know?"

"I didn't..."

"They're both miserable without you. You really hurt Lance."

"*I* hurt Lance? I don't know what he's been telling y'all but he... *he's* the one who blew me off."

"He didn't dump you or blow you off Jordan. Sweetie, he *couldn't* call you." She stated matter of factly. "I thought you knew."

"Knew what? Everyone's telling me these things and I…"

"Jordan, my dad wouldn't allow Lance to call or see you anymore. After your fight, when Lance came home three hours late, my dad flipped out on him. At Thanksgiving Lance finally snapped. He and my dad got into an extremely physical fight. Lance was hospitalized for it, separated his shoulder, broke his arm and two of his ribs. Dad told Lance if he ever saw or talked to you again he'd kick him out of the house. He won't leave Wyatt and mom alone with him Jordan and *that's* the only reason why he blew you off."

"Why wouldn't he just tell me that?"

"Because he's an idiot." She stated with an exaggerated sigh and a shake of her curly head. "Supposedly, he wrote you a letter. Sweetie, Lance is in love with you but he didn't have a choice for his actions. I probably would've thought the same thing after the fight you two had." She explained sadly. I began to comment as tears rolled down my face, but she continued. "Lance wanted to tell you he loved you first, but you beat him to it and he felt like a jerk. He thought you deserved this perfect moment for him to utter the words and that's why he took off. It's hard for him to express his feelings. He told me he wanted to say it a thousand times, but never could. You just have to be patient and read between the lines.

Jordan, he's miserable and he hates himself for hurting you. He possibly would've told you all this at the mall or even tonight, if you'd let him. Don't get me wrong though, I probably wouldn't either. I just can't stand to see my little brother hurting because he has NEVER been like this over a girl and *that's* why I'm intervening."

"It doesn't matter, we obviously can't be together if you're dad…"

"Is an asshole and is gone." She shrugged. Jess's phone rang and she giggled as she showed me the text message Lance had just sent her.

314

Just leave her alone please. You're making me

look like a pathetic loser

"I'm such a bitch." I mumbled as her explanation soaked in. Lance and his family had been through Hell, because of me, and I ditched him the first chance I got.

"No, you're not." Jess admitted. "You were clueless and just thought you were dumped. None of us think poorly of you for it."

"Thanks." I mumbled, as I spun on my heel and rushed off to where Lance had been standing earlier, but he was gone. I frantically looked everywhere for him.

"Maddie, did you see where Lance went?"

"No, why? Jordan…"

"I need to talk to him."

"No, you don't." She replied as she rushed towards me. I shook her away.

"I have to." I murmured, as I fought back tears. Maddie didn't look happy, but she nodded and pointed towards the far end of the gym.

"I don't want you to hurt anymore J." She murmured as she shook her head. "But I saw him go out that way. Please be careful."

"Wait for me?" She nodded and made a gesture for me to hurry. I rushed out to the parking lot, pushing through people and not caring if I was being rude. I finally saw him headed for his truck while he talked to his friends.

Chapter 46

"Lance! Lance Bowman!" I hollered. He ignored me at first, but finally spun around.

"So my sister talks to you and you finally wanna give me the time of day?" He asked icily. "I don't want your fucking pity Jordan."

"Is it true?"

"Does it really matter now? It's been months, I thought you were *over* it."

"It *does* matter asshole. It would matter fifty years from now Lance, because I'll *never* get over you." I admitted in a sad voice.

"Does your boyfriend know that?"

"Obviously not, because he didn't think I deserved to know the truth about the shit going on his life. My boyfriend didn't think I could handle it, apparently. And if you're accusing me of seeing someone else, call me crazy, but I'm a little hesitant to get hurt again."

"I never meant to hurt you." He mumbled as he slowly moved closer to me.

"Is it true Lance? Is *this* because of me?" I asked as I gently touched his arm.

"No." He lied as he looked down at the ground quickly.

"Why didn't you tell me?"

"How could I? Do you have any idea how hard this is for me? I wouldn't have *ever* told you if it wasn't for my sister's big mouth." His eyes flew up to mine, they were so full of pain and frustration that my knees practically buckled.

"And risk never getting me back?" I asked in shock.

"It's not something..."

"You could've told me, could've explained that you *couldn't* see me. I deserved better than you never calling me again."

"You deserve better than me."

"I don't want anyone but you."

"Then why are you with Keller?"

"I'm not."

"You were with him before and at the mall, I saw you kiss, so what am I supposed to think?"

"Whatever you want I guess." I shrugged. "I'm an idiot for thinking you ditched me because of your dad, maybe that's what you want everyone to think. Apparently the reality is that you got laid and decided I wasn't worth the trouble anymore."

"Jordan." He sighed.

"No Lance. What the fuck? All your family is coming up to me and saying how bad *I* hurt you, but apparently *you're* lying to them too! All I want to know is why you took off that night, why did you run Lance? Why did you break my heart?" I cried. Lance looked back at me sadly, but he didn't answer.

"Fuck you then. I *gave* you my heart and soul; that wasn't easy for me. I fell for you because you're this amazing and perfect guy, but out of nowhere you turned into the biggest asshole I've ever met and I can't figure out why!" Lance was still silent, staring down at the ground, kicking at the dirt with his muddy boots. I let out an exasperated sigh, trying to cover the sound of my heart shattering. As I stood there, staring at his handsome face I knew I didn't want to lose him forever. And I opened my mouth to let the stupid fall out.

"I know you're going through a lot right now, according to your friends and family." I added sharply. "So if you need a friend, then I'll be that for you." Lance's eyes darted up quickly as he looked at me in shock. He was the only guy I trusted with my demons and I knew he felt the same about me. I missed our talks; I missed having someone who knew everything about me. I wondered if he did too. I acted on impulse and grabbed Lance's shirt, pulled him towards me and kissed him passionately. All those emotions raced to the surface again, tears filled my eyes just as quickly as the heat took over my senses.

"I love you Lance Bowman and I always will. So when you catch up and realize I'm worth fighting for, then call me. Unfortunately, I'm the dumbass who'll drop everything." I whispered tearfully before I walked away. Lance didn't say anything, he just watched me go and that hurt more than anything.

I knew Alicia and Maddie were waiting for me nearby, I didn't have to look I just raced towards where they were parked and jumped inside.

"Are you okay?" Alicia asked softly. I shook my head, clutched my stomach and sobbed.

"I realize he's your cousin but it would be really fantastic if you'd run that fucker down right now." Maddie hissed as she glared out the window.

"How can he not come after her?" Alicia mumbled. "How can he…?"

"Just drive, please!" I cried. Alicia didn't hesitate to put the car in gear and tear out of the parking lot.

"Do you want to go back to the house?" Maddie mumbled. "We can just go hang out, just us three."

"I need alcohol and lots of it." I hissed.

"We can do that. I'll text Caleb and…"

"No, I'm fine. I will not let that bastard hold me back any longer." I growled, wiping my eyes and taking a deep breath. "Let's go to the party. Fuck him."

"Fuck him." Maddie repeated. "You deserve so much better than that." I nodded my head. I could tell Alicia was trying not to look me in the eye, I knew she was torn on how to react to the whole situation, but I didn't care. It was time I realized that Lance Bowman didn't care about me in the same way that I cared about him.

Chapter 47

Keller's family had purchased a home just outside of the Callatin gates where they could stay, on the rare occasion, when they visited. Keller used it often, to take girls back to and to throw parties. He had planned another big party for tonight, it was supposed to be to celebrate the win against our rival, but since we lost it was pretty rowdy with ridiculous drunks.

"Thanks Brennan." I grinned as I grabbed a bottle out of his hand and chugged it quickly.

"Um, you want another one?" He asked, chuckling as he shook his head.

"Three more, at least." Brennan nodded and scurried away. I found Zack next and eased his Styrofoam cup out of his hand as he talked to my brother.

"What'cha drinking?" I queried as I sniffed it.

"Jack and coke." He answered with a raised eyebrow.

"You got more?" He nodded his head. "Good, because I'll be finishing this."

"What's gotten into you?"

"I am officially single, because that asshole Bowman decided I'm not important enough to be privy to the shitty parts of his life."

"Jordan." Alicia sighed hesitantly.

"What does that mean?"

"It means nothing." I grumbled. No matter how pissed off I was, I wouldn't air Lance's dirty laundry because that wasn't fair. "He let me walk away from him again, therefore he doesn't deserve me." I took a long pull from Zack's mixed drink and didn't stop until it was completely gone. I handed the cup back to Zack just as Brennan came up with three bottles for me.

"Triple fisting?" Zack asked flatly. "This isn't going to end well."

"Who knows Zack, maybe I'll get drunk enough to sleep with you and not remember how bad it'll hurt when you ditch me the next day." I mumbled as I chugged another bottle and started off

"Why do you think Zack would do that to you?" Caleb questioned angrily, stopping me effectively.

"Because, like all males, he thinks with his dick and nothing else." My brother opened his mouth to respond, but Zack stopped him.

"She's not going to listen right now, she's not ready to." He stated with a shake of his head.

"Zack's right." Maddie added.

"I'm still here assholes." I spit before I walked off. I needed to get away, needed to find someone who wouldn't tell me I was wrong, who wouldn't make me slow down or stop wallowing in my misery. I needed someone who put their desires before mine, I needed to find Keller James.

"Jordan!" Quinn Altrip yelled as she waved me over to where she stood with a group of girls, girls that were normally Keller's entourage.

"Hey!" I grinned. "Where's all the excitement at?"

"Keller's on the back deck with a bunch of the soccer team, I'm sure it's about to get really fun back there." Quinn stated.

"They were bringing out the liquor a few minutes ago." Sage Qualls announced as she swayed inside the house. I followed the girls until we were through the expansive, barely used, house and on the back deck. Someone had pulled one of the glass top coffee tables outside and lined all of Keller's parents expensive liquor on it.

"Who's playing?" Ben Seetar asked.

"What are we playing?" I queried with a flirtatious grin.

"Shots until we puke." Ben grinned as he winked at me. What a stupid game, I thought to myself.

"I'm game." I purred. Ben and a few others boys started pouring liquor into shot glasses and immediately handed me one. Keller took a step forward, not to stop me, but so he could watch and be the first to catch me when I face planted.

I stood next to a few soccer stars, two football players and Sage. She would bow out before long, she just wanted to look like she could hang. *I could hang.* My mother was an alcoholic, I came from a long line of them and I was going to tap into that genetic history so that I could forget about my broken heart and start over tomorrow.

Chapter 48

Keller

Twelve shots. Twelve shots of liquor were passed out to five different people and Jordan was still going strong. She was swaying as she sat, she didn't look good at all.

"She's had enough." I told Ben as I held a hand out to him.

"Pretty sure she can tell me when she's done."

"When she stands up it'll hit her all at once."

"Let her go Keller, she's having a blast and so are we." Ben reached down and squeezed Jordan's thigh, she barely noticed.

"I'm not cleaning up her vomit when she blows, she's done. She's hanging with guys three times her size, she'll get alcohol poisoning before we even realize it."

"Like you'd clean it up." Ben chuckled. "When did you get a conscience anyway?"

"Excellent question." Jordan slurred, her angry blue eyes piercing right through me.

"Sue me for caring about you J." I mumbled.

"You only care about yourself Keller." She stated evenly. "Everyone knows that." I pretended not to notice the few nods from the people surrounding me.

"C'mon J." I sighed, as I took her by the hand and helped her up.

"Thanks for ruining our party, Keller." Ben lit as he waved me off. They should be thanking me, ten more minutes and she'd be puking all over the place. I rolled my eyes, flipped him off and led Jordan inside the house. She was dead weight behind me, barely able to walk without running into people and things.

"I'm not done forgetting Keller." She hissed as she plopped into an open chair in the den. "I need more shots."

"If he walked away after a kiss from you, then he's an idiot and he doesn't deserve you." I hissed, falling down to my knees in front of her.

"But he's all that I want." I sobbed.

"*He's* all that you want?" I asked disgustedly, covering it with false hurt. Jordan nodded her head and focused on her drink.

"I'm sorry Keller." She sighed as she looked up at me. "I didn't mean to hurt your feelings. It's just that…I don't know, maybe this is all a result from losing my virginity to him. Maybe these are just pretend feelings or something. I don't know. Whatever it is, I can't fucking think straight."

"I think the alcohol is helping with that." I chuckled as I reached out and touched her face. "What you feel for Lance is lust. It's completely normal for a chick to feel like she's in love with her first. Ask anyone." Jordan nodded as she tipped her bottle and took a long pull from it. *That's it J, chug it down. That's what I want, for you to be trashed later so I can take advantage of the situation.* I thought to myself. "What you and I have, baby, is the real thing. We have a solid foundation; common goals, common lives, we're meant for each other."

"Meant for each other. Schmeant for each other." She giggled airily. "It's all a load of crap. I'd be better off if I just acted like a guy and fucked everything in my presence. After a while, I'd have to build up an immunity to feelings, right?"

"I suppose." I answered warily. I'm certain this is going to backfire on me any second. "There's only one way to find out."

"You're right." She agreed as she stood up quickly, faltered and fell back down. "Where's Zack? He's the best one to tell me if that's true?"

"Zack? Are you fucking kidding me?" I exploded.

"He fucks three girls a week, he'd know right?"

"I guess. You're not..."

"Keller, Zack would die laughing if I ever propositioned him."

"I highly doubt that."

"I don't." She giggled. "I'm tired. And lonely. And...h...never mind."

"And what?" I smiled cockily. She narrowed her eyes at me, before taking another long drink of her beer.

"Wouldn't you like to know." She chortled. I raised an eyebrow and moved closer to her.

"Oh, I definitely would." I flirted in a slow, quiet voice. "I'm thinking you should know that I'm more than qualified to help sort that out."

"I'll bet you are." She nodded with a roll of her eyes. "But I'm not..." She let out a sigh and looked away. "Obviously, I'm not very good because..."

"He's a redneck plowboy who's partial to his cows Jordan. He wouldn't know what was good if it was slapped to the back of a tractor with flashing lights." I spit drily. "Please don't tell me you would let that jackass dictate your self-esteem."

"He's the only..."

"I know. But that can quickly be remedied." I offered as I took her hand in mine and squeezed it. "C'mon Jordan, I can give you so much more than him, in more ways than one." I stared down into her baby blue eyes as I touched her cheek gently. "And obviously, I care about you more than he ever has. I'm here and he's not."

"Keller." She sighed as she shifted closer to me.

"I've got all night babe." I murmured softly, running a finger down her cheek. "One night is all I'm askin', one night to show you how good we are together." Jordan didn't answer, just closed her eyes and leaned into me. I took that as a yes so I used her hand to help her off the couch and led her to a nearby vacant bedroom.

I couldn't believe this was happening. Sleeping with Jordan? Seriously? That would put me to a whole new status at school, especially if there were witnesses. Not to mention, I'd have a hold on her tighter than the plowboy. How sweet is that?

"I've been wanting this for so long Jordan." I lied softly as I pulled her into me for a kiss. She kissed me back.

"Me too Lance." She sighed. Her entire body tensed as she pulled back and looked at me with wide eyes. "I'm so sorry Keller."

"It's okay." I lied as I pulled her in for a hug. "It takes time to get over someone. Look at me, it's been months and I'm still not over you."

"Maybe we shouldn't..." She began, but I pulled back and looked at her sadly.

"Please Jordan, just stay the night with me? If nothing else?" I begged. I really should win an academy award for this crap. I'd settle for sex though. She started to shake her head no and I backed off. I plopped down on the bed and buried my face in my hands. I heard her exhale before she started towards me. No girl can resist a guy who is heartbroken, because of her. "I'm sorry."

"Keller, honey. Please don't do this."

"I'm sorry." I repeated slowly, shaking my head. I looked back at her with watery eyes. "It's just that you're the first girl...the only girl that I've ever liked so much. I really thought we had something. I know I come on too strong, but it's how I was raised. I just wish…I just wish that you'd give me another chance."

"I'm not ready."

"I know that. And I'm willing to wait Jordan. I'd wait forever if I have to. That's how certain I am that we should be together." I lied hurriedly as I reached to grab her hand again. "I just miss you so much. It hurt like Hell to see you and Lance together."

"Keller please stop. I can't handle this." She admitted nervously. "Please. I didn't…I don't."

"I'm sorry I'm blubbering like an idiot. I'm just out of my element when it comes to you."

"I know the feeling." She mumbled as she leaned into me. "I do care about you Keller."

"I know." I smiled as I bent down and pressed my lips against hers. Say a few sweet things to make her think I'm

336

pining away for her, start kissing her while she's trashed, and

she's mine. There's no telling how far I can ride this one.

Chapter 49

Zack

"Have you seen Jordan?" Alicia asked worriedly as she grabbed my arm. I flashed a smile as I shook my head.

"No ma'am." I drawled. "But I'd lay bets that she's passed out in a room somewhere sleeping off her heartbreak."

"That's just it. I don't think she's doing it alone." She admitted nervously as she bit her bottom lip and looked away quickly. She crossed her arms in front of her chest self-consciously, but it only made her ample cleavage that much more noticeable. I made sure she saw me ogling, before I looked back up at her face. She shot me a dirty look, but she was more concerned about her roommate.

"There's no guy here stupid enough to take advantage of her while she's drunk."

"You're wrong. I saw her and Keller all cozy on the couch about twenty minutes ago. Now I can't find either of them. The bedroom down the hall is locked. And Kaya told me she saw them both go in there, but Jordan could barely walk."

"That son of a bitch." I growled as I stormed towards the room.

"My thoughts exactly." Alicia grumbled as she hurried behind me. I grabbed the doorknob and jerked at it, it was locked. I heard Keller yell a muffled Go away from the other side, but I didn't listen. I don't trust Keller James at all, especially when it comes to Jordan. He's a manipulative bastard who does whatever it takes to get what he wants, it's painfully obvious that he wants Jordan and will stop at nothing to get her. I'm not entirely positive that he wasn't completely behind the incident with Collins.

While Alicia paced behind me and fretted about finding Caleb and Maddie, I heard her phone go off. I was too busy picking the lock to worry about anything else. Most people thought this skill was because I was meant for the dirty life, my family certainly did when they jumped at the opportunity to get me away from the less than stellar crowd I used to run with. However, lock picking has certainly come in handy when it comes to Jordan.

"Oh my God." I heard Alicia gasp behind me as she showed me a text message. Or rather a picture message. It was a selfie of a barely dressed Jordan and Keller kissing with the caption "Guess who's back together?". The next message was half porn of the two, all sent originally from Jordan's phone. Alicia pointed to the screen, showing it had been sent to Lance and all of his friends, as well. It didn't take a genius to see how drunk she was or that she wasn't participating on her own free will.

"Go find Caleb. I do not want you to see what I think might be happening on the other side. I especially don't want a witness to my killing Keller James." Alicia noticeably gulped as she nodded slowly back at me.

"If he's hurting her Zack, I'll be your alibi. That son of a bitch." I put a finger to my lips to shush her as I turned the doorknob this time; I heard the latch click and I motioned Alicia away. She was gone before I turned around to creep into the room.

On the bed lie Jordan passed out. Eyes closed, snoring softly while Keller was doing business on the other end. Rage filled my entire body and it took everything in me not to pounce the little weasel. Unfortunately, if I attacked then the whole party would be drawn to the events that were playing out before me. Yeah, Keller would be ruined at CA, but so would Jordan. I would risk my life to make sure that girl didn't suffer the embarrassment of this mess.

"What do you think you're doing?" I asked in a tight voice, as I flexed my fingers at my side. Keller's head jerked up, his eyes narrowed and he practically growled.

"We're kind of in the middle of something Bentley."

"No *you* are." My eyes flicked up to Jordan. "And by the way Jordan looks right now, I say that you have about two seconds to get the fuck away from her before I outright kill you. Oh, and about two minutes before Caleb flies through the door and double kills you."

"She's my girlfriend. I can do…"

"The fuck she is." I laughed rudely. "And that doesn't give you the right to do anything to her, you worthless son of a bitch."

"You're just jealous."

"Of you? Not a chance in Hell. Of the fact that she's crazy in love with Lance Bowman and the bastard doesn't even know what he's got, Hell yes."

"Leave Bentley." Keller repeated as he started to go back to his business.

"Are you fucking kidding me?" I spit as I charged. In one swoop, I grabbed him by the back of his shirt and threw him into the wall. He stuttered for only a few seconds, long enough for me to throw a blanket over Jordan, before his face darkened with rage and he charged at me. Keller didn't even make contact though, as much as I was itching to fight him I was glad to see Caleb storm in and pick Keller off like the fly that he was. I was too enraged to think clearly and I'd probably go to jail for killing the bastard.

"What the fuck is going on?" Caleb hissed, his angry face millimeters from Keller.

"Jordan and I were…were…" His eyes darted towards me for help. "Zack just came in like a psycho and attacked me."

"Tell the truth Keller." I growled.

"Caleb." Maddie said softly. "Keller needs his ass beat right now, but it's only going to draw attention to Jordan. You can't touch him."

343

"It's not my fault she was all over me." Keller shrugged cockily. "You can't keep your sister on house arrest for life Caleb. She wants me. I want her. It's inevitable."

"She wants you all right. She's stone cold passed out." Alicia snapped from the doorway. "Take his phone Zack and give it to me." I did as she said and handed her his iPhone. After a few seconds, she threw it at him. "I know you sent that video and pic to Lance. If it went elsewhere, you will pay Keller."

"What video?" Caleb asked hoarsely. Maddie shook her head. I grabbed Keller by the shirt and pinned him against the wall.

"You better be damned glad Caleb stepped in. Next time, you're mine." I hissed with a wicked grin.

"In your dreams." Keller scoffed, but flinched when I faked a punch.

"Oh yeah. You're definitely my little bitch." I laughed. Keller glared as he left the room, but he couldn't do anything else. It would be social and absolute suicide to do so.

"What the Hell just happened?"

"Don't worry about it." I instructed airily. "I stopped it. I took care of it." Caleb eyed me carefully then nodded his head in appeasement. Caleb knew that Jordan meant the world to me and I would do whatever it took to keep her safe.

"We need to get her dressed." Alicia muttered as she walked towards her friend. "I overheard Ben say she had at least fifteen shots before Keller pulled her away."

"Fifteen? What the fuck? She…"

"We'll get her dressed and make her puke when we get home." I offered. "If she doesn't do it on her own."

"All this over a fucking guy?"

"She's in love with him Caleb." Maddie sighed. "She falls hard, you know that."

"It doesn't." He began, he growled and shook his head while his fiancé and Alicia pulled Jordan's clothes back on. She barely stirred. "Could you stop screwing around and convince her that you have a thing for her? I can't take much more of this."

"She won't listen or believe it until she's ready." I responded with a shrug. "If she decides Keller James is an option again though, I will lock her up in the basement until she believes me."

"She's pretty out of it." Alicia interjected worriedly. "Do you think we should take her to the hospital?"

"No, it would end her career at Callatin." I stated.

"My aunt is a nurse, my dad is a doctor…should we…"

"We'll watch her, get her to vomit and…"

"I don't feel comfortable." Alicia began.

"I'm not going to let anything happen to her Alicia." I spit as I crossed over to the bed and picked Jordan up into my arms. "Unlike your cousin, I'm in love with this girl and would give anything to be in his fucking place right now." Alicia took a step back and inhaled sharply.

"He loves her too." She mumbled.

"Really?" I snapped.

"Let's just get her home." Maddie interrupted, pushing me gently. I looked down at the girl in my arms. She was a beautiful, happy, caring and amazing person. She would do anything for anyone and any guy would be lucky to have her attention. I was grateful Bowman couldn't see that because it left the door open for me, eventually. However, it didn't mean that I didn't want to beat the holy Hell out of the jerk for causing her so much pain that she risked her own safety.

Chapter 50

Lance

I should have seen it coming. However, it still felt like I'd been sucker punched with a knife. I was excited to see the text from Jordan, but then to watch that shit. Unreal. If I thought there was a chance Jordan was telling the truth, thought she did love me, it was gone now. How can someone be so cold as to send that? Especially, after all that she'd learned tonight. Was it all just a game?

"You okay?" Chopper asked as he fell down on the couch beside me. Everyone else had long since passed out. They had all gotten the same picture message, I forced them all to delete the video before they saw anything though. I don't know why, I should've let her reputation be ruined since she obviously didn't care about it.

"What do you think?" I snapped sarcastically as I leaned back into the couch and chugged the bottle of whiskey I'd yanked out of the cabinets.

"I think...that Jordan had nothing to do with that message for starters. But I know you're going insane right now. It doesn't take a genius to figure out how you feel about her, Hell we all know. Even if she did send it, just imagine how bad you hurt her to turn into that kind of spiteful bitch."

"I hurt her?" I scoffed, taking another drink of the Jack Daniels. "She's the one who moved on, went straight back to Richie Rich and gave me the finger."

"She didn't go back to him. Alicia said Jordan's been single, been praying for you to wise up."

"Obviously, Alicia doesn't know everything."

"They're roommates. Lish would know better than us. Besides, from what I know from convo's with Jo,

Alicia's right. She's crazy about you and devastated that you blew her off."

"I didn't…" I growled through clenched teeth as I sat up.

"You did."

"What the fuck does it matter now? She screwed that bastard and I can't…"

"Jordan is not like that and you know it. You should know it better than anyone." Chopper scolded with a shake of his head.

"I thought I knew her better than anyone." I admitted softly. "Obviously, it was just a game."

"Stop the pity party. And I know it may suck, but maybe you should watch that video again. See if you see the same thing I did."

"What? Did you see Bentley getting her from behind?" I spit as I stood up and started out of the living room.

"I should punch you in the face for that." Chopper spit as he jumped off the couch and took a step towards me. "Jordan's a good girl. She's a *great* girl and you, of all people, should know that. How can you say shit like that about her? Maybe you're not as crazy about her as I thought. Maybe you *were* playing games."

"Fuck off Chop. We all know who got played and it sure as Hell wasn't her." I stormed out of the house and onto the back porch of Drew's house. We'd been party hopping for most of the night, celebrating Drew's accomplishments. Of course, we'd ended up here and I'd had delusions of Jordan coming home with Alicia and being able to talk to her. No such luck. I'd probably…Hell, I don't know what I'd do right now if I saw her. I was pretty disgusted by the entire thing.

I fell into one of the Adirondack chairs on the back deck and buried my face in my hands. How had I gotten myself into this situation anyway? How had I gone from no attachments to feeling as if my left arm were ripped away when Jordan and I were apart? It wasn't right. It wasn't natural. Maybe dad's been right all along, you should never let a woman know your weaknesses, she'll burn you to the ground with them every time.

"Hey cousin." Alicia mumbled halfheartedly as she came outside and plopped into a chair beside me sometime later.

"Tell me that lying…"

"Don't finish that sentence." She warned as she stood up and towered over me. "Jordan didn't send those messages Lance. Why would you, even halfheartedly, believe she would do something like that?"

"Someone sent them. You can't tell me that she didn't know about it."

"I *can* tell you that, because it's the honest to God truth." She sighed as she fell back into the chair.

"Now you're in on the games? What the Hell, do you Callatin bitches stay together or what?"

"You get one. Call me a bitch again and see if I don't give you a black eye." Alicia retorted. I chuckled and shook my head. "I don't even know why I'm trying to tell you this. You don't deserve her." She sighed in exasperation and stood up.

"Thanks cousin." I said drily. "Nice to know that I don't deserve a manipulative, lying…"

"Shut up." She hissed. "Jordan is none of those things and you know it. She's in love with you, idiot and God only knows why. You're a fucking bastard as far as I can see. After you blew her off, for the fiftieth time, she got completely trashed. Keller, of course, took advantage of the situation and tricked her into the bedroom with him. What you didn't see, for obvious reasons, was that Jordan was trashed in the pic, and the video. As a matter of fact, she's completely passed out in the video. What you saw is Keller…"

"Alicia, if this is some kind of game."

"What kind of sick and twisted person…" She took a deep breath, exhaled and then pinned me with a steely glare. "Believe what you want Lance, but I'm telling the truth. Keller sent the texts. I can only pray we're the only people he sent it to. Jordan knows nothing. She didn't even stir when Zack carried her out of the party, out of the truck and into her bed. As far as she knows, she passed out in her own private pity party over you. Again, I can't see why."

"Why should I…?"

"Look at the texts again, from a different point of view." She sighed. "You'll see." I didn't say a word, just chugged more of the bottle of whiskey. Alicia shook her head and started into the house. She stopped before opening the door. "I know she hurt you Lance, because you think she should have waited around for you. I also know that you hurt her more by keeping secrets from her. She loves you. You love her. I don't' know why you just can't tell her that. Tell her the truth and get back to where you want to be, with each other." Alicia went inside and I remained in the chair. I stared out at the yard in front

354

of me, losing focus quickly. I took another long pull from the bottle of whiskey, felt it burn all the way down and closed my eyes to try and think about anything other than Keller and Jordan together.

After twenty minutes, I lost the battle and pulled my phone out of my pocket. I opened the first text message and stared at the picture of Jordan and Keller. It was hard to tear my eyes away from the fact that she was barely dressed, but when I looked at her face, I saw exactly what Alicia was talking about. She was trashed. In addition, when I checked the video, I concentrated on Jordan only. She was passed out cold.

Rage filled my entire body as I gripped my phone and the whiskey bottle. I will kill that bastard if he did…if he…I couldn't even think of what he could've done to her. Surely, Alicia would've mentioned that. I jumped up and raced inside.

"Took you long enough." Alicia sighed as she sat at the kitchen table bent over a book. She looked exhausted. I just stared at her, unable to speak the horrible thoughts that were racing through my head. "Zack stopped it before much could happen." She answered sheepishly. "He didn't...rape her, but he..."

"What was he doing? Does she even know?"

"She knows nothing. She was out cold, as I said earlier. As far as the rest of us are concerned, she will never know."

"But if she doesn't know what Keller is capable of then,"

"Trust me when I tell you that she knows *exactly* what Keller James is capable of." Alicia replied with a disgusted look. "Why do you think she dumped him in the first place?"

"When?"

"They weren't back together Lance. Keller may try, but Jordan isn't falling for it." She shrugged. "Not to mention that she was holding out for you" She rolled her eyes as she stood up and closed her book. "I'm going to bed cousin. It's been a long night and I'm beat."

"Will she talk to me?"

"Obviously not tonight." She snapped as she started out of the kitchen. "But the band is playing at a bar tomorrow night in Carbondale."

"What bar?"

"You can figure that out on your own. If you want her back Lance, work for it. Act like it. I'm not going to help you; I won't be responsible for you hurting her anymore."

"You're not…"

"It doesn't feel that way." She mumbled softly. She turned around and looked at me sadly. "I've always wanted a sister Lance. Always. I've had friends before, but nothing like Jordan and Maddie. They are my *best friends* and I will not let that be ruined because you're a selfish asshole."

"I was protecting her."

"No. You weren't. You are a typical guy who was terrified when she said the L word, you just used everything else as your excuse. You could have told her *everything*, but you didn't. You were protecting yourself and nothing more."

"Alicia." I started angrily. She put her hand up in the air and waved me off.

"I'm done. I'm going to bed. If you feel I'm judging you unfairly, then prove me wrong." Alicia walked out of the room and I heard her bedroom door shut shortly after. I buried my face in my hands and tried to rack my brain to figure this whole mess out.

Chapter 51

Jordan

The band had a gig at a bar nearby and I needed to look older than fifteen, so I pulled on a black micro dress, sexy black heels and let my hair flow down my back in wild curls. I knew I looked well over twenty-one and incredibly freaking hot. I thought being ogled and hit on by hoards of college guys would boost my ego and make me feel better about Lance, but it didn't.

The show went awesome and after three encores, we finally finished loading up the van, but it did little to console my broken heart. We were about to head for home when Izzy grabbed my arm and pointed at a familiar truck in the parking lot.

"Isn't that your ex?" She asked excitedly. Lance had been sitting on the tailgate until he saw us. He was wearing khaki dress pants, a white button up shirt and wasn't wearing a hat, I didn't know why he was dressed so out of character.

I stared at him as he stood up, grabbed a bouquet of flowers and walked towards me with a nervous smile.

"Oh my God, he came back." I breathed excitedly as I stripped my shoes off and sprinted towards him, jumped into his arms and planted one Hell of a kiss on his surprised mouth.

"Jordan, I…"

"Sshh, you don't have to say anything." I whispered as I put a finger up to his mouth. "You're here now and that's all that matters to me."

Lance just stood there grinning back at me, his arms wrapped tightly around my waist and I knew I was back where I was supposed to be. I kissed him again and when I pulled away, he handed me the beautiful tulips.

"Can I take you home?"

"No." I answered quickly. His face dropped and I giggled as I smiled back at him. "You can take me somewhere and kiss me for a while first."

"Good." He smiled as he stared deep into my eyes. He carried me to the truck, stealing sweet kisses as he did. He opened the door to his black Ford and placed me on the leather seats before he followed behind me.

As Lance started the truck, I called to tell Caleb that I'd be late.   "Where do you wanna go?" Lance asked once I hung up.

"Just drive." I instructed as I snuggled into his chest.

"I've missed this. I've missed you." He admitted sweetly as he kissed the top of my head, while we pulled out of the parking lot and headed down the road.

"Me too." I answered quietly.

"I'm really sorry about everything Jordan. I shouldn't have acted the way I did." Lance blurted out a few minutes later. "I *am* crazy about you and that night in my truck I don't know what freaked me out more; the fact that you said exactly what I was about to say or that you said it first."

"Why didn't you tell me this that night, instead of running off?"

"I was embarrassed."

"Don't ever be too embarrassed with me, Lance. You can tell me anything, I thought you knew that."

"I did. I do. It's just…I'm too proud and complex sometimes. That's why I *didn't* tell you about everything else." He stated softly. I nodded my head in understanding and snuggled even closer into his chest. I fit into his arms perfectly; I was ready to focus on that and nothing else. We could only apologize and explain so much. In reality, he didn't even have to do that as long as he just held me in his safe and warm arms all night long.

"So where'd you learn to play the fiddle anyway?" Lance asked to break the heavy silence that had fallen in the truck.

"Pops." I grinned as I sat up and looked back at him. "My mom's father, I was his little buddy and he loved that thing. He was always messing around with it on the front porch. At night, I'd climb up on the swing and just watch him in awe. Finally, he taught me to play too. Boy did my dad's parents hate that."

"You were amazing." He chuckled, "You never manage to stop surprising me."

"I'm good like that." I flirted, winking at him as I leaned forward and kissed him softly.

"Do you know what bothers me the most though?" Lance asked a few minutes later, as he pulled down our familiar dirt road; make out road I'd started calling it. "You and Keller. At the mall, I wanted to tell you everything, but when I saw him I figured I lost my chance. Then last night at the game…"

"First off, Keller was being a friend and forced me to get out of the house and *that's* why we were together. At the game, I wanted you to think we kissed but I assure you, we didn't. I needed to get back at you, wanted to hurt you as bad as you hurt me." I told him sheepishly as I ducked my head.

"You did."

"But I'm here now and that should be all that matters. If I wanted Keller James I wouldn't be in this truck with you right now, I'd be with him."

"It still bothers me."

"Trust me Lance." I sighed softly as I moved closer to him. "I broke up with Keller for a reason. I've been down that road and I will not go back down it."

"Why do you say it like that?" He asked looking at me nervously. I shrugged my shoulders. "Why did you break up?"

"Because he's a very controlling and clingy person. I wasn't myself when I was with him."

"Controlling how?" Lance asked in a tight voice.

"As in he dictated what clothes I wore. He *bought* all my clothes. He had a schedule set up for me when I was supposed to do certain things; he scheduled and paid for hair and nail appointments, facials, spa days whatever. He shanghaied my birthday party and took us skiing in Tahoe as my present, totally what he wanted." I explained airily. I sucked in my breath when I realized all I'd said. I looked back at Lance's wide, defeated eyes.

"He bought your clothes?" I shrugged indifferently. "Just a few or?"

"It's not important."

"It kind of is."

"Lance." I sighed as I reached for him. He backed up quickly. "It's not important."

"I need to know Jordan. I want to know what I'm up against."

"You're not *up* against anything Lance. As I said before, Keller is not even on my radar."

"But you're on his and he will do whatever it takes to get you back."

"No, he won't. He can have any girl at Callatin. Ninety eight percent of the female population at school thinks I'm the biggest fool in the world for dumping him on his ass."

"Why? He's an ass."

"That's not important there." I shrugged. "All that matters to the girls at CA is that he's hot, he's super rich and that he spoils his girlfriend rotten. I'm on a hate list at school, because of Keller."

"How did he spoil you?"

"Lance, stop."

"No. I want to know. What did he buy you?" I shrugged my shoulders and stared out the windshield, nervously playing with the diamond tennis ankle bracelet Keller had given me as a gift. "Tell me." I rolled my eyes and looked back at him disgustedly.

"He bought me clothes. He bought me a computer. He bought shoes, accessories, and a few dozen other things. I didn't keep a tally."

"Accessories like jewelry? Like the expensive ankle bracelet you're wearing, or the earrings?" He asked as he shifted uncomfortably in his seat. I nodded my head. "And the clothes that look like they came off the cover of a celebrity magazine?" I nodded my head again, my eyes not meeting his. "Just a few or...?"

"Basically my whole wardrobe Lance." I sighed. "Does that make you feel better?"

"No it doesn't." He spat. "I didn't think you were like that. I thought..."

"Had you listened then you would have heard me say that I broke up with Keller because he was turning me into someone I'm not. He showered me with expensive gifts and I shoved the majority of them back in his face, but he has a way of not taking no for an answer. I didn't ask for those things. I didn't want them. I didn't expect them, but that was how Keller was raised; you show your affection by blowing wads of cash on someone and that's what he did. It's all he knows."

"Then why the fuck are you with me? I can't give you any of that; I wouldn't even know where to begin."

"I'm with you because you're nothing like Keller James." I exlained in a low, icy tone. "You did a damn fine job with my Christmas present Lance. Honestly, it was worth more to me than any gift I've ever received in my life." Lance sat back in his seat and rested his arm on the doorframe before putting his hand to his head.

"I can't give you…"

"It's not about what you can give me monetarily Lance. I don't care about those things." I whispered. Tears pricked my eyes and I let them slowly fall down my cheeks. "Why can't you understand that? Why do you think I'm such a horrible person?"

"I don't think that Jo." He admitted softly as he reached for me. "I just...it's hard for me to understand why you're even here right now. I'm nothing special, at all. You're too good for me."

"That's ridiculous." I protested with a shake of my head. "I am not too good for you. Why would you even think that?"

"I'd be blind and stupid not to." He spit. I pulled away from him and leaned against the passenger side door. I shook my head in disbelief as I stared back at him.

"I just don't understand why you would think that way, Lance. How can we be a couple if you feel like that?" I asked sadly. Lance's face dropped as he closed his eyes and inhaled.

"I don't know." He mumbled. "I'm nothing from nowhere Jordan. A farm boy with nothing and no future."

"You *have* a future Lance, you just have to figure it out for yourself but with that mentality, you have no future. You are one of the smartest people I know. And you're not just book smart, you're street smart and mechanically inclined. You adapt, you survive, you're honest and hardworking. You're a caring person. You have all these attributes that round you into this amazing person. You're someone that I admire, that your friends and family adore and respect. You can do anything you want Lance and your life will be golden, do you know why?" He shook his head. "Because it'll be real. It'll be something that you earned, not something that was handed to you. If you do nothing more than stay on the farm for the rest of your life, it won't make you any less of a person, because you did it out of duty, out of honor and no matter what, you are contributing to a legacy that's grown for decades and will continue to do so.

Do you know how many people don't know crap about their family? Me included. Do you know how many people would give millions of dollars to know one iota of the family history you do? Not just that, you live amidst your traditions and history every single day, Lance. That's amazing."

A smile tugged at the corner of Lance's mouth, revealing his lone dimple. He shook his head and let out a chuckle. "Only you could make farming sound honorable."

"It *is* honorable Lance. I don't know half of what you do in a day, but I know that you bust your ass from dawn till past dusk, no matter what the weather. I know that when you slack off it doesn't mean someone else will chip in, it means you have double the work the next day. I don't think I could do what you do. I don't know anyone who could."

"It's life. It's not honorable."

"It is to me." I admitted softly as I looked down at the slinky dress I was wearing. "If you could see things from my eyes Lance, you'd know without a doubt, why I fell for you."

371

Lance reached his hand out and took mine in his before pulling me into him.

"You sure do know how to make a guy feel good about himself." He murmured with a sly smile.

"That I do." I flirted in a thick voice. "In more ways than one." Lance chuckled softly as I climbed on to his lap, straddling him. I touched his face softly and stared back into those muddy brown eyes. The same amazing eyes that had been keeping me up at night, since the first time I looked into them.

"You know I can't think straight when you do this." He sighed as he helped me settle on to him. "I can't focus on anything but you."

"That was my intention." I drawled as I kissed the corner of his mouth. "Don't fuck this up again okay? Three strikes and you're out; this is your last chance."

"What?"

"You blew three chances to ask me on a date and *I* had to give *you* my number, that was strike one." I admitted.

"Is that right?"

"Yes." I nodded with a seductive smile. "Now are you going to take advantage of the barely dressed hottie in your lap or what?"

"Hmmm." He teased.

"You're an ass!" I exclaimed as I swatted at him playfully.

"I am." He mumbled sadly, as he took my face in his rough hands. "But I'm gonna be better. I can't lose you Joey, you're the best thing in my life."

"Then kiss me dammit!" Lance laughed and kissed me hungrily, he didn't stop for hours. I slipped though; I was so caught up in him that we made love again.

"I'll see you tomorrow, right?" Lance breathed in my ear as he held me on my front porch. I nodded, relishing the feel of those warm arms wrapped around me again.

"Do you really have to go tonight? I wish you'd stay. I'm not ready to let go of you."

"I do have to go." He tipped my chin up and looked directly into my eyes. "But I'll be here tomorrow, first thing. I've missed spending all day with my girlfriend. We'll probably have to swing by the house; Wyatt has been missing you something fierce."

"I'd like that." I giggled as I leaned my forehead against his. "So I'm your girlfriend again?"

"I thought you always were."

"I hate to admit this, but I always thought I was too." I said. "It won't happen again though."

"I know it won't. I don't plan on anything coming in between us ever again."

"Promise?"

"I swear." He whispered before he bent down to kiss me hungrily. "I've already decided that my life sucks without you in it."

"Mine too." I sighed. "I love you." He nodded and kissed me again.

"Sweet dreams darlin'." He drawled before he left my arms and headed to his truck. "I'll call you in the morning and let you know what time I'll be here." I nodded and waved before I headed inside the house on cloud nine.

Chapter 52

I floated out of my bedroom and towards the bathroom early the next morning. I was on an amazing high, really. My mind kept flipping back to Lance's kiss, his touch and then my stomach would go into jelly.

"How was the show last night?" Zack asked as he caught me after my shower.

"Amazing."

"Good. I thought we were going, I'm still not sure why we didn't end up there." He chuckled.

"No worries. You guys don't have to go to every one of my gigs, it's not a big deal."

"We're supposed to support our friends." He looked at me evenly, gauging my mood I guess.

"True, but I'm not at all of your baseball games."

"You're at all the ones you can be at." He shrugged. "What time did you get in last night? I tried to wait up for you."

"I know." I mumbled as I looked down at the ground. "I saw you on the couch, put a blanket over you." He nodded his head and chuckled. "It was pretty late. Lance showed up and we talked."

"Oh yeah?" His voice was flat, his jaw tight as he looked back at me with no emotion on his face. "How'd that go?"

"Good." I smiled, hugging myself tightly. I don't know why it felt wrong to tell Zack this, it just did. "He's going to be here soon to pick me up." Zack nodded.

"So you're back together then? Even though…"

"I don't need a lecture Zack." I sighed. "There's so much that you don't know about and…I just…I love him too much to turn my back on him when he needs me. When I need him so badly."

"Jordan." He started.

"I need to get ready." I mumbled as I slipped into my bedroom and shut the door. I knew my friends would react this way, but I didn't care. I grabbed my phone off the bed and checked the time. I had a missed call from Lance, I let out a curse and hit the redial button. It went directly to voicemail. I sent him a text, but there was no response. My stomach started hurting, I didn't have a good feeling about this at all.

My phone rang at around noon, Lance's ring tone filled my bedroom. I dove to answer it.

"Hey." I grinned, forcing the shooting stomach pains out of my head.

"I'm so sorry darlin''." He sighed into the phone. "Something came up and I can't hang out today."

"Oh. Is everything all right?" I asked, trying to disguise the disappointment in my voice.

"It's fine. Nothing for you to worry about." There was no inflection in his voice, I waited for him to continue, but he didn't.

"You're not going to tell me what it is?" I asked, not masking the irritation in my voice.

"No. It's family crap, I can't get into it right now." He muttered. "I'm sorry to stand you up. I'll make it up to you though. Next weekend or something, okay?" Non-committal answers, no commitments for the next weekend; I'd be an idiot not to realize he was blowing me off again. My temper flared as I clutched the phone in my hands.

"So you get laid last night and you can't bother to mess with me today?" I hissed. "Is that all you wanted; one last roll in the hay before you dumped me for good?"

"What?" Lance laughed sarcastically. "You're a trip, Jo."

"Not funny." I spit. "You disappear from my life for a month, then strategically come back, get laid and totally blow me off the next day without even an explanation. The least you could do is make up some pathetic lie so you wouldn't be shoving my stupidity back in my face." Tears rolled down my cheeks. I was an idiot.

"Damn it Jo, don't start a fight with me right now. I realize how this looks, but it's not how it is. Okay? Trust me."

"Trust you?" I asked feigning a sweet voice. "I did that once Lance Bowman and you disappointed me then."

"Jordan." Lance begged in a broken voice. "Please don't do this now. Please don't. I will call you tonight and explain everything, okay darlin? We'll talk tonight. I promise I'll call you around eight o clock, just like normal."

"Fine." I growled as I hung up the phone before he could reply or I could break down. I was thoroughly confused now. It's like he runs hot one minute and cold the next...or however that saying goes. I'll give him the benefit of the doubt, if he doesn't call at eight tonight and explain everything, then I'm officially done with him.

Maybe.

Chapter 53

Two hours later, I went downstairs and tried to pass the time by hanging out with Caleb and the others. For a while, just Zack and I hung out; which happened a lot. I wouldn't complain though, he was definitely fun to be around and he kept my mind off reality. I was more than thrilled with the fact that he didn't ask why I wasn't with Lance.

Zack and I flirted all day before I finally retreated to my room to do some homework and get ready to head back to campus. The academy was very strict and everyone but seniors had to be back on campus by ten o clock on Sunday nights, unless the school is notified prior.

At five till eight, my phone went off, signaling that I had a text message. My entire world was shattered as I read it.

I don't think we should see each other anymore. It's been fun but that's it, I should've left it alone the first time. Please don't contact me or my family ever again.

My heart sank.

I reread the message a hundred times and grew more devastated each time. It didn't sound like Lance at all. The words conflicted everything he'd said to me the night before. I was confused, hurt and furious all at the same time. I didn't know how I could've been so wrong about him.

Despite the message's request I did try and call Lance. After everything, I deserved more than to be dumped via text message. I prayed it was some horrible mistake as his phone rang, but he never answered. I didn't want to seem psycho so I hung up without leaving a voicemail.

Lance and I had been more than boyfriend/girlfriend. He was one of my best friends. The two of us told each other about our demons; our secrets that we'd never told anyone else outside of our families. We could talk about anything and everything, without any fears. We'd spend hours on the phone talking and it all had disappeared.

I called Maddie immediately. She was already hanging out with my brother, but she ditched him to console me.

"I should just call him. It's probably a misunderstanding. It's probably a joke. He wouldn't dump me after we had sex, Lance isn't like that." I'd repeated that sentence a hundred times that night, each time I'd jump up for my phone and try to call him. Maddie had confiscated it, finally, and shut it off.

"You need to calm down, take a few days to think about what you want to say." Maddie instructed as she sat down on the bed and slung her arm over on my shoulders. "If he says not to contact him, then maybe that's what you should do. If he can dump you in a text message sweetie, he's not worth your time."

"No, if he's done with me then he should have the balls to tell me so."

"You're absolutely right." She sighed.

Chapter 54

Lance

"You think it's too late to call again?" I asked, looking down at my watch and seeing that it was after midnight. "She's got school tomorrow."

"No, not after what happened between you two. She's probably waiting up for you to call anyway." Sawyer offered. "If you don't talk to her before we get home, then I'll personally help you sneak on that campus after school, or during, whichever."

"Thanks Teems." I chuckled as I dialed again. Straight to voicemail, my heart sank. I don't understand this at all. I realize she was pretty upset by my brush off earlier; which I completely regret, but I told her I'd call at eight. My phone had been missing at that time, Drew finally found it at quarter after. I had been calling ever since and each time, it went straight to voicemail.

I tried to call her phone a few more times that night and never got another answer. I left a few voicemails, but she never returned them. If Alicia wasn't at the hospital with me, I would've called her to get through to Jordan.

"You can talk to her tomorrow." Sawyer reassured me an hour later. "You goin' to school in the morning?"

"I don't know." I shrugged. "It really just depends on what the doctors say tonight. They haven't really given anyone an all clear yet." Sawyer nodded and stared out at the parking lot. "*You* have to go tomorrow, so you really need to get the Hell out of here." Sawyer shrugged his shoulders and looked down at the ground. "It's okay. You've been here all day bud and you didn't have to be."

"It's my family too." He answered somberly. "But you're right, I do need to go. If anything changes or y'all need anything, just call." I nodded my gratitude and Sawyer loped off to his car. Chopper and Coop had been with me all day as well, but they'd left hours ago at their parent's insistence. I knew if it were up to them, they'd all be sacked out in the waiting room with me.

I tried Jordan one last time and got the same result, voicemail. I took a deep breath, stood up and headed back inside to the ICU where they were waiting to transfer my sister upstairs to the maternity wing.

Unbeknownst to my family, my father had been released from jail. Apparently, my mother hadn't shown up to the hearing to enforce the Order of Protection and the judge took that as a sign to drop the charges. I had been out in the barn, doing as much as I could when my mother stuck her head in to let me know that she and Wyatt were headed into town to meet Jenn and Rob for brunch. I was invited, but I was eager to be with Jordan. I had missed her more than I realized. I promised mom that we would stop by later, for dinner and she was gone.

I was in the truck headed to get Jordan when the phone rang. It was Coop, telling me that his brother had just called to tell him my father was released and headed home. He cursed and then told me that my family had been in an accident, he was on his way to get me to take me to the hospital.

My drunken father had hit my mother, sister, brother in law and nephew in a head on collision. He was trashed. He was treated and immediately taken back to jail. The rest of my family lay in hospital beds trying to figure out what the Hell had happened to them.

Mom has a lot of bruises, scratches and a nasty concussion. Rob broke his arm and suffered a concussion, as well. Wyatt was okay, thanks to his car seat, and Jenn had the most damage; she's been in and out of consciousness all day, losing a lot of blood and they've been having a lot of problems with losing the baby on the monitors. From the moment of impact, she began having contractions. An hour ago, her water broke. This wouldn't be a bad thing if she was farther along, but she's just barely 34 weeks. The doctors assured us a baby can survive that premature, but there could be a lot of complications; especially after the accident.

Why didn't I tell Jordan any of this? I don't know. I was so freaked out; I had called her on my way to the hospital. I really just needed to hear her voice, needed her reassurance and I wanted her to be here with me; I need her to stand beside me but instead, I pushed her away. I was vague and an absolute jerk about the whole thing. I didn't know where my father was at the time, didn't know he was involved in the accident until I walked into the emergency room. I was terrified that he'd show up, see us together and attack my girlfriend. When he saw me in the waiting room at the hospital he came at me, I couldn't risk him doing that to her. I couldn't handle her seeing that nasty side of my life. Seeing it and hearing about it are two completely different things.

"Hey." Alicia greeted me softly when I walked into the waiting room. She stood up and crossed over to me immediately. "They're taking Jenn back for an emergency C-section." My whole body tightened and my aunt rushed over to me.

"Now that doesn't mean anything bad, Lance. C-sections are perfectly normal nowadays. Honestly, after all Jenn's been through today they probably figured it would be the easiest on her and the baby." I nodded and plopped down in one of the uncomfortable chairs.

"Did you get a hold of Jordan?" Alicia asked, plopping down beside me. I shook my head.

"No. I didn't. Since Drew had my phone, I didn't call her until quarter after eight and I guess she assumed the worst." I explained through clenched teeth. "I've been trying ever since, but her phone's shut off."

"I'll try tomorrow." Alicia offered. "Otherwise, I'll explain things when I get back to the dorms tomorrow night. I still don't know why you didn't tell her to begin with."

"I was freaked out. I'm lucky I even thought to call and tell her I wouldn't be showing up for our date."

"Yeah, that wouldn't have went over well either." She laughed drily. "I can talk to her if you want, but I know things will go over better if it comes from you. She was a little perturbed that everyone else had to explain why you were MIA recently." I nodded my head in agreement and took a deep breath.

"I'm just not very good at this whole thing. You know? I was embarrassed. Why would anyone want to get involved in that kind of a mess anyway?"

"She loves you, which I still don't understand." Alicia teased as she playfully bumped into me. "Rob went back to scrub up for the delivery and dad said it shouldn't be longer than twenty minutes before they bring the baby out. You want to head up to the baby floor?"

"Yeah." Fifteen minutes later, my niece, Ella Jane, was carried into the nursery where the nurses began to frantically work on her. A liaison stepped out after a few minutes to tell us that everything was fine, mostly just a precaution since she's so early.

Now all I had to do was wait and that's the worst thing of all.

Chapter 55

On Tuesday, I climbed out of my truck in the Mencino County High School parking lot and looked around. My friends were all standing around Chopper's beat up old Bronco, smoking cigarettes and laughing. I had skipped school yesterday, but my mother forced me to return today.

"Did you talk to your girl yet or what?" Coop asked as I approached. I just shook my head.

"Straight to voicemail every damn time. I even tried the house, but whoever answered said she was sick and not taking calls."

"What are you going to do?"

"Skip out at lunch and go see her." I shrugged. "If I can figure out how to sneak past security."

"I've got that one for you." Sawyer smiled. "Mom said she's got a few deliveries there today and they usually let her go all the way up to the admin building to drop them off. If it's after hours, then right to the dorm. I told her we'd take care of it for her."

"You're the man Teems, I owe you." I grinned. "Owe you big."

"When are Jenn and the baby coming home?" Chopper asked. "When I left yesterday no one knew."

"Jess called me on my way here and said they told Rob it would probably be Friday and they could all go home together. Ella's doing great and they don't foresee any problems."

"Who the fuck is that?" Cooper interjected as he pointed towards a yellow Porsche Boxster as it pulled into the parking lot.

"What the fuck?" I growled recognizing the flashy sports car immediately; Keller James. My heart immediately dropped. Is that why I can't reach her on her cell phone? Did something bad happen, and he's here to break the news to me?

"Is…" I started as I rushed towards where Keller had slid to a stop. Keller's face was angry and distorted as he charged at and knocked me backwards.

"WHOA!" Chopper yelled as he started for Keller. All the boys hung back momentarily, they knew I could handle myself against this scrawny rich boy.

"What the fuck is wrong with you?" I yelled as I landed a punch on Keller's jaw and took the opportunity to push him off me.

"You stay the fuck away from her, do you understand?" Keller yelled as he stood millimeters from my face.

"What?"

"Stay the fuck away from Jordan, *do you understand?*"

"No I won't. You have…"

"Do you really think she's still your girlfriend after you dumped her in a text message?"

"What are you talking about?"

"You fucked her Saturday night and then you dumped her by text on Sunday." He yelled as he reeled back and swung. I ducked out of his way and landed another blow in his stomach. Keller stumbled back, obviously winded and just glared.

"I did not break up with her. I don't know what you're talking about."

"She got a text message from your phone on Sunday, saying it was over."

"That's ridiculous, I didn't send that. I wouldn't do that." I rambled, I tried to focus and watch the rich boy at the same time. "I didn't even have my phone until after eight o clock."

"Then who fucking sent it to her?" Keller retorted, obviously not buying my story.

"I'll take care of that. It wasn't me, though."

"Regardless, you stay away from her. You've hurt her enough as it is. She's fucking devastated, I wish I knew why. It's not like *you're* anything great." Keller said with a confident laugh. "*I* am right for her. You are nothing, *I* am everything. I can give that girl the world and you'll only show it to her from the back of some broken down tractor."

I was seeing red, my ears roared and without thinking, I took another swing at Keller, this time connecting with his eye. The boy flew backwards onto the ground and just chuckled.

"She's already mine. She's already made up her mind about you Bowman; she's done with your lame ass." Keller laughed before he climbed back in to his car and sped away.

"He's got a lot of fucking balls." Coop said.

"I have to talk to her." I mumbled as I stormed towards my truck.

"How are you going to get on campus?" Sawyer hollered after him.

"I don't know. I'll figure something out. I'll meet you at the flower shop in thirty minutes, if I don't figure something out before then."

I tore out of the parking lot and headed for Callatin Academy, immediately calling Jordan's phone. It wasn't shut off anymore, it rang a few times before going to her voicemail. I cursed repeatedly and continued to call. She's probably in the middle of class and can't answer, but surely if she sees I called a hundred times she'll rethink everything. I had no idea what I was going to do or even what I would say if she answered. I just knew that this could not be the end of our story.

Chapter 56

Keller

I came to a stoplight, pulled down the vanity mirror and inspected the damage from Lance's fist. The redneck packed a punch, that's for sure. My eye was already starting to swell and my jaw was red as pain shot through it, but it was all worth it.

The light turned green and I started towards the academy again. I grabbed the phone, made some arrangements and then smiled wickedly to myself as I pulled through the campus's wrought iron gates. As I parked the Porsche, I looked down at the phone in my passenger seat; Jordan's phone. Maddie had given it to Caleb for safe keeping Sunday night and I had swiped it from him. It was on silent, but every ten seconds or so, it would light up with Lance's number. Pathetic redneck. Won't he ever learn that he should just stick with the cows and leave the women to the real men?

I laughed out loud and picked up the phone, deleting all his calls with a flick of my fingers. This was my chance. I was going to get Jordan Donaldson back, no matter what. Once we were back together, she'd realize how silly she was for falling for the plow boy. She was going places and he obviously wasn't.

I skipped all my classes that day and then snuck over to the girl's campus before Jordan was finished with practice. I'd ordered flowers for her and just wanted to make sure they looked expensive and gorgeous.

When I arrived, a note was taped on her door and another vase of flowers sat next to mine. They paled in comparison, of course. Who buys tulips when it's not Easter? I picked up the card. Lance, I should've known.

I love you Jordan. Please call me so that we can fix things between us. I don't want to lose you again. Love, Lance

I smiled as I found a nearby trashcan and emptied Lance's flowers and card inside. I grabbed the envelope off the door and read the letter inside.

I'm sorry about Sunday. I should've told you on the phone what was going on, but I was a little freaked out. I missed you all day. I needed you all day. I saw Keller today. He told me about the text. I don't know what's going on, but we need to talk. Drew had my phone, which is why I didn't call you on time, but I did call you. I'm going crazy. I miss you. I love you Jordan, Please call me as soon as you get this so I can make things right. Love Lance.

I chuckled. "Pathetic." I mumbled as I threw that letter in the same trashcan. What a pathetic loser. That was money well spent. He's blaming his cousin for the text message, that's too bad. It was pure luck I ran into that townie slut while I was at the mall. It couldn't have fallen into my lap any easier. She couldn't have been any easier, either. I overheard the girl talking to a Drew, when she was finished I threw a smile and a little charm her way and learned that she was going to meet him around seven thirty tonight. I buy her the expensive outfit she's eyeing and take her back to the Porsche and within minutes, I have her willing to do whatever I ask of her. Really wasn't that hard once she realized who I was plotting against; seems Jordan and Kelcie have had a run in before and she'd love nothing more than a little payback. How sweet it is. I get a blowjob, the plowboy pushed out of my way and no possibility of being connected to this little scene. No one would believe I'd stoop so low as to hook up with a townie so if she ever tries to pinpoint me, I'll be in the clear.

Voices interrupted my thoughts and I quickly picked up my vase of expensive roses and pretended to be setting them down when Maddie turned the corner.

"What are you up to?" She asked evenly with a raised eyebrow.

"I heard about what happened and I knew Jordan would be upset, so I just wanted to leave her these."

"No. You're trying to move in on her."

"What if I am?"

"She needs time Keller." Maddie sighed. "And I think you're wasting yours. You're not good enough for her."

"But the plowboy is?"

"I didn't say that either." She hissed. "Obviously any son of a bitch who would break up with her in a text message isn't good enough for her. You don't deserve her and neither does he."

"Well that's Jordan's decision, not yours."

"Maybe so, but I have a lot of influence."

"You wouldn't."

"I would." She spit defiantly. "She's my best friend and you treat her like shit."

"What if I tell you that her dumping me this last time showed me the error of my ways? What if I tell you I realize she deserves better than I was giving her? What if I mentioned there'd be a five thousand dollar shopping spree in it for you, if you talk me up?" Maddie's eyes widened before she burst into laughter.

"Five thousand dollars? Is that all? Daddy does better than that every weekend. Give it up Keller; I'm one girl you can't buy." She rolled her eyes. "Get lost, now."

"No. I'll just wait around till Jordan gets back from practice. Why isn't she with you anyway?"

"Because she didn't go to practice. She didn't go to classes today either. Which you would've known had you not skipped out as well. What in the Hell were you doing anyway? And why do you have a black eye?"

"Don't worry about it. So Jordan's in her room? Is she sick?" Maddie grabbed my arm and yanked me away from the door. When we got a little ways down the hall, she spun back around and eyed me angrily.

"She's upset Keller. She's devastated, actually. Her first love dumped her in a fucking text message. She's broken hearted and humiliated, to say the least. She was too depressed to go to classes today. I doubt she'll go tomorrow either."

"First love." I snorted. "You're kidding right? I was…"

"A boyfriend, nothing else." Maddie snapped. "Leave Keller, or I call security."

"Fine, I'll leave. Make sure she gets those roses. I'll be back to check on her tomorrow too. I won't stop until she talks to me and sees that she's better off with me."

"Get over yourself Keller." Maddie retorted as she flipped around and marched back to her room. She picked up the roses and carried them inside with her, too polite to chuck them into the trashcan as she wanted. Good girl, Maddie. That's all I needed was for her to see the flowers and see that I care. The rest will fall into place in no time.

Chapter 57

Maddie

That conniving little fink. I brought the flowers inside the room and let him think I'm delivering them. I saw that smug smile. Jordan's not even here though. It's a good thing she got the flu and decided to stay at home so she wouldn't infect the rest of us, but Keller does not need to know that. If he knew she was at home he'd be all over it, bothering her when she really needs rest and time to heal over Lance Bowman.

I picked up my phone and speed dialed my boyfriend. He picked up immediately.

"Keller is up to something." I announced quickly.

"Hello to you too, Maddie." He chuckled. "And what makes you think that?"

"He was waiting around outside our door doing something. When I came up he was putting flowers out there for Jordan. He said he wanted to make her feel better because of Lance."

"I'll bet he does." He grumbled.

"My thoughts exactly. He thinks she's here with me. I didn't tell him otherwise. I thought if I did he'd be at the house in a heartbeat trying to worm his way in. She doesn't need that Caleb; she's really vulnerable right now."

"I know Maddie." He sighed. "I won't tell him any different either. I'll tell Zack not to either. You think he was just dropping off the flowers?"

"No. Lucy texted to say that two guys were messing around outside my room. I hurried over, but Keller was the only one here. She would've recognized Keller. I even sent her a message back asking if it was Keller she'd seen and she said no."

"No idea what he was doing then?" Caleb asked and I knew he was mentally going through the number of things Keller James could be plotting.

"None." I sighed as I grabbed the vase of flowers and carried them back outside. I went to the nearest trashcan and tried to fit them inside, but it was bursting over so I hurried down to the next one. "I just trashed the flowers though."

"Good girl." Caleb chuckled. "We'll keep him away from Jordan as long as we can. I'd hate to see her go right back to that jerk because Bowman did a number on her self-esteem. Especially when she'd be a heck of a lot better off with Bentley."

"Me too. That reminds me; how'd Keller get a black eye?"

"Black eye? I don't know. He skipped out of class today, maybe he got jumped or something. He does tend to run his mouth."

"That's no joke." I chortled.

"I'll try to get it out of him. Maybe Bentley finally gave it to him and I just haven't heard about it yet."

"Maybe." I giggled. "But if he did, Zack would've already texted and called you to see his handiwork."

"Very true." He chuckled. "Is Alicia back yet? Have you asked her what the deal is?"

"Nope. Her and Jordan must've gotten the same flu bug. Jayden told me there was a family emergency on Monday and that's why she wasn't here, but then she said Alicia came down with the flu bug too."

"Family emergency? You think that's why Bowman bailed on her Sunday morning?"

"No. He wouldn't have sent the text if that's all it was." I let out a loud sigh and plopped down on my bed. "I really wish she didn't keep finding the biggest losers on the planet. I thought Lance was different. He had us all fooled."

"That's for sure." Caleb said on the other end. "I really wish dad would've let me lock her up in her room and keep her away from the male population."

"Oh shut up." I giggled. "She'd have broken out and you know it." Caleb grunted his agreement on the other end. I leaned back into the pillow and tried to think of ways to help Jordan out of her funk. She'd fallen hard for this one and it would be tough to pull her back up. There was a knock at my door that yanked me out of my thoughts and conversation with Caleb. I pushed myself up and hurried over to the door.

"Hey Maddie. I was emptying the trash and saw some things for Jordan in it. I know she's not here, so I didn't know if someone else threw them away out of spite." Lily, the late night janitor asked as she stood in front of my door, trash cart behind her.

"Roses?"

"No, tulips actually. Kind of out of season, so I thought it was weird." She explained, tucking her flaming red hair back behind her ear.

"Tulips? Those are her favorite." I raised an eyebrow and peeked behind the woman. "Where were they?"

"In this can right here." Lily stated as she turned around and pointed at the gorgeous pink flowers that were now broken and destroyed from the can. She pulled out the card and a nearby letter.

"Lance." I breathed. "What the…?"

"Lance sent her flowers?" Caleb interjected quickly.

"Oh shit. Sorry babe, forgot you were there." I laughed as I transferred the phone to the other ear. Both pieces of paper were covered in something pink and sticky, I wasn't touching them. I grabbed a pen off the dresser inside and went back to the notes from the trash. A brief peek and I was flabbergasted. "He says he loves her."

"So?"

"He's never said that before. Something about he did call and seeing Keller. I think it says he's sorry and they need to talk. It's illegible."

"When did he see Keller?"

"Today possibly. That would explain the black eye." I mumbled. I looked back at Lilly and smiled. "Thanks a lot. I'll let Jordan know he sent them and what happened. You have no idea how amazing you are." Lily's face lit up as she nodded and started back down the hallway.

"Are you going to tell Jordan?" Caleb asked. "Because I don't think we should. I haven't seen any missed calls on her phone, except from Keller. He hasn't called. I think he's full of shit."

"Does Keller know where the phone's at?"

"No. I don't think so. I've never mentioned that I even have it." Caleb said with a groan. "Someone is fucking with my little sister's head and I will kill whoever it is."

"Chill out turbo." I laughed. "I won't tell her right now. I'll wait until I talk to Alicia and see what she says about everything. However, the culprit of tossing the flowers is most likely Keller. I think maybe they're both playing games with our girl." I sighed. I wanted to strangle both boys just as much as Caleb did. I hadn't known Jordan for that long, but she was more like a sister to me than my own. She was my best friend, the only real friend I've ever had and I hate it when someone hurts her like this.

My conversation with Caleb drifted away from his sister, but she was in both our thoughts, I knew. An hour later, I signed off with him and looked around the room. It was the first time in a long time that I'd had the room all to myself and it was a little weird. And I was a little more than lonely. I sure hope the girls get better soon; I can't stand the quiet much longer.

Chapter 58

Alicia

"Hey stranger." Maddie smiled when I trudged into the room Thursday morning. "Feeling better?"

"Enough to maybe make it through the day." I shrugged as I dropped my bags into the floor and fell onto my soft bed. "I had no other choice though. I can't even imagine how far behind I am in all my classes."

"Well, I'd say that Jordan took amazing notes for you and would help you out but she's just as bad off, if not worse than you."

"She's sick too?"

"Among other things." Maddie sighed. I was about to comment on that sigh when Jordan came through the door.

"Someone please tell me why I'm here." Jordan grumbled as she too fell onto her bed. "Because, I sure as hell don't want to be. I really just want to stay in my bed, hiding under the covers for the rest of my life."

"I feel the same way." I added with a weak chuckle that turned into a phlegm cough.

"Hey girls." Jordan smiled weakly. "I just came to crash for a few hours. Dad called in a half day for me. I just can't miss anymore Anatomy."

"Brennan's been taking notes for you, of course." Maddie singsonged.

"Love him."

"Maybe you could give him a *real* chance now that you're single." Maddie stated excitedly. "He's definitely cuter than he was freshman year, he's super sweet and he just *adores* you."

"Single?" I coughed. "What are you talking about?"

"You don't know?" Jordan asked as she sat up in bed and looked back at me quizzically. I shook my head and sat up as well, propping myself against the headboard. Now that I looked at her, I could see the red rimmed, puffy eyes and I realized they weren't a sign of the flu. She'd been crying. A lot. "Lance and I are no longer together."

"What?" I gasped. "Why not?"

"Because he's an asshole." Maddie explained quickly as she rushed to Jordan's side sympathetically.

"I take the SOB back on Saturday, screw him and on Sunday he stands me up."

"He called."

"Oh yeah, he did do that." She snapped sarcastically. "But it still doesn't change the fact that he's an asshole *or* that he stood me up."

"How can you say he stood you up?" I asked disgustedly. "You can't seriously have dumped him because he chose his sister being in the hospital over you. Are you really that fucking selfish?"

"Hospital?" Jordan whispered, her eyes were downcast and I felt a sharp tug of guilt for yelling at her.

"You didn't know? He said…" I sighed. "He said he was going to call you and if he didn't get a hold of you, then he'd tell me. Aunt Sarah, Rob, Jenn and Wyatt were on their way to brunch when they were in a head on collision. They all pretty much walked away without a scratch but Jenn started cramping and having contractions."

"Oh my God. Is she all right? Did she…"

"They did a C-section around one o clock Monday morning. The baby's fine, but tiny. They think she'll come home tomorrow. Lance was trying to call you up until then." Jordan's eyes darted to Maddie before they landed on me again.

"Why didn't he tell me that?" She asked softly, her voice thick with tears.

"Jordan stop." Maddie said firmly. "Don't forget what else he did. Don't let him get off that easily."

"What are you talking about?" I asked, a little irritated by Maddie's tone.

"He broke up with her in a text message."

"What?" I gasped. "No, that's not possible. When?"

"Sunday night."

"What time?"

"Around eight." Jordan whispered.

"He didn't have his phone until after eight, he said. So it *couldn't* have been him." I protested.

"Alicia don't." Maddie warned, glaring at me with her emerald green eyes. "Don't stick up for him. Who else would've sent her a text and why?"

"I don't know, but it wasn't Lance. I know it wasn't. Jordan, he was so distraught over being short with you on the phone and then when he couldn't get a hold of you..."

"But why wouldn't he tell me his family was in an accident? Why didn't he want me to know that?"

"Because he's an idiot, for one." I admitted quickly. "And second of all, he called you on his way to the hospital. He was freaked out."

"Or he really didn't want me there. Didn't want me to know for some reason. Maybe he's lying to you too, so he can pull one over on both of us." Jordan murmured. She looked back at me as tears rolled down her cheeks. I rushed over and enveloped her in a hug. I'd love to say that Lance isn't that type of guy, but I wouldn't put anything past him. He has a bad reputation for screwing girls and then blowing them off. I thought Jordan was different, but maybe I was wrong too. Maybe Jordan's right and that's what he wanted, for us both to believe so he could get what he wanted.

"I'm sorry Jordan." I said softly. "We'll figure out the truth okay? I'll get the truth out of someone."

Ten minutes later Maddie and I left Jordan to her tears while we hurried to our first classes.

"Maybe it's better this way." Maddie said.

"What is?"

"That they're not together anymore. He did totally abandon her and that alone makes him not worthy."

"I agree that he's a piece of crap for that, but there were circumstances you don't know about Maddie. I don't agree with how he went about things, but he was trying to protect her.

He really loves her. He may not say it, but I can tell. He's a totally different person with Jordan."

"He sent her flowers." Maddie blurted as she motioned for me to follow her to her locker. "Jordan doesn't know yet and I'm leery of telling her. Lily actually found them in the trashcan. He put on the card that he loved her. Then there was another letter that said something about seeing Keller, he was sorry and he loved her. But that's really all I could read."

"Why would you let her think he dumped her if you knew he sent flowers?" I asked in shock.

"I know it looks bad." She sighed as she bent down to pull her books out of her locker. "But I'm trying to protect her. You didn't see her Sunday night Alicia. I thought we were going to have to take her to the hospital. She wouldn't stop crying; she just lay in bed and stared off into space. Hell, we couldn't get her to eat anything until Tuesday, which could have to do with her flu, but...I think it's more of her depression over Lance. What if the flowers were a fluke or a hoax? They *were* in the trash. And what if he was telling her he was sorry for dumping her in the text message, but nothing else? I couldn't read enough of the note to know the truth. I don't want her to get her hopes up and then him slam her back down again."

"Sawyer's family owns the flower shop in town so it couldn't be a fluke or a hoax. Sawyer probably delivered them himself or Lance even." I said thoughtfully as she closed her locker before we headed down the hall to where mine was. "I'll call the guys and Lance and try to figure things out. But you're probably right; we should wait to tell her anything. Maybe I am wrong and Lance is a jerk and used her, but I have a hard time believing that. I mean, I know he's a jerk but he wouldn't hurt Jordan again. This last month absolutely killed him."

"It's killed her too and I don't know how much more she can take Lish." Maddie mumbled sadly. "She fell hard for him and he's got a habit of leaving her hanging."

"All dumb luck. Maybe. I don't know. I'll do some digging and I'll get back to you at lunch if I find out anything." Maddie nodded and then said goodbye as she hurried off to her class. I wasn't far behind, but I whipped out my phone and sent a quick text to Sawyer asking him about the flowers and Jordan and Lance's break up. If anyone would know the truth, it would be Sawyer. I hope that this is all a misunderstanding that would be fixed by tonight.

Chapter 59

Jordan

"Keller, what are you doing here?" I gasped as I saw him setting a vase of flowers down when I opened my door to head to class.

"I...I just wanted to check on you, cheer you up maybe." He stammered as he looked down at the ground, obviously hiding something.

"What happened to your face?" I asked as I gripped his chin and forced him to look at me. I'm not an idiot. I knew his shy act, was just that; an act. If Keller had a black eye, whether he got jumped or not, he would wear it as a proud badge of honor and muck the details to make him come out to look a lot better than he should.

"Nothing. It's nothing." He mumbled, pushing my hand away.

"That's not *nothing*, Keller James. What happened?" I asked, stupidly falling for his bullshit.

"I saw Lance last night." He sighed after a precise hesitation. My eyes grew wide, he saw Lance? Did he know what happened? Maybe Keller could tell me everything was just a big mistake.

"You did? Where?"

"I...are you sure you want to know, Jordan?" I nodded hesitantly and he continued. "I went in to town to grab something to eat after practice. I saw him and some girl making out, so I called him on it."

"What?" I asked in a broken voice, tears filled my eyes as my heart sank and broke in to a million more pieces.

"I'm sorry, I wish I hadn't seen it. I wish I didn't have to tell you this."

"What happened Keller?"

"I went up to him and asked him about you. He pretended not to know you. The girl got up and went to the bathroom and he said you were just a conquest, a bet he had with his friends. So, I punched him. I walked out, left and then his friends chased me down and jumped me."

"What?" I asked in shock. "That doesn't sound like…"

"Luckily, a cop drove by and they stopped." Keller shrugged. "I'm sorry Jordan, I wish…"

"Are you okay?" I asked. Something wasn't right about Keller's story, like the text message, it didn't sound like Lance or his friends at all. I tried to cover up how upset I was anyway, until I could figure things out. I didn't know why he would make something like this up, knowing how bad I was already hurting.

"I'm fine. I'm just worried about you. I feel so horrible." He admitted as he moved closer to me.

"I'm fine Keller. I told you."

"I know." He said, as he wrapped his arms around my waist. "But I know that's a load of crap. You lost your virginity to him, you loved him and he did this to you, it's unbelievable."

"I'm over it, I really am." I lied in a hoarse whisper.

"Well, I got you some flowers. I thought maybe it'd make you feel a little better." He said as he held up the vase of two dozen, fresh cut and gorgeous red roses.

"Keller, you didn't have to, really."

"I know, but I wanted to. You deserve better than this, Joey. You deserve to be treated like a princess and I just really want to do that for you." He stated sweetly as he tipped my chin up. "Promise me you won't go back to him. Promise me, that you won't call or talk to him. He's just going to use you again."

"Keller, Lance isn't…"

"Please Jordan. Please, promise me you won't. He's an asshole and he's just going to keep hurting you over and over if you let him. Caleb's going to beat the Hell out of him for you and me, next time he sees him."

"What? Keller…"

"Don't argue with me Jordan. He's no good for you, he's an ass. He's just going to keep hurting you, if you let him." Keller rambled, feigning worry as he looked at me and smiled. "I was thinking, maybe you and I should get back together. You know, if Lance does come back around and finds out we're together, then you won't look like you even cared about what he did. That'll burn more than anything; you'll be able to get back at him, sort of."

"Keller…" I sighed in exasperation. Was this his ploy? Was that why nothing was making sense, because Keller was making it all up just to get me back? I was overreacting, Keller James wasn't like that. Lance, on the other hand, I found out on our first date was capable of screwing a girl and then ditching her without a second thought. I was an idiot to pursue a relationship knowing that and then I went and fell in love with him, like a moron.

"C'mon Jordan, we'll just start back where we left off. I was going to ask you to be my girlfriend again the weekend of the game and then Lance came along. It'll be like picking up where we left off, so what do you think?" Keller

asked, before leaning into plant a surprising kiss on my mouth.

It's not like kissing Lance. It's not the same. I thought. I

immediately cursed myself for thinking that way. Lance was a

jerk, Keller was going out of his way to take care of me, I

shouldn't be so picky, so naïve and so stupid.

We were interrupted by Maddie, who had gone to another

room when she saw Keller. I heard her clear her throat and

turned to see her standing there, looking skeptical with one

eyebrow raised and her arms crossed in front of her chest.

"Maddie." Keller grinned, "Have you met my

girlfriend?"

"Girlfriend?" She asked, the shock I heard in her

voice was the same that resounded throughout me.

"Um no, Keller." I interjected, shaking my head

vehemently. "I'm not ready to be *anyone's* girlfriend. I don't care how good your offer sounds, I just can't do it. It's going to

take a long time before I can even think about it."

"Jordan." He sighed, his voice growing a little

angry. I watched his eyes dart back to Maddie questioningly.

She just glared at him. "Fine. I thought I'd try to make things a

little easier on you. But you know best, I guess." I nodded my

head and gave him a hug and a thank you for the flowers. He

offered to escort me to the cafeteria for lunch but Maddie quickly

intercepted and rushed me back into our room.

"Stay away from him, he's up to something."

"Maddie, you're paranoid."

"No, I'm not. Keller is up to something. He was

never this sweet and thoughtful when you two were a couple,

why start now?"

"I think he's just trying to be my friend."

"So he can get in your pants." She hissed. "I don't

trust him. And don't believe that shit about Lance until you hear from Alicia first. Alicia will know the truth. Or maybe you should call Chopper. You two are pretty close and you said he instant messaged you on Facebook the other day, right?"

"Yeah, but I didn't answer. I didn't know what to say, especially if he busted out; sorry Lance is such a jerk, I don't know why he dumped you or has been screwing someone else the whole time." I muttered.

"Now *you're* paranoid." She lit. Maddie reached down and gave me a big hug. "I'm sure Alicia's right and this is all just a really big misunderstanding."

"It always is and it's always someone else who has to make me understand it. I just kind of wonder if it wasn't for meddling friends and family, if Saturday night would've even happened. Maybe I'm better if everyone backs off and lets him grow some balls." Maddie just nodded and bit her bottom lip in thought.

432

"Let's go grab some lunch and then reintroduce you to the living world." She teased. "We'll find something to keep your mind off your heart for now."

"Easier said than done." I sighed as I leaned into my best friend and let her lead me out of our room. I really wasn't looking forward to rejoining anything but Lance Bowman, or my bed right now, but I knew my friends wouldn't see it my way.

Chapter 60

I sat on the sidelines of the Varsity basketball game the next night, fully outfitted in my cheerleading uniform, but trying to nurse myself back to full health. Maddie wasn't having me even attempt more than cheering from the bleachers since I hadn't really ate anything since Sunday. I was a little wobbly and lightheaded, to say the least. Luckily, I'd started my period on Wednesday, but now the cramps were getting the best of me as well. I just couldn't win.

It's not easy for me to just sit back and watch, I'd much rather be in the thick of things. Maddie bribed me with a to go cup of a mixed drink, one in which no prying faculty, staff or parents would ever smell the alcohol. Needless to say, I was on the sidelines getting tanked. And for good reason.

Alicia had come back to our room around nine o clock last night saying that she'd spoken to Drew, Sawyer, Chopper and Cooper and all had been shocked about the text message.

They'd also told a different story about Keller's visit to Lance, saying that Keller showed up in the school parking lot looking for a fight, and he found one. Alicia blocked my comeback of them lying for their friend by saying she'd asked around and at least five other people; unconnected to Lance and his friends, had seen the Porsche, seen the blonde get out and start swinging at Lance. Alicia said that Chopper invited us to a party that night so we could talk and get things straightened out; Lance wouldn't be there though, they were dealing with more family issues and Jenn was coming home today and so on.

According to all the boys, there was no way in Hell Lance Bowman was cheating on me, but when I called his phone earlier this afternoon it was a giggling female who answered.

"Hi, um, I was looking for Lance Bowman."

"I'm sorry." She giggled. "He is indisposed at the moment. I'm also sorry to be the one to tell you that he is madly in love and completely off the market."

"Oh he is, is he?"

"Yup, he's finally found the one and there's no deterring him." She sighed. "Spread the word."

"I'll do that." I hissed as I slammed down the phone. Obviously, if she were talking about me, she would've realized who I was when I called. My name, picture and phone number should have come up on the screen of his phone. Obviously, everyone is worthless liars or he's running more game than anyone realizes.

Which led me to the place I was at now. The game was over and I was piss drunk, pissed off and looking for answers. I played it cool around Alicia and Maddie though, if they knew my true condition they'd keep me locked in my room for my own good, but now was the best time to find out the truth and confront Lance if I had the chance. I wasn't above going to his house. No siree, I would totally do that to get my point across.

"Hey J," Keller grinned as he plopped down in the vacant seat beside me as the game neared the end.

"Hey Keller." I quipped drily.

"What's up?"

"I'm confined to the bleachers. I'm pretty miserable, that's what is up."

"You want to go to Donovan's party with me? I'm getting ready to leave soon."

"I'm already going to a party."

"Where? I didn't hear of anyone else having a party other than Donovan."

"We're in a school of four hundred plus, there's more than one party tonight."

"But Donovan's is the only good party." I rolled my eyes.

"We're meeting up with Alicia's brother and friends."

"You mean Lance?" He questioned angrily, his fingers gripping the seat tightly.

"Unfortunately, no."

"Unfortunately? Jordan, you need to stay away from that bastard. He attacked me. He used you as a bet."

"I'm not an idiot Keller." I hissed as I moved closer to him. "I know you're not that reliable of a source." His green eyes narrowed as he glared at me. "And I can't just break all contact with Lance Bowman, there are things you don't know and my heart is too involved. He would have to fall of the face of the earth for me to stay away from him, our lives are too intertwined."

"That can be arranged." Keller growled under his breath.

"Excuse me?" I gasped, thinking that I couldn't have heard him right.

"I said that can be arranged, just say the word J and Lance Bowman can disappear as soon as tonight." His grin turned wicked and I backed up slowly.

"I won't ever say the word asshole." I spit. "We can be friends Keller, nothing else. I've told you that before, I'm just not interested. Our time passed a long time ago."

"No, it didn't." His eyes were sad and frustrated all at once. He shook his head, bit back the words that were itching to come out. "You're a fool, Jordan." I rolled my eyes and turned away as he stood up and stormed off.

"Asshole." I grumbled.

"What was his deal?" Zack asked. The game had ended and I hadn't even noticed because I was so caught up in Keller's ridiculousness.

"It's Keller, he was being his typical pouty, assholey self." I shrugged with a loud sigh. "Nice game."

"Thanks." He grinned as he looked down at me. "How you feel?"

"So so." I rolled my shoulders and looked around. I held up the cup I was drinking out of and grinned. "This is helping."

"I don't even know how you can stomach that." He shook his head and held a hand out to help me up. I took it and felt him pull me into him. "Hanging at the house tonight with Cale and me?"

"Nope. Maddie, Alicia and me are hanging with Chopper and the others."

"And Lance?" He questioned evenly. I shook my head.

"He's apparently got crap going on and won't be there." I shrugged. "Chopper wouldn't lie to me about that." He nodded his head and watched me carefully.

"Dang, I was kind of hoping for a quiet night in with the five of us."

"On a plus side, it'll be a quiet night with just you and Caleb." I giggled. "I know how much you've missed that." Zack rolled his eyes and swatted at me playfully. I darted out of his way with a laugh before I winked at him.

"Make sure you guys have a DD, okay?" Zack asked seriously as he pulled me back into him. "I don't know why but I have a really bad feeling in my gut, those feelings usually aren't ever wrong." I looked back at him worriedly.

"What do you mean, a bad feeling?"

"I don't know. Something just doesn't feel right." He sighed. "You'll think I'm crazy, but I got the same feeling before both my grandparents died."

"You're freaking me out a little." I breathed.

"It's probably nothing to do with you, I just...I worry about you. I hate seeing you get hurt."

"I hate seeing me get hurt too." I mumbled sadly as tears stung at my eyes. "I can't live in a bubble forever though, right?" He nodded and pulled me into a hug. I closed my eyes and leaned my head against his chest. It felt really nice to be wrapped in his strong arms and feel the security there.

"You could just hang with me all night." He breathed in my ear. "Please?" I pulled away and shook my head. I felt like a hundred people, ninety of them females, were shooting death glares my way.

"Either choice I make right now is dangerous." I mumbled. "I have to know the truth Zack and I'll only get that from Lance's friends. I can't move on if I don't know the truth, right?" He nodded his head. "I'm thinking your gut feeling is that I'm about to get jumped in the parking lot." Zack chuckled, shook his head and looked around.

"You have an active imagination." He winked. "Can you find out the truth quickly and then come back to the house? I just...I need your advice on something and..."

"I will, but just make sure you're waiting up for me, okay? I'll be back by curfew, if not sooner."

442

"I'll wait up." He grinned as he reached out and took my hand in his, he gently squeezed my fingers and gave me another hug, "I could just carry you out of here and lock you up in the house, you know that, right?" My face grew flush as the wrong images flipped through my mind.

"I've had enough to drink to make that sound like an amazing idea that won't cause a million problems later on."

"I don't want you drunk J." He breathed in my ear. "I want you to know and remember everything I do to you." My eyes grew wide, my stomach dropped and I started to pull away. "All the problems you expect are only there if you put them there."

"It would be…"

"Amazing."

"I'm not…"

"You think too much." He chuckled as Tate Donovan hollered at Zack. He pulled away and looked down at me. "I'll see you later I guess." He sighed as he reached down, kissed the top of my head and went off with his friends. I didn't know what his game was, didn't know why he flirted so much with me, made such a big show of it, unless he was trying to make someone jealous. That was probably it. Obviously, kissing me on top of the head wouldn't be something he would do if he were serious about anything he'd just said.

Chapter 61

Alicia drove the three of us to a party out in the sticks. There were many winding roads and I'm lucky I didn't lose the little lunch I'd had earlier today. When we pulled up to the party, I searched for Chopper or someone that I knew. And I immediately found *him*; Lance was over by his truck, engulfed in PDA with a buxom blonde. Remy. The little bitch.

"I will kill him." I growled when I saw him grinning from ear to ear and laying on his patented charm to someone else. That smile was reserved for me, not some trashy little bimbo.

"Jordan, wait." Alicia protested as she grabbed for my arm and looked around to see what I saw. "I'm sure it's not what it looks like. Just wait a second." I was beyond rational thought. Waiting would be the right thing to do, but I just wanted to cause him as much pain as he caused me. My heart was breaking all over again as I watched the little tramp lean into him and whisper something in his ear. I could barely hear Alicia and Maddie tailing behind me, trying to calm me down as I stalked towards my boyfriend. I could only focus on the rage roaring in my ears, the sounds of my heart shattering and the jealousy that was wrapping its way throughout my body and causing my fists to clench tight.

"Jordan." I heard Lance gasp as an uncomfortable smile crossed his face. I shot him a dirty look before I grabbed the blonde by her hair and yanked her away from Lance. Then I turned on her, still gripping her hair I was inches from her frightened, pale face.

"You keep your filthy hands off of my boyfriend. Do you understand me bitch? You have five seconds to get the Hell out of here before I rip you into little trampy pieces. And if I ever catch you with him again, I *won't* issue a warning." I hissed.

"I wasn't...I didn't."

446

"Don't speak to me you little whore. Get the fuck out of here before I make it impossible for you to eat anything but liquids for the next year." I let go of her hair as I tossed her to the side. She skittered quickly away, pushing through the hordes of people who had gathered to see the show. I turned on Lance before I could lose my nerve, I wasn't ready to lose my cool, more, in front of fifty people, but I was too drunk and too far pissed to back track now.

"What was that?" Lance gaped. "I was just talking to her. About you."

"About me? Is that right?" I asked in a syrupy sweet drawl as I inched closer, a fake smile plastered on my face. Some people yelled and screamed when they were furious, but not me. I spoke in a low, even tone that would make the offender think nothing was wrong. In fact, a lot of the group had started to thin out, thinking the show was over. "Were you telling her about fucking me and then hightailing it out of your truck so fast that my head was spinning? Did you mention that you broke up with me in a text message, you sorry son of a bitch? Or were you just telling your little slut that you could finally be together because your stupid ass girlfriend was out of the picture?"

"What are you talking about?" He shot, lowering his eyebrows as he took a step closer to me. His arms went out to me, begging me to come into him. I took a step back and glared.

"You know exactly what I'm talking about. Was that her? Was that the bitch you've been cheating on me with, or is there more?"

"I'm not cheating on you." He said feigning disbelief and hurt.

"Oh that's right. We're not together anymore, are we?"

"Of course we are. I told you, there are some things going on…"

"Things going on, huh? Like what, Lance honey, some other girl screwing you better than me? I thought you were so busy with the farm and school that you couldn't get out of the

448

house. Of course, Saturday night when you were trying to get me horizontal you were singing a different tune. Looks like it was all a big ass lie, wasn't it?"

"No." He stated through clenched teeth as he took another step towards me. "I haven't been out of the house in a month."

"But how many girls have been *in* your house, servicing you Lance? I know how you were before we met; I find it hard to believe that you've gone this long without getting any. Hell, I'm sure you were getting it on the side the whole time, weren't you? That's why you weren't pressuring me."

"Are you accusing me of something?"

"Yes, dumbass, I'm *accusing* you of being a pathetic son of a bitch." I hissed as I leaned in closer to him. "You were right Lance; it *is* over between us." I spun on my heel and stomped away.

"Asshole." I heard Maddie mutter as she rushed after me.

"You're beyond pathetic Lance." I heard Alicia say. "Why can't you fight for her? Tell her she's wrong, tell her the truth!"

"What in the Hell?" Lance called after us as Alicia turned away and jogged to catch up.

"I'm not going to cry. I'm not going to cry." I kept repeating as Maddie grabbed my elbow and hurried me to the car. "Get me out of here. I need a beer and something to fucking punch." I stopped dead in my tracks, causing Maddie to lurch forward. "No, scratch that. I'm going to punch that sorry bastard."

"Jordan!" Maddie screeched, lunging for me as I marched back to where Lance stood in shock. "Alicia, help me!" Alicia hadn't reached us yet so she stopped cold and waited to block my path, taking up a football stance.

"Hey there sweetheart." I heard Chopper drawl as he swooped in, wrapped his arms around my waist and pulled me close to him. "How about we take a detour?"

"Let me go Chopper." I growled trying to push away from him.

"Not until you calm down." He said with a firm shake of his head. "Just walk with me. Let's get away from the crowd, have a little talk and then I'll let you go beat the bloody Hell out of Lance if you still want to."

"I don't want to talk. I don't want to walk. I just want to beat the bloody hell out of that worthless piece of shit."

"Keep it up and someone's gonna call the cops. Just chill out for a second."

"I don't care." I hissed as I yanked myself away from his strong grip. "I'm sick of being cheated on and treated like shit. It's about damn time I stood up for myself."

"I agree, but Lance isn't cheating on you. There's shit you don't know Jordan." Chopper sighed.

"I've heard enough of this bull shit." I spit through clenched teeth as I stormed away. I was still fighting mad but my drunk was wearing off, I needed to get away before I stopped being pissed at Lance. Punching him in the face or the balls would feel good. He deserved that. The third time we'd slept together and the third time he'd totally blown me off.

"Jordan, please stop. Just listen to me. I don't know what the Hell led to this but…" Lance rambled as he jogged to catch up with me.

"Get the Hell away Bo. Just let her simmer or she's gonna deck you." Chopper warned as he hurried to intervene.

"Let her hit me." He said to his friend, when he turned to look at me his jaw met my fist.

"Worthless piece of shit." I muttered as I walked away. Coop and Drew were hooting and hollering their praise of my right hook when I heard Lance's voice again.

"Damn it Jordan, would you just stop?" That was a blow to my ego. My hardest hit and it didn't hinder him for a second. Damn. Maybe the alcohol impeded my strength?

"Fuck off." I growled, as I picked up my pace. "You would think the jack ass would learn his fucking lesson. If he doesn't think I'll fucking knock him flat on his ass he's got another thing coming." I muttered to myself.

"I deserve it." Lance admitted at my ear, his hand going down as he tried to link his fingers through mine.

"Get lost Lance." I hissed, smacking his hand away from mine and trying to push him off in the process.

"Come on darlin'. Please. Just stop and let me talk. I know I've been an ass, but there's a lot you don't know. I would never cheat on you and this business about breaking up, I don't know *what* you're talking about." He rambled helplessly as he continued to touch me and reach for a way to pull me back to him.

"I do. We're through Lance. Over. Done. Don't call me again." I hollered back, not even bothering to turn around and look at him. I knew if I did look into those brown eyes my resistance would be gone and I'd believe anything he told me. The safest thing for me right now was to put as much distance between Lance Bowman and me; it was the only way to protect what was left of my heart.

Chapter 62

"The Hell we are." I heard him growl, seconds later his strong arms were wrapped around me and tossing me over his shoulder as if I were a rag doll. "We are not over until we talk."

"Fuck you!" I screamed as I kicked, punched, flailed and screamed more. His grip remained strong; as he tried to set me down in front of his truck, I began hitting him harder.

"Chopper!" Lance howled. "Help me out here buddy."

"I'm not going near her. She'll give me a black eye."

"She won't hit you. She's pissed at me. Find out why."

"Jordan." Chopper began softly. I stopped focusing my anger on Lance and pierced Chopper with an upside down glare.

"Do not talk to me like I'm about to murder fifty thousand people."

"I'm not." He gasped in disbelief. "I'm just talking to you like I normally do."

"No, you're not. Tell your asshole friend to put me down before I fucking hit him in the balls."

"He won't put you down until he knows you're not going to run. He just wants to talk and clear things up."

"I'm *done* talking to him."

"Then tell me."

"NO." I whispered, realizing I sounded like a two year old, I took a deep breath. "Ask Lish for my phone. She'll show you what the bastard did and then maybe you'll deck him too." Alicia jogged over with my phone held out. Chopper took it, read the message and then handed it to Lance.

"And you think Lance would be so stupid as to break up with you? And even to do it in a *text*?"

"Who else would've sent it? It's from *his* phone."

"I didn't send that." Lance gasped as he put me down on the ground. "Jordan, I would never break up with you in a text message." I snorted a sarcastic laugh before making a loud buzzer sound.

"The correct answer should be 'I'd never break up with you Jordan.'" I spit, trying to steel myself against the watery reserve plucking at my eyes. "Then who fucking sent it Lance? Huh? It only makes sense. You barely acknowledge that I'm your girlfriend for a month. You show up out of nowhere Saturday night spouting all the right things so you could get some, and *you did,* and then you fucking disappear again."

"I didn't disappear. If anyone did, it was you. I've been trying to reach you since Sunday night. I've left voicemails and text messages, but I haven't gotten anything in return." I made the loud buzzer sound again.

"Again, the correct answer would be 'I didn't come to see you Saturday night and pour my heart out, so that I could get some Jordan." I bit sarcastically as I dropped my voice a few octaves to mimic him. He gave an exasperated sigh and rubbed his hands across his face. "Keller said he caught you making out with a blonde the other night and I come here to find a blonde Remy hanging all over you, and you grinning from ear to ear like you just won the biggest prize in the world. Oh and there was the call I made to you this afternoon that was answered by some giggling idiot who said you were hopelessly in love and off limits. What is it Lance? You just prefer to dump me without telling me, is that it?"

"Keller is a lying sack of shit." Lance spit. "He came to school to attack me and I was surrounded by the guys, no one else. Remy is a very good friend of mine, as you know, and

458

she must've answered my phone earlier, without me knowing. We've been talking about you all day; when she said I was off limits, she meant because you were my girlfriend. I didn't dump you. I told you there was stuff going on, I thought you understood." He rambled, again trying to ease himself towards me. His eyes searched my face, tried to lock onto my eyes, but I wouldn't let him. I couldn't look at him; if I did, I knew it would be all over.

"Obviously not, asshole. I do *not* get ignored Lance Bowman, I will not be treated like shit and be put on the back burner while you play the fucking field."

"I am *not* playing the field." Lance roared as he scooped me up into his arms again. "What do I have to do to make you see that I only want you?"

"Lance, put her down." Chopper instructed under his breath. "Why don't you take her home? Curfew is soon. Maybe you two can figure this out on the drive."

"I'm not going anywhere with him." I hissed as Lance set me down again. This time he positioned his arms on both sides of me and made himself an impenetrable wall. I tried punching and pushing him out of my way but it was as if I were a teeny, not even irritating bug. Damn him.

"Jordan, honey, you came to find out what the hell was going on, did you not?" Chopper asked as he pulled me away from Lance and the others, his voice barely above a whisper. "I know for a fact that he would never dump you, especially not via the phone. That boy is in love with you, he's been having a rough time at home. He didn't want to get you involved in his drama, so he hung back till it cleared up. He's too fucking proud. I told him to tell you. We *all* told him to tell you, but he worried he'd lose you for that alone."

"It's one thing for *you* to tell me all this Chopper. Because you, Alicia, his family, all you guys are telling me things, but *he* won't fucking talk to me." I cried, tears spilling down my cheeks. "What the fuck is the point of being his girlfriend if he won't tell me anything? He can't trust me?"

"He's a cowboy Jo, plain and simple. Cowboys are proud. They don't show their emotions, they don't talk about them and they sure as Hell don't air their dirty laundry. *Especially*, to the woman they love."

"Shut up Chopper. He doesn't love me. Stop trying to smooth things over for him."

"Look at me." Chopper demanded as he pulled me a little further away so no one could hear us. "I've known that boy all my life. I know things about him no one else does. He is my best friend, the brother I never had. He is head over heels in love with you, Jordan. But he's an idiot. He's a dumbass because he's too scared to tell you that. Too scared that you'll break his heart. His daddy tells him all the time that if a woman knows your weaknesses she'll use it against you, and he truly believes that. You are his weakness, sweetie. You and only you. There's only one thing in the world that would keep him from you; that's the thought of completely losing you or you getting hurt and he's been faced with both. Just listen to him, okay? Let him talk, let him grovel and beg forgiveness. But please forgive him, because it will honestly kill him if he loses you."

"I could never break his heart, Chopper." I whispered, looking away quickly and wrapping my arms around my body in a hug. "Because I'd be shattering mine in the process. I love him so much that it hurts."

"And you're breaking mine by crying." Chopper said softly as he pulled me into a bear hug. "I love you to death girl and I just want to see you guys happy. Being apart isn't making either of you happy, so go to him. Just a ride home, okay? If he tries anything funny, call me and I'll kick his ass. Not that I doubt your capability."

"I love you too, Chopper." I sighed as I hugged him tighter. "If Lance dumps me for punching him, will you take me?"

"In a heartbeat." He chuckled. "But it's going to take a lot more than that to get rid of Lance." Chopper put his arm over my shoulders and led me back to the truck where our

mutual group of friends stood like bodyguards.

Chapter 63

"You don't have to go with him Jordan." Maddie said, pushing her way to the front. "I don't care what his reasons are, there's no excuse for the way he's been treating you. You have fifty guys knocking on your door for a date, and fifty of them are better than this loser."

"Maddie." Alicia started as she put her hand on my best friend's arm. She shook her head and whispered something in her ear. "Go Jordan. Just call if you need us, we'll be there in a heartbeat, okay?" I nodded my head, still unsure of what I was doing. Lance took a step forward hesitantly, his big brown eyes pleading with me for a chance. He extended his hand and I slowly took it. He opened the truck door and helped me inside so carefully that I felt like I would break at any second. I don't know, maybe I will.

"Lance." Chopper interrupted as Lance started to climb inside the truck. "You tell her. You tell her everything or I won't bail your ass out again. Got it? Because Maddie's right, if you can't tell her, there are fifty guys, fifty thousand guys who will and more. She deserves better than what you're giving her."

I didn't look, but out of the corner of my eye I could see Lance nod before he closed the door.

"If you're gonna hit me again, can you do it now? Before I start driving?" Lance asked with a sheepish smile.

"I hate you." I said, staring out the windshield. "I want to kill you, so I'll wait until there aren't any witnesses."

"Fair enough." He mumbled as he started the truck and threw it into gear. The rumble of the engine was the only sound in the cab for at least five minutes. When Lance came to a stop at a deserted four way, I lost it. My fists started flying, more than half landed on his solid chest, but a few hit his face before he was able to wrangle my arms and pull me into him.

"I hate you." I repeated in a sob as the tears flooded onto his shirt. "I hate you."

465

"Please don't. Please don't hate me. I can't…"
He said in a broken voice. I yanked myself away and stared back
in disbelief. I had to see for myself, I had to see what I was
hearing. Sure enough, Lance was crying too. My defenses were
gone as I plowed myself back into his arms and twisted my arms
around his neck.

"Whatever it is. Whatever happened, we'll fix it,
okay? We'll fix it. We'll fix us." I soothed.

"I hate what I did to you. I hate that I hurt you,
that I made you think such awful things about me. I hate myself
for…"

"Lance. Stop. Please stop." I cried. "Just tell me
what happened." I leaned my forehead against his and stared
back into those sad, sad eyes. "You can tell me anything baby,
and it won't change how much I love you. Okay?" He nodded
slightly, but I could see how hesitant he was and that hurt more
than anything.

"It's my dad." He said. "When I came home late, that night, he blew his top. He banned me from seeing you, talking to you, anything that had to do with you, was done. I didn't believe him, but…when Wyatt was talking to you that day, he went after Wyatt. I was outside, my mom tried to stop him but he threw her into the wall, knocked her unconscious. I came inside and Wyatt was screaming, he was in hysterics and had welts all over him. My dad was outside, headed for his truck and said he was going…" Lance stopped and looked down at my lap, like he couldn't find the words. I put my hand up to his face before I kissed his tears softly. He took a deep breath and continued. "He said he was going to your campus to have a talk with your dad. To have a talk with you. Then he laughed and pulled his .22 out from under the truck seat and said he'd do whatever it took to keep us apart. And up until then, until he attacked Wyatt I'd been trying to figure out a way to see you, to still be with you without him knowing but after that…I couldn't let Wyatt suffer because of me."

"Oh Lance. He wouldn't…"

467

"He *would* Jordan. He pointed it at me first. Said if Luke hadn't left, if my mother wasn't still grieving, he'd kill me. He was so trashed."

"What did you do?"

"Nothing. I just stood there, like an idiot. Which pissed him off even more. Another day, he found my phone and saw we were still texting. He attacked us all, even Chopper, he was the person the cops were chasing. He was headed to the bar, for you. I tried to stop him. I lost it. I attacked him. I blacked out." He rambled sadly. "*I blacked out on my own father.*"

"You didn't have a choice. He had a gun pointed at you Lance. He hurt your mom, he hurt Wyatt. You did what you had to do. I know you'd do anything to protect your family." He just nodded his head as I continued to try and soothe him. "It's good to talk about it though, right? Makes you see it differently, makes you understand why you weren't in the wrong. Tell me what he said Lance."

"No. It's not important."

"Yes it is. Tell me." I said a little louder, sitting up a little straighter. He shook his head again and I started to climb out of his lap. "If you can't tell me everything Lance, then there's no point in me trying."

"No. Please." He said as he pulled me back to him. "Jordan. Please don't make me. It's horrible. It's sick." He repeated. I just stared back at him, waiting and he finally gave in. "He said…he said that he'd make sure that you knew what it was like to be laid by a real man. He said he'd find out if it was your sweet little…you know, that had me doing tricks." I was appalled, disgusted and frightened all at once, but my face was a mask of indifference. I couldn't let Lance see my emotions when he was so afraid of telling me that. But I was also proud, so proud and grateful to Lance for protecting me from that monster. "I couldn't let him near you, even if he was bluffing."

"Is that what happened to your arm? And your eye?" I asked, finally commenting on the broken arm and black eye I immediately noticed when I first saw him tonight. Lance nodded his head slowly.

"This is better than it was." He shrugged nonchalantly. "My face was his punching bag. The last few weeks I've been in and out of the hospital. He was released from jail, drove drunk right into my mom and the others. He almost killed Jenn and the baby."

"And where is he now?"

"I don't know. He's supposed to be in jail, but..."

"Has he...has he come around?" Lance just nodded his head.

"I try not to leave the house too much. I'm scared he'll come in when I'm not there and hurt mom and Wyatt. Mom lets him run the farm, says it isn't right to take away his way of life. But Rob or someone is always there, or mom and Wyatt are gone."

"Where are they now?"

"With Jenn."

"Where are you staying?"

470

"At home."

"No. You'll stay with me tonight."

"Jordan." He sighed.

"No. I don't want to let you go." I mumbled softly as I buried my face in his chest. It would be so easy to just let everything fall to the wayside, to let it all go and just focus on making him feel better. That would've been best. But I was still so hurt that he didn't feel like he could tell me any of this, like he needed to ignore me for the last month. I pulled away again and scooted off his lap.

"I don't want to let you go either." He said as he tried to pull me back to him.

"Lance, that was weeks ago. All you had to do was tell me what happened, I would've understood. I would've laid low. And then your family gets into an accident, Jenn and the baby are hurt and you couldn't even tell me that. I just don't understand it. Are you embarrassed by me? I just don't understand how you can throw me to the side like I don't matter. I'm in love with you and it's like you don't even care about me."

"Jordan. No." He sighed.

"Can you drive please? My curfew is in twenty minutes and we're still at least fifteen away." I stated icily. Lance nodded; his hand hovered over the gearshift. He finally put it in drive, but his hand found mine immediately after. He quickly interlaced our fingers, tightening his grip when I tried to pull away.

"I was embarrassed." He mumbled.

"Why?"

"I was in the hospital. I have a broken arm and a black eye from my *father,* Jordan." He said drily.

"You don't need to be embarrassed in front of me."

"How would I answer your brothers, or your friends?"

"You could've left that to me. You're an asshole, Lance Bowman. We made love, again. I told you that I loved you and not only did you flip out, but then, the last month you've been blowing me off with no explanation. I thought you…and then I get the text message."

"I didn't send that message."

"So you say. But how do I know that? *How* do I know that you're not just trying to save face right now? It'll be all over school by Monday that you dumped me in a text, that I went psycho on you, no girl will come within a mile of you by then."

"*I did not send that message.* My phone was missing Sunday night, now I know why. I don't want to break up with you. I just didn't know what to do with everything. I didn't know how to tell you any of it. I was mortified and scared. I'm still scared my father will find out we're together and come after you. I'll never forgive myself, if that happens. And Sunday it had nothing to do with embarrassment and everything to do with

473

me being freaked out. I needed you so bad, all day, and that terrified me. I've never had to rely on anyone else, my family relies on *me*. I thought I made that clear in the note I sent with the flowers."

"I didn't get a note." I said sharply as Lance pulled the truck to a stop again. "I didn't get flowers from you either." I added. "Why *don't* you want to break up with me Lance? Obviously, it didn't bother you to be away from me all this time. You didn't miss me, like I missed you, because you never called or texted. I barely heard from you. I've been single for a month, more or less. Hell, if you *were* my boyfriend I wouldn't be the last to know about any of this. All your fucking friends know. Shouldn't your girlfriend know too? Shouldn't your girlfriend have been called to the hospital to take care of you? *Yes*, she should have. So *obviously,* I am not your girlfriend."

"Stop it. Stop it Jordan. You *are* my girlfriend. You will always be my girlfriend, because I will *never* let go of you."

"You already did." I said softly as I let go of his hand and looked out the passenger side window. "I gave you my heart Lance. I would do anything for you. I *never* let my emotions take over. My grandma always said emotions are your weakness, if you let them get the best of you, then you're weak to everyone you meet. You can't ever take back that kind of crazy. And I can't take back what I did today. Fuck. I made a mess of everything."

"No. No, you didn't. I'd be hurt if you hadn't reacted that way, it would've meant that you didn't care I know you went after Remy because you thought she was after me, I know you hit me because I broke your heart. I know you came to try and fix things because you love me."

"What's the point Lance? Of course I love you. I have for a long time. But I can't..." Lance's hand went up to my face; he cupped my chin and turned it towards him.

"Damn it Jordan. I love you. I love you, darlin''. Please tell me that it's enough to keep you." My bottom lip quivered as I stared back into his face, praying he wasn't bull shitting me. There was nothing but love and sincerity in those eyes and I knew that I was Lance Bowman's forever. There'd never be anything that could change that. I turned and looked out the windshield, trying to control the emotions that were rushing to the surface. As I did, I noticed a big black mass.

"No." I mumbled, as the mass got closer. As it sailed through the air towards us, I couldn't do anything. I was frozen. "NO. Lance." I screamed before I heard the crunch of metal and everything went black.

Chapter 64

Lance

Pressure. So much pressure. I feel like I'm underwater. No maybe, I'm just stuck under a thousand pounds of Chopper or something. I feel wet and sticky. Humidity? No, something else. I smell gas. Gas and something else. Alcohol? Fuck, is that pot? Surely, Jordan didn't have that, did she? I tried to shake my head, shake away the darkness that blanketed me. So dark. I can't see anything, but an eerie black, as I fight to the surface of whatever is trapping me down. I felt like I was fighting, punching, kicking and tearing into everything. I struggled until I could see a hint of light, hear the screams. Screams. Who's screaming? Why screaming?

Jordan.

She was screaming. I remember her saying no, then screaming my name. She was still screaming my name. I fought harder. I kicked, punched, pushed and tore even harder than before. I had to get to her. Had to see why she was screaming.

I gasped for air as my eyes flew open. What? Where am I? What is this? Grey. Hard. Fuck. It's the road. It's gravel. I picked my head up slowly; it feels like it weighs a million pounds, like a heavy balloon or something. It feels like someone pounded it with a jackhammer. Yikes. Where in the Hell am I? I looked around some more. Is that my truck? It looks more like a Transformer or something as I realize that another vehicle has become a part of it.

Jordan's screams pierce my epiphany again. I look around. Yelling her name. Yelling for help. Just yelling. I finally see a heap nearby. I call her name, the heap answers. No. That can't be Jordan, that can't be *my* Jordan. The mass looks like something out of a horror movie, I can't exactly tell what it is, but I drag myself towards it. Every inch of me hurts; I can't feel anything but the need to get to Jordan.

478

Blood. So much blood. Lots and lots of blood surround the mass that's now only a few feet away from me.

"Jordan?" I croak, half near hysteria. "Jordan darlin'."

"Lance." She whispers. "Lance, I smell gas. We're gonna die. The truck is going to blow up." Her sweet, melodic voice was gone, replaced by a hoarse, throaty sound of shock and fear. "What happened?"

"I don't know." I mumbled as I tried to look around again, tried to look at anything but the bloody, disfigured mess in front of me. She was right, there was gas. It was close. I could also hear more screams, coming from my truck. That's when I saw there were more people. More people in the other vehicle, trying to move around. Moaning, screaming, and trying to get out. On the other side of Jordan, I saw her cell phone. I pulled myself closer to her and grabbed it. Surprisingly, it was in the best shape of anything nearby. I dialed 9-1-1 with bloody, trembling fingers.

"There's been an accident. It's bad." I slurred into the phone. I peered at a nearby street sign and mumbled a number before I fell onto Jordan's limp body. I tossed the phone away, knowing Jordan's dad had GPS installed into it. I hope someone will find us, soon.

"Lance." Jordan whimpered beneath me. "I'm scared."

"Me too." I said. "Help's coming." I hope. I pulled myself up, propped myself up on my bad arm, it hurt the least of anything right now, and surveyed the damage. Jordan's leg was lying in an awkward position, as was her arm. Her beautiful face was scraped till there was barely anything left, but blood, a mix of raw, peeling skin and gravel and oh, oh god, is that bone?

"Don't leave me, okay? Please don't leave me."

"I'm right here." I said.

"I don't want to die." She said. "I didn't get to tell Keller to go to Hell for lying to me." I chuckled. I couldn't help it. We were broken, bruised, bloodied and barely hanging on and she was cracking jokes. I looked down at her and saw her eyes flutter into the back of her head, her breathing became shallow.

"Jordan. Stay awake." I begged; even though I could barely keep my eyes open myself.

"Lance. I love you. Promise me. Promise you'll always love me, no matter what." She whimpered, her voice broken into labored, uneven breaths. "I can't move. You need to move before the truck blows up. You need to move somewhere safer."

"I love you too. I promise. But I don't need to, nothing will ever change the way I feel about you." I admitted as I searched for her hand, once I found it, I grabbed on to it. "I'm not going anywhere. I won't leave you." I heard more screams coming from the vicinity of the mangled vehicles, so I looked up. From the underside of my truck, I could see a small flame. I cursed and then prayed to God to save us, to protect us. It didn't

take long for that tiny flame to engulf itself and gain control of

the metal and consume everything in it. "Hold on Jordan. Close

your eyes." I whispered, as I pulled myself over her just in time

for the world to explode.

"Jesus. Jesus Christ." I head an unfamiliar voice

mutter. "What in the Hell happened?" The voices moved closer,

but that's all they were, disembodied voices. I couldn't see

anything. I couldn't fight to the surface of the darkness. I was

too tired. Too weak. Too scared to see what was on the other

side. "I've got two!" The voice hollered, his voice filled with

exhilaration when he added. "They're alive! I've got two,

alive!" Was he talking about me? Was he talking about Jordan

and me? Or was I gone and just hearing this in my post

traumatic/pre out of body moment?

Someone was tugging on my body. Little bursts of

pressure underneath the searing pain that had taken over. I could feel myself being moved, but I wasn't doing it on my own. I knew that. Suddenly, I felt as though something had been lifted off me, but I wasn't sure. I hadn't noticed it before. It didn't feel like much now, anyway.

"Can you hear me, son? Hello? Can you hear me? Are you awake?" Another voice repeated. "He looks like he's coming to. This one's out. No movement. There's a pulse…low, thready. Let's get him moved and work on the other quickly. I don't want to lose anymore tonight."

"I've never seen anything like this before. God, this one's messed up. I think I'm going to be sick."

"Don't think about it. I can't afford you getting sick. Help is on the way. When the others get here you can puke your insides out all you want, not now." The voice said sternly. There was more pulling and tugging on my body, I started to feel the darkness receding. I tried to shake free of whatever was holding me down, whatever was keeping me from surfacing.

"Hey bud. Can you hear me?" I heard a groan, weak and hoarse. Was that me? The voice kept talking, I kept following it. Using it as a beacon to guide me through the thick, whatever it is.

"Jordan." I gasped when lights and shadows began to appear in front of my eyes. "Jordan."

"Is that your name? What's your name?"

"No. Where's Jordan? Where is she?" I repeated slowly, gasping for every breath.

"She? Was she still in the truck?" The forty something paramedic asked me with no emotion on his face whatsoever. I shook my head; at least I think I did. It hurt. But he repeated his question.

"Under me."

"That's Jordan?" He asked, pointing at the mass of clothes, blood and carnage nearby. I nodded. I think. "What's her last name?" I mumbled a reply. He tried to ask more questions; my name, address, phone number and the details of how we ended up taking a nap in the middle of a back country road. I wasn't much help. I felt myself being lifted up and I started to fight, to flail pointlessly.

"No. No. Help her. Help her. I told her I wouldn't leave her." I said in broken and almost unrecognizable sounds. I was screaming now. Screaming her name as they strapped me down and started towards the ambulance. I made a promise. I couldn't break another promise to her. I couldn't leave her. I was belligerent and pissed, no longer paying attention to the searing pain and numbness that had taken over.

"JORDAN!!!"

Chapter 65

Chopper

"Why in the Hell is my mom calling me?" I asked when I recognized the house number flash across my screen. I still had an hour before curfew. At the same time, Maddie's phone started trilling as well.

"Hey mom. What's up?" I said into the receiver.

"Oh thank God." She bellowed.

"Um. Okay."

"Chopper, I need you to come home right now. Where are you?"

"At a party, down by Trollings. Why? What's wrong?" At the same time I heard a group of kids walk by saying something about cops being everywhere because of a bad accident down the road.

"There's an accident."

"Why are you calling me, mom? There are accidents every day. I'll just take another road home."

"No honey." She began in a broken voice. "The scanner...the scanner."

"Oh Jesus." I moaned, when her words finally made sense. Lance was in that accident. They hadn't left that long ago, it had to be them. I prayed it wasn't, but judging from mom's freak out, it most definitely was. "You called because you thought I was in the truck?"

"Honey. Come home now. Come home now, I just need to see that you're okay." My mom pleaded, her voice thick with tears.

"Where was the accident mom? Where was it? Is Lance..."

487

"He's alive. There are five…" She sobbed. "Oh Chopper."

"I'll call you when I know something. I love you." I stated hurriedly before I hung up the phone.

"I can't get a hold of Jordan." Alicia panicked. "Try Lance, Chopper. Caleb called Maddie and said Jordan hasn't come home yet. She's never late without calling." Her voice had become shrill as she came to the same conclusion that I had.

"There's an accident." I mumbled as I charged for my Bronco. "The scanner said Lance's name."

"Oh no." I heard Alicia gasp at the same time Maddie inhaled loudly.

"Come on, I'll drive."

"What's up?" Sawyer asked as he approached the group, a beer can in hand.

"Lance and Jordan were in that wreck."

"No. No, that's not possible." Sawyer said angrily. "They said the truck exploded. That's not possible." Alicia grabbed Sawyer's arm and tugged him behind her as we all rushed to the truck.

It didn't take long to race to the scene. I wasn't exactly sure where mom had said the accident happened, but it didn't take long to see the lights, the helicopter, or the blazing fire up ahead. I could hear the girls behind me gasp and sob in horror. I think Maddie called Jordan's brother and told him what she knew, but to be honest, I was on autopilot. I was numb. It was all like a horrible nightmare. I was just going through the motions.

"Why do they need a helicopter?" Someone mumbled before I heard Lance's screams. Without hesitation, I threw my keys at Sawyer and rushed towards the gut wrenching sounds.

"Whoa buddy!" A tall, massive black cop yelled as he held up his hands and took a defensive stance in front of me. "You can't go any further."

"That's my friend. I know them. Those are my friend's in there."

"I'm sorry son, but you can't...there's nothing left."

"No. No. My brother, my friend, Lance. I hear him screaming. Please." The cop glanced over his shoulder, taking in the scene inside the ambulance where Lance was thrashing about, screaming Jordan's name. "I can calm him down." The cop nodded once and stepped with me towards the ambulance.

"Gentlemen, this young man is a friend. See if he can help you out."

"Bo. Bo. Lance. Bud. It's Chopper." I mumbled, raising my voice as I went. I tried not to look at anything, but it was next to impossible. My stomach clenched at the blood and clearly broken bones, but the worst was hearing him scream her name with such pain and terror. I moved closer, against my will, so that I was in his line of sight. "Bo. Chill out." He immediately stopped screaming, the vehicle filled with an eerie silence as he tried to focus on me. His eyes were distant, full of pain and something else, that I couldn't make out.

"Chopper?" He winced. "Jordan. They won't let me see Jo. I promised."

"It's okay bud. I'll go. You do what they tell you, so you can take care of her. Okay?"

"Chopper." He gasped, reaching for me slowly. "Tell her she's beautiful. *No matter what you see.* Tell her."

"Will do." I said, forcing a smile at him. "You gonna be all right? The guys are by the Bronco. Do you want one of them to ride with you?"

"Call mom." He gasped as he fell back against the stretcher, wincing in pain. His eyes were fluttering, rolling back into his head and his breathing was so labored and wheezing it sounded like a flat tire. "I promised I wouldn't leave her. I told Jo I wouldn't leave her. I left her. Again. I left her again." He rambled as he moved his head back and forth. "I can't lose her. I can't lose her."

"She's fine Bo." I lied. "She's fine. And you're going to be fine. We'll see you at the hospital, okay?"

"Tell her I love her. She doesn't know. She doesn't know." He mumbled as his eyes rolled into the back of his head and he let out a howl of pain, before the machines began beeping erratically.

"You need to go." A female EMT said sternly as she rushed to Lance's side, the other EMT slammed the doors behind me as I hurried to the other stretcher. I could hear the helicopter getting closer as I neared Jordan. I stopped dead in my tracks the moment I focused on what I was seeing. This time, my stomach heaved and I fought back the urge to puke when I took

in the horrific sight in front of me. Had I not known better, I

wouldn't have recognized her. She resembled a character out of

those scared straight videos they show you in drivers ed, the

carnage was something that I'll never be able to get out of my

head.

"Is she…"

"She's in and out of consciousness." A dark haired

paramedic said with a grim smile as he looked up in the air to

check the Helicopter's whereabouts. The wind picked up, letting

us know it would land soon.

"Jordan. Jo, sweetheart?" I asked timidly, my

voice was weak and shaky, so I cleared my throat and repeated

her name.

"Where am I?" She asked weakly.

"You've been in an accident sweetheart." The

paramedic said as he moved into her line of sight. "We're

waiting for the helicopter to land so we can get you to the hospital."

"Helicopter." She repeated as if she was trying to make sense of things. "Lance?"

"He's in another ambulance." The paramedic said. "Remember, I told you a few minutes ago that he was fine. He was worried about you, but they're taking good care of him."

"Jordan?" I repeated when the paramedic looked up at me and nodded. She didn't move her head, her eyes darted towards me as she tried to focus, and I could tell there was no recognition at all. "Hey gorgeous. It's Chopper." I said softly, moving a little closer to her. "Lance asked me to check on you and to tell you he loves you."

"Lance." She mumbled, almost like a question as her eyes fluttered closed.

"She's got a bad head injury." The paramedic stated his lips in a tight line. "She's in serious shock as well. She's lucky to still be alive."

"Will she be okay?"

"No guarantees. You should know that both your friends are in serious danger. If you're not a praying man, I'd turn into one." He explained as he nodded for me to leave. The helicopter hovered overhead and began its descent downward. "We'll be taking them to Mencino County Hospital. You can meet us there." I nodded back at him, took one last look at Jordan before I scurried away.

"How bad is it?" Alicia asked warily as she clutched on to Maddie for dear life. I shook my head and turned around to watch them load my best friend and his girlfriend up on the helicopter. Crazy thoughts raced through my head, wondering what to do next, if I could really go to the hospital and risk hearing someone tell us that neither one of them made it. That Jordan did, but Lance didn't. Or vice versa. I couldn't take

losing anyone else. I couldn't handle losing another brother. Oh
Jesus. I picked up my phone and called my mom back.

"Chopper honey, please tell me you're on your
way home."

"No mom. We're headed to the hospital. They're
flying Lance and Jordan to Mencino. I don't know if mom, if
Mrs. B. knows yet. Can you call her? No, can you go to the
house and get her? I'll try Jess and Jenn, but please mom, can
you get to her before someone else does? She needs you."

"Deb and Laura are on their way over here now."
She said quietly, referring to Cooper and Sawyer's mothers.
"And Alice already called Sara."

"I'll meet you at the hospital then." I said quietly,
signing off before she could protest. I looked back at my friends
behind me and wondered what the Hell we were supposed to do
next. Maddie and Alicia were basket cases, sobbing and wailing.
Sawyer was catatonic, his eyes darting from the helicopter, to the
ambulances, to the fire trucks and then to the crash scene. The

only sign of emotion was that his knuckles were paper white as they gripped the door of the Bronco. Cooper and Drew had come up to the scene at some point and both were staring in wide-eyed horror.

"We should get to the hospital." I mumbled. "They're taking them to Mencino, for now. Maddie, you should probably call Jordan's family and let them know." The dark haired girl's eyes flitted to me cautiously, as if she didn't know where the voice was coming from. She gave a slow nod, but her eyes were still glued to the scene in front of us. "Load up guys. We need to get there before the ambulance takes off or we'll never get out of here." There was a varying round of nods and muffled agreements before everyone started to climb into the Bronco and Drew's truck. I barely heard Maddie in the back seat, taking deep breaths before she picked up her phone to call Caleb. She was stronger than I gave her credit for; she told Caleb that his little sister was being flown from the scene of an accident in a helicopter as calmly as if she was saying she just had the flu. I gripped the steering wheel tightly; knowing I had to make the same phone calls as well. I searched through my phone book for Rob's cell phone number and reluctantly pressed the send button. Five minutes later, I had notified him and he'd promised to get Jess and Jenn to the hospital immediately. I cursed under my breath and sent up a silent prayer; begging God to let them all get to the hospital before it was too late. I prayed it wouldn't ever be too late, but they needed to say their goodbyes if they had to.

"Chopper." Sawyer interrupted my thoughts in a strangled whisper. "I don't know that I can handle this, bud."

"Me neither." I mumbled. I took a deep breath and looked back at the girls in my rearview mirror. The two of them were huddled together, hugging for comfort and quietly sobbing and praying. "They're going to be fine. They have to be."

"I hope you're right." I heard Sawyer say softly.

Chapter 66

Maddie

It seemed like it took hours for us to arrive at the hospital, but as we did the helicopter was already flying away from the building. Chopper pulled the Bronco into a slot and put the vehicle in park, but no one got out. We all sat there, too scared to be the first to move. Too terrified to be the first to find out that we lost our friend forever.

Chopper finally opened his door and as he climbed out, he opened mine as well. I stared at the hand he offered to help me out, before I finally took it. Sawyer followed suit and helped Alicia out as well. Except when Chopper pulled back, showing a friendly sign of comfort I noticed that Sawyer didn't. He kept his hand linked with Alicia's as they somberly started for the emergency room doors. Something silly for me to notice at this moment, I know, but thinking about that kept my mind off other things.

A group of women came rushing toward us in the parking lot, calling out the boys names. At the show of emotion, I'm guessing it was their moms. Five minutes later, a tall broad man staggered into the ER looking around as if he were lost. I almost wondered if he was some drunk who had accidentally wandered off the street; his brown eyes flicked over me in disinterest, but they pierced through Chopper as if he were the devil himself. Chopper stood up quickly.

"Mr. Bowman." He cleared his throat. Alicia's mom jumped up quickly and hurried towards the man, tugging on his arm to lead him outside. Chopper fell into the chair and exchanged glances with his mom. "He's drunker than a fucking skunk. Probably doesn't even know why he's here." I heard him mumble to Drew.

"Mom will take care of him."

"The police need to. He's going to start trouble; especially if he finds out they were together."

"It's too public." Drew muttered.

"That's what you think." I felt incredibly out of place and stared down at my phone to ease my fear. The ER entrance doors slid open again and Caleb, Mr. Donaldson and Zack rushed in. Caleb beelined for me and I jumped up and fell into his arms.

"*What* in the Hell happened?" He growled. "Why was she with him?"

"I told her not to go." I murmured in his solid chest. I shook my head and dismissed those thoughts quickly. "They were talking. He was taking her home and explaining his side of the story to her. Someone at the party said some kids were hill hopping or something, whatever that is. When they flew over the hill, they landed on top of Lance's truck."

"How bad is it?" Zack asked quietly, standing there awkwardly looking around. I put an arm around him and pulled the two boys into an empty corner while Mr. Donaldson was at the admitting desk.

"Bad. Chopper said it's bad. Lance was screaming. And they took Jordan out in the helicopter. It can't be good if she had to be flown here." I mumbled.

"I'm going back. You kids stay out here for now." Mr. Donaldson said sternly, shooting Caleb a look that told him not to even think about arguing. Surprisingly, my boyfriend didn't. He just nodded and pulled me closer to him. When the doors opened, an eerie howl pierced through the room. Lance was still screaming Jordan's name. I fell against Caleb again and the sobs racketed through my body as the screaming stopped suddenly.

The whole room was quiet for a long time, as we waited for some word on how the two of them were doing. By now, we'd heard bits and pieces saying that there were four other people involved in the accident; none survived, all were our age.

Caleb's body was rigid with fear and worry. He tried his best to comfort me to keep his mind off things, but he was a ticking time bomb. I was grateful Zack was here to help me corral him.

"What in the Hell was she doing with him Maddie?" I heard him ask again softly. I didn't answer, thinking he was just talking. "Why would she get back in a vehicle with him and listen to his bullshit? All he does is use her and throw her away again. She deserves better than that redneck little prick." Caleb's voice got louder as the insults towards Lance continued. Everyone ignored him, knowing he was just lashing out at whatever seemed worthy. "That worthless…"

"That's enough!" Chopper yelled as he jumped off his chair and stood in front of Caleb in barely two steps. I gripped Caleb's shirt, knowing this was not what he needed right now, but I wasn't strong enough. My boyfriend jumped up as well, his eyes bore into Chopper as the two stared each other down, mere inches from the other. "This is not Lance's fault and I've had enough of listening to you bash him. He's on his death bed and you're…"

"That bastard could've killed my sister." Caleb growled.

"No the dumbasses in the other car almost killed your sister. They were just in the wrong place at the wrong time."

"She shouldn't have been with him. She should've been with Maddie and Alicia. She shouldn't have been anywhere near you fucking assholes and she shouldn't have even been within ten feet of that son of a bitch." Caleb spat. Every other word out of Caleb's mouth was a curse or derogatory remark about Lance, Chopper yelled again.

"I'm about to lose another brother and all you can worry about is badmouthing him. That boy would die himself, just to take her place; to save Jordan's life. And if she doesn't

504

make it, he *will* die. If you want to run your fucking mouth take

it elsewhere, because I am not above beating the shit out of you

right now. Especially if his mom and sisters walk in this room

and you start talking shit again." Chopper warned as he grabbed a

hold of Caleb's shirt and pushed him against the wall. Caleb

blinked in surprise, but it wouldn't last long.

"He's right Caleb. It's not Lance's fault. And

blaming him is not going to help Jordan." Zack said quickly as he

tried to get in between the two boys. "You'll feel like an ass later

if you don't stop." Caleb looked back at Zack with wide eyes,

surprised to see himself in this position.

"Let's go outside honey." I murmured, tugging on

his arm. "I'm sorry." I said softly to Chopper as I pulled my

boyfriend and Zack outside for some fresh air. As soon as we hit

the parking lot, Caleb fell to the ground and began sobbing. I

looked back at Zack helplessly; he stood rooted to the asphalt as

if a giant portal to Hell had just opened up. I grabbed Caleb in a

hug and tried to comfort him as best I could.

A few minutes later, my boyfriend had quieted down and I could hear snatches of conversation in the parking lot. Muted references to a restraining order and someone not going inside. I recognized Alicia's mom's voice immediately and wondered who she was talking to. There was a lot of arguing and when I heard the male voice say he warned that little bastard to stay away from the rich whore, I knew whose voice it was. Lance's dad was blaming Jordan now. I prayed that Caleb didn't figure that out, that he couldn't hear the conversation as well as I could, because there really would be a brawl this time.

Sometime later, Lance's mom and sisters finally arrived and that's when all Hell broke loose. As far as we'd heard, both Lance and Jordan were critical but stable, in the middle of life saving surgery. Lance's father started raising Hell because he wasn't allowed to go back.

"All that boy needs is a good ass whooping. If you'd have let me discipline those boys the right way from the beginning Sara we wouldn't have one in the grave and the other

on his way. This is all your fault." He screamed. Chopper flew

out of his seat and rushed over. "I told him to stay away from

that little cunt and look what happened. It'll be the best for

everyone if they both die in there." I watched in horror as

Chopper squared up to the old man.

"Shut up Mr. Bowman. This is no one's fault

here. Why don't you go back outside and cool off?"

"Are you sassing me boy?" Mr. Bowman cackled.

"I sure as Hell didn't think you had any balls in all that lard."

Chopper didn't so much as wince. Mrs. Bowman put her hand on

Chopper's shoulder and murmured something to her husband,

just as Cooper, Sawyer and Drew stalked over to their friend.

Mr. Bowman didn't notice and seemingly forgot about the rest of

us in the room as he lifted his fist to his wife. I stared in absolute

horror as I watched, my mouth gaping open.

"Go outside and sober up." Chopper said through

clenched teeth, putting himself in between Lance's parents. This time the drunk Mr. Bowman glared at Chopper and looked like he might lay him out any second. The ER entrance doors flew open and two police officers rushed inside. I recognized one as Cooper's older brother; I'd met him once before.

"That's enough." Coop's brother bellowed. "You're done here, Bowman."

"Fuck off." Mr. Bowman cackled as he looked back at the two young men, daring them to try and take him away.

"You're breaking the restraining order."

"My son is in there." He growled. "They don't know if he'll make it through the night and you won't let me be here?"

"No. I won't. I have been called to your house three times in the last month because you've beat the Hell out of that boy, so don't try and pretend like you give two shits about him!" Coop's brother growled as he got up in his face. "Make a

508

move old man, I'm itching to get a piece of your drunk ass. Only

a pathetic son of a bitch would go after his wife and kids, let

alone a helpless three year old. You lay a hand on anyone in

your family again and I'll make certain you're locked away for

life."

"Just because you wear that little two dollar

uniform doesn't make you more than a sissy momma's boy

Cooper." Mr. Bowman laughed as he lunged for the officer. In

one swift movement, the old man was handcuffed and his face

slammed into the tile below him. As they yanked him out of the

hospital, I don't think Mr. Bowman knew what had just

happened.

My eyes darted around the room to see if everyone else

was just as shocked as I was, but each person had rushed to Mrs.

Bowman's side; engulfing Lance's family in hugs and a show of

support. I looked up at Caleb and saw the comprehension etched

on his face.

Now we knew why Lance had been acting the way he had. It all made sense now. If they survived this mess I would make sure Jordan knew the events of tonight, so she could understand that the love of her life hadn't really dumped her; he'd had no other choice.

Chapter 67

Zack

I should have trusted my gut and made Jordan stay with me tonight. I should have never let her leave my arms. I looked around the waiting room in disbelief. The tiled room was poorly lit and full of people praying for good news to come walking out of those doors. I could only beg God to let Jordan walk out of this okay.

My stomach hurt so bad with regret, anger and just pure fear. The second Jordan didn't walk through the door at five till midnight, like she always did, I knew. I knew something bad had happened. I knew my whole entire world was about to shatter.

"Did you call Kyler?" I mumbled. Caleb shook his head, Maddie followed suit. I nodded my head, gestured to my phone and walked out of the emergency room doors. I couldn't bear to be in that somber room any longer, I would suffocate. I called his cell phone and waited, holding my breath until he answered the phone.

"What's wrong?" He grumbled drowsily into the phone. Why had I chose to make this phone call? All words flew out of my brain and I stood there mute. "Zack, you better not of butt dialed me while you're fucking some random chick."

"Jordan."

"Jordan? You're calling to tell me you and Jordan…"

"No. Jordan was in an accident. They flew her to Mencino." I rambled quickly. "It's not good Ky."

"How not good?"

"They flew her by helicopter, that should tell you something."

"Zack." He growled.

"She was in a truck with Bowman, headed home. There were some kids hill hopping and apparently, they landed on top of the truck. Somehow, Lance and Jordan were thrown from the vehicle and then the cars exploded."

"So…"

"The kids in the other vehicle all died. Jordan and Lance are in surgery right now, but they're not optimistic about their survival." Tears rolled down my cheeks. I didn't realize I was crying until Kyler's breath hitched.

"It's bad?"

"Yeah."

"I'll call my Commanding Officer." He mumbled. "I don't…I don't know that I can come home and…"

"I'll keep you posted. Caleb's a mess. Thank God for Maddie." Kyler was quiet on the other end. "I'm sorry Ky, I don't know why I thought I should be the one to call you…I…"

"I'm glad you did." He admitted quietly. "Make sure…make sure she knows…"

"I'll tell her you'll be here as soon as you can. I…"

"Thanks bro." We hung up without another word. I stared at my phone, desperate to find some sort of comfort. I could call any number of females in my phone, they'd be here in a flash to let me bury my fear and anxiety in them, but I couldn't. It was my stupid reputation that made Jordan steer clear of me, I couldn't fall back on it now. She would need me when the worst of this was over and I couldn't fuck that up.

My phone rang, my brother Nick's face flashed across the screen. "How do you always know when to call?" I asked with a quiet chuckle.

"I had a bad feeling."

"Me too, but I let her leave anyway."

"What's wrong?"

"It's Jordan."

"Your roommate's sister? Your friend?"

"Yeah." I breathed. I retold the story of what I knew and my brother shared his bad feeling story with me, telling me that I kept popping into his head. I could go weeks without physically talking to my brother, but it never failed, if I needed him he would call and just know. Spilling my feelings to him about J helped a little, eased my fears but I was still a wreck when I walked back into the waiting room.

Chapter 68

Keller

I walked into the hospital carrying a dozen of the most expensive pink roses I could find. Jordan had been in this God awful place for the last four days and it was the first time I'd come. Up until now, she hadn't awakened. No one would know the full extent of her injuries until she did. I'd come up to our dorm room yesterday and overheard Caleb and Zack talking about Jordan and Cancer. Something about them finding a stomach tumor and the accident was somewhat of a lucky break; it could've went unnoticed and untreated otherwise. When I asked for more details, neither of the boys were talking.

I cringed when I got to the extended stay ICU floor and saw Lance's friends and family littering the waiting room. He must be close by too. I flashed them all a smug smile and sauntered towards the room number the nurse downstairs had given me.

Son of a bitch. Chopper and two women, I'm guessing to be Lance's family stood inside of the same room and I immediately saw why. Lance and Jordan were sharing a room. Their beds were pulled close together, hands clasped limply. I gave a disgusted look and an eye roll, not caring if anyone else saw it. Pathetic. Did they think that would help or something?

"Who are you here to see honey?" An older woman in pink scrubs immediately asked me.

"Jordan." I said rudely, as if I would visit that lame redneck in the next bed.

"Well, you'll have to wait outside dear. We're about to clean her up and check her dressings. It'll take about ten minutes and then you'll be able to stay until visiting hours are over." I nodded my head and walked back out of the room, but not before I heard Lance's mom offer her assistance to the nurse. Chopper followed me outside.

517

"Nice of you to stop by." He stated icily.

"Who are you, the welcome wagon?" I lit with a bark of laughter. Chopper eyed me carefully.

"As a matter of fact, I am and you're *not* welcome."

"You have no say over Jordan's visitors."

"He's right, Keller. You're not welcome." Maddie interjected from behind me. "The flowers are nice, but you don't need to be here. I gave you the benefit of the doubt before, but she's been here for four days and you only now show up?"

"I've been busy and I couldn't get off campus."

"Bullshit." She coughed. "I'll let Jordan know you stopped by."

"Is she up?"

"No, but when she does I'll tell her." Maddie said quickly, through clenched teeth. "It's family only anyway, they shouldn't have let you up here."

"What are you doing here then? And what about this lard ass over here?"

"Sister in law." She smiled sweetly. "And Lance's brother."

"What about the others?" I asked. "Bentley's been here all week."

"All family members." Maddie grinned. I rolled my eyes and shook my head in disbelief.

"Well, I'm not going anywhere."

"Keller." She sighed. "I'm pretty damn sure you're behind most of the shit that went on the week before. I'd lay bets to say that you sent that message to Jordan somehow and that you threw those flowers and the note from Lance in the trash as well, but I can't prove anything. I just know that you're up to something and you can pretend you're this great guy who is a changed man, but I know better. Jordan does too."

"Conspiracy theories are really unbecoming Madeline." I drawled. "I believe they're causing worry lines in that perfect little face of yours." Maddie rolled her eyes and pushed past me.

"Watch your back Keller and stay out of Caleb's way." I rolled my eyes this time and headed towards the elevator. No I wasn't leaving, but there's no way in Hell I was about to breathe the same air as the townie losers. The nurse said ten minutes, so I'll go downstairs have a little smoke in the parking lot and then come back up to see my girlfriend. Because she will be my girlfriend again.

Twenty minutes later, I sauntered back into Jordan's room. Mr. Donaldson looked happy to see me and hurriedly went out of the room to take a break, saying he knew Jordan was safe with me. The beds were separated now and the curtain pulled around Jordan's bed to give us privacy. I'm guessing they were stripping Lance's bed and clothes off now, because I could hear someone behind the pulled curtain on the other side.

I sat in the chair looking around, texting and checking up on my email and stocks with my phone. If I sat here for twenty, thirty minutes I'd have fulfilled my duty for the day. Come back later in the week, do it again, and then make sure Jordan knew of it when she woke up. I wanted to make certain she knew I was here for her when it wouldn't benefit me in the slightest.

Jordan stirred in the bed and I quickly dropped my phone in the chair and leaned closer to the bed. I wasn't sure if this was normal though. I didn't know if she was really just unconscious, because they had doped her up so much or if it were more. Her eyelids fluttered and I knew I was a lucky SOB.

Five minutes later Jordan was groggily looking back at me, trying to focus.

"Hey J." I drawled slowly and softly. I took her hand in mine and feigned worry and nervousness. "You're awake." She just watched me closely and quietly. Can she not talk anymore? Did the accident do brain damage or what? "Do you need something to drink? Do you need a nurse?" She shook her head and continued to look at me, no recognition on her face whatsoever. I pretended to be hurt, but underneath, I was jumping for joy at my luck. "Do you know who I am baby?" She shook her head slowly. "I'm Keller. I'm your boyfriend honey." She nodded her head in agreement, then cocked her head to the side.

"Boyfriend? My boyfriend?" She asked softly in a scratchy, throaty voice. I nodded my head.

"Yeah sweetie. Oh baby, I love you so much. I've been worried sick. I've been here day and night, watching and waiting for you to wake up, Jordan." I rambled. Jordan gave a small smile and squeezed my hand. In an excited rush, I leaned forward and kissed her quickly.

"Jordan?" A female voice asked as the curtain was ripped back. Lance's mom stood on the other side grinning excitedly. She rushed over to hug Jordan and pulled away. "I'll call a nurse, sweetie." She said as she pushed the button. She looked her over quickly, checking her monitors and so on before she realized Jordan was looking at her questioningly.

"Do you know who I am, sugar?" She asked, leaning down to touch her cheek gently. Jordan didn't answer, because the nurses rushed in.

"Well look at you." The nurse from earlier said excitedly. "Do you know where you're at sweetheart?"

"No." Jordan said softly as her dad raced into the room.

"Do you know who this is sweetie?" She asked. Jordan shook her head. "Do you know this young man here?" She asked, pointing at me. Jordan nodded her head.

"Yes. That's Keller. My boyfriend." She murmured as she reached out for my hand and pulled me closer to her.

"No. I thought…" The nurse said, but was interrupted by a grey haired doctor that walked in the room.

"Nurse, are you questioning my patient's memory?" He teased. The nurse shook her head quickly and looked back at Lance's mom. "Good, because if that's what the young lady says, then we mustn't argue."

I really liked this doctor and judging by the seriousness on his face. He wasn't joking around. Jordan and I were officially back together.

Chapter 69

Jordan

"Can you tell me what your name is?" The tall, grey headed doctor asked as he leaned down to look at my eyes with a light thing.

"Jordan?" I asked hoarsely.

"Are you asking me?" He questioned as he moved the light back and forth, holding my chin in his hand, so I wouldn't move my head to follow it.

"He...um, *Keller*, said my name was...I mean, he called me Jordan. And so did she." I said pointing to the middle aged brunette who was hovering over me. "Are you my mom?" I asked, tilting my head curiously as I studied her aging face closely. The woman's beautiful face dropped and she shook her head slowly.

"No sweetie. I'm Lance's mom." She responded with a thick drawl.

"Who is Lance?" I asked quietly after a minute's hesitation. The name sounded so familiar, it slid off my tongue easily and made the uncertainty I'd been feeling the last ten minutes fade away quickly. The woman's eyes darkened with sadness and tears before she forced a smile. She started to answer, but Keller jumped in.

"He was in the accident with you sweetheart. He's just an acquaintance."

"Acquaintance?" Someone gasped from the back of the room. "He's hardly an acquaintance." Keller's hand tightened around mine, I looked back at him questioningly and he flashed a movie star grin at me.

"So you don't know your name then?" The doctor asked, snapping his fingers so I would pay attention to him again. I turned my head slowly back to him and then closed my eyes. I tried to push out the unfamiliar sounds and faces that were

526

hovering in the room, tried to focus on the simple question he was asking me, but everything was blank.

"No." I sighed. "No, I don't know my name." The room grew awkwardly silent. The doctor gave me a small smile and then turned to look at the others in the room.

"We are way over capacity in here." He said irritably. "Immediate family only please; for both patients." I shot him a confused look, but he didn't notice. The room quickly thinned out, Keller remained. "That means *you*, too." The doctor said eyeing my boyfriend with a glare.

"I'm her boyfriend." He laughed as he shot the doctor a dismissive glance. "I'm staying."

"No. You're not."

"Do you know who my father is?" Keller asked in disbelief, his face tightened with irritation.

"Unless he signs my paycheck, I don't care. It's hospital policy for only immediate family to be allowed into ICU.

Now under the circumstances, we've been incredibly lenient, but don't push me and ruin it for everyone else." Keller glared back at the doctor.

"Step outside for a while, Keller." A balding, middle aged man with piercing green eyes said sternly. "The doctor knows what is best for Jordan and that's all that matters right now."

"Yes sir." Keller said quietly with a nod. He leaned down and kissed me roughly on the lips before he walked out of the room, glaring at the doctor the whole time. The balding man remained. Standing next to him, was a gorgeous dark headed guy with bright blue eyes and a stocky build. His eyes and face were puffy and tired, his muscled body taut with tension. Again, I knew I should recognize these two men, but as I closed my eyes; there was nothing but emptiness.

"Now that it's quiet I want you to relax, close your eyes like you're doing and *think*." The doctor said softly. The room was eerily still, the sound of machines working nearby was the only rhythm I could sense. A few minutes later, the doctor

spoke again. "Okay, now open your eyes and look at these two

men behind me. Do you recognize them?" I looked both of them

over thoroughly, but it didn't help.

"No. No sir, I don't." I said. The second the

words were out of my mouth, I could see the pain cross through

both of their eyes, but they remained stoic. The doctor looked

back at the older man and nodded. The man walked timidly to

my bedside and sat on the edge of it.

"I'm your father, sweetie." He said softly, as if he

were talking to a frightened child. "Your name is Bethany Jordan

Donaldson, but you go by Jordan. This is your older brother,

Caleb, behind me and your oldest brother Kyler is in Maryland at

the Naval Academy. Do you remember either of them?" I shook

my head again. What in the Hell was wrong with me that I

couldn't remember my own family? What happened to make me

forget them altogether? Anxiety welled up in my stomach and

panic started to grip the rest of my body so quickly that I began shaking. Tears streamed down my face. Neither my father nor brother moved, they watched in open-mouthed horror.

"What's wrong with me? What happened? Why don't I know who I am? Why can't I remember my family? Shouldn't I know that much? What's wrong with me?" I rambled incoherently as I tried to yank the wires and needles out of my body. I was terrified and ready to bolt out of this horrible nightmare as soon as I could. Surely, that's all this was; a nightmare. Who can't remember their family or even their boyfriend?

"Jordan." The doctor said as he hurried towards my bedside. I saw him push something before my father and brother joined him in trying to hold me down. Even with three grown men above me, I was still thrashing wildly. I felt a prick a few minutes later, after much shouting, and before I knew it, the world was dark again.

Chapter 70

Caleb

"What happened?" Maddie asked as she rushed to my side the second dad and I stepped out of the room. I was out of breath and freaked out so I moved out of her way, leaned against the wall to try to catch my breath. I bent down and rested my palms on my thighs, hoping to calm down and get a grip on myself. "Answer me Caleb. Is Jordan alright?"

"No." I replied hoarsely, my voice thick with tears. "She's not okay. They had to sedate her. She doesn't even know who I am Maddie." My girlfriend's arms went around me quickly as she pulled me into a tight embrace.

"Oh Cales." She sighed. "It's going to be okay. She's probably just in shock from the accident and everything;

the doctors said it was possible. I'm sure she'll wake up again and remember everything."

"Then how in the Hell did she remember *Keller fucking James* and not her own brother…or her own father?" I snapped. Maddie didn't even flinch, she just held me tighter.

"Because that's what he told her." Someone hissed from behind us. I turned to see Lance's mom standing there, tears rolling down her cheeks. She looked around the waiting room quickly. "He told her that he was her boyfriend. Why would that boy lie to her like that? Or is that true? I know Lance and Jordan were having problems, but…"

"No ma'am." Maddie interjected. "Keller and Jordan are not…were not together. Even when she thought Lance dumped her, she wouldn't give up."

"Then why?"

"Because he's a conniving bastard." Maddie bit under her breath. She looked up at Mrs. Bowman apologetically.

532

"Don't worry; we'll get everything straightened out. We'll tell Jordan the truth as soon as she wakes up."

"No, I'm afraid you won't." The doctor interrupted as he walked out of my sister's room, studying his clipboard. He looked up at me directly then let his gaze roam the rest of the waiting room. "If Miss Donaldson wakes up, and her memory has returned, then we have no worries, it's possible this is just a post traumatic type of amnesia or it could be more severe. Miss Donaldson did suffer a blow to the head and the EMT's on scene said she was thoroughly confused, continuously repeating herself, which they accounted to shock, but it is possible that it is more deeply rooted."

"So you're saying that she might never remember us?" My father asked.

"Unfortunately, yes. Amnesia is a very difficult thing to predict. It's possible that in a week or so, all of her memories will be restored. Sometimes it takes longer, sometimes less. *Sometimes* they never come back and the person lives with a big black hole in their memory banks of everything that happened before the head injury. As for your daughter, it's hard to tell. We'll run more tests and see if there's anything suspicious, anything that was missed in the preliminary checks. Nevertheless, I'm advising that for now you allow your daughter to remember her life on her own. Telling her things is really not helping at all because she'll never know if she remembered those things on her own or not. There'd be no way to judge her progress. If she believes this young man is her boyfriend then it's best to let her figure out on her own that he isn't. Otherwise, we could be dealing with a lot more trauma in the future."

"No. No way." I spit through gritted teeth. "There is no way I will allow my sister to believe that conniving little bastard's lies. It's not right and he will hurt her worse than telling her the truth could."

"I beg to differ. If you *truly* care about your sister, Mr. Donaldson you will adhere to my instructions." The doctor said sternly. I clenched my fists and took a deep breath, the only thing that kept me from losing it was Maddie's soft arms

534

wrapping around my waist and the soft whispers to calm me in my ear.

"As of now, there should be no more than two people in Miss Donaldson's room at a time. I think all the visitors overwhelmed her, rather than reassured."

"I'll take the first shift." Keller said nonchalantly as he flashed a smug smile and floated past us. Maddie placed herself in between my roommate and me before I could attack.

"Now, I also believe that it would be in your daughter's best interest if we refrained from telling her about the cancer we found. Let us take care of the meds and treatments until it's necessary, or she's ready to hear it." The doctor said quietly to my father. The rest of the waiting room was still in an uproar and were not paying attention to the private conversation. This was probably for the best, we didn't need the whole world to know that they'd found a tumor in Jordan's stomach; especially since we weren't allowed to tell her anything about it. My dad nodded and the doctor handed him a card with contact numbers on it before he sauntered back down the hall.

"So I'm supposed to just sit back and watch that creep move in on my sister while she's vulnerable?" I hissed as I gestured towards Jordan's hospital room. "I'm supposed to let him lie and use her?"

"Let him think he won Cale." Maddie said in my ear. "He'll get cocky and complacent, but when Jordan does remember everything, then he's going to be one sorry little SOB." I just nodded my head and fell back against the wall again. I slid down it slowly and buried my face in my hands.

Today was one of the worst days of my life. I would venture to say it was worse than being five years old and walking into the bedroom to find our mother had committed suicide. Just a few days ago, I was lecturing my sister about finding a nice guy to date rather than her current ex-boyfriend, Lance Bowman, who she couldn't seem to stay away from. I was chastising her about being home in time for curfew, even though it's not enforced.

When she didn't come home, my world shattered with a phone call from Maddie calling to tell me that Lance and Jordan had been in a horrendous accident caused by stupid kids who were 'hill hopping' and soared right into Lance's truck on a back road. All those kids were dead and Lance and Jordan had been clinging to life ever since. If I ever doubted Lance's true feelings for my sister, they were cemented when I arrived at the hospital and could hear the boy screaming her name with such agonizing terror that *I* almost broke down and cried.

At our request, they had put Jordan and Lance in the same room together; hoping the contact and nearness would help them heal faster. Oddly, their stats were always best when someone pushed their beds closer and allowed them to touch; hold hands or just be close to one another. I don't understand it; I don't think anyone else did either.

Now my sister was awake, but she didn't even know who I was. Her own brother. We've been close as siblings can be since we were little and now she doesn't even know who I am? I thought them finding a tumor in her stomach was the worst God

would hand us, but I was clearly wrong in epic proportions.

Chapter 71

Jordan

For the last twenty-four hours I'd been sedated, it was the only way I could deal. I didn't know who I was, didn't know where I was or how I'd gotten here really. All I knew is that I had an extremely hot boyfriend, who I felt a little uncomfortable around, and many people who seemed to be genuinely concerned about me.

Keller wasn't around much, which I was grateful for. I could feel the underlying tension in the room when he was near and I didn't like not knowing why no one seemed to like him. He didn't seem to notice it though.

I found myself looking over at Lance, the boy who was driving the truck, as often as possible. I wanted so badly to learn why I was in the truck with the handsome guy. My heart fluttered when I looked at him, it hurt not knowing who he was. For some reason, my body seemed to know him, even if my mind didn't. His family and friends were great, fussing over me as if I were one of them.

Late that night, a few minutes after the nurses had made their most recent round, I forced myself to sit up in my bed. It hurt like Hell, my body screamed in agony, but I'd been dreaming about the guy who shared my room so often that I had to get up and see if it was really him that I was fantasizing about. I also knew it was my only chance to get close, his mom had left when the nurses came in, saying she'd be down in the cafeteria grabbing something to eat. I'd have thirty minutes at least, I hoped.

It was a slow process; it took me at least ten minutes to move my feet to the floor and even longer to stand and walk over to his bed, even though it was only a few feet away. My breath caught once I hovered over him, he was torn up pretty bad, but I could see the gorgeous planes of his face, the stubble that would soon turn into a beard if he didn't awaken soon. I lifted a battered hand, hesitated before I gently touched his face and immediately jerked my hand back. It was like a static shock.

"Who are you to me, Lance?" I whispered quietly as I moved my hand down to grasp his. I intertwined our fingers, felt the heat and spark soar throughout my body and was amazed when I saw a smile form on his mouth. I felt a tug and looked down in shock; did he just squeeze my hand? That's impossible, right? Hadn't I just heard the doctors telling his family that he was in a coma, that his body wasn't responding to anything else? They weren't optimistic about his progress. In fact, I specifically heard the doctor tell Mrs. Bowman that the nurse would bring information about long-term care facilities so they could discuss their options; they didn't think he'd ever wake up, although he was breathing on his own volition. If that happened, I may never find out what this boy is to me and why I was in the truck with him in the first place.

I could feel myself weakening as I stood there, I'd pushed myself too hard, but I couldn't sever the connection with Lance. It's the only thing that seemed familiar since I awoke. My knees gave out and I fell against the bed. I was too tired to cross the room; I guess I could take a small nap here, just to build my strength back up. In five minutes, I'll get back up and make my way back to my own bed, but for now, it won't hurt to crawl up next to Lance. No one would ever know but me.

Chapter 72

"Jordan." I heard a female voice whisper in my dreams. "Jordan honey." I felt a shake and I reluctantly woke up. "Sweetie, let me help you to your bed. You'll have visitors soon and…" It took me a second to focus and realize that Mrs. Bowman was talking to me. I looked around groggily to see that I was curled up next to her son. My face flushed immediately. "It's okay sweetie." She smiled as she squeezed my shoulder. "I don't mind. Lance does best when you're close to him."

"Why?" I asked softly. Her brown eyes grew sad as she forced a smile and shook her head.

"Let's get you into your own bed, okay?" She asked as she took a hold of my elbow. "I can't believe you made it all the way over here on your own anyway. You haven't been out of bed in days. Your leg is broken and…"

"I don't know how I did it either." I mumbled. She smiled and gave me a small hug before she helped me over to my bed. I fell onto it, out of sheer exhaustion and fell back asleep without another word.

"Hey baby." Keller greeted me sometime later that afternoon. I was in and out of sleep all day, but he'd always wake me up the second he arrived. "Any idea when you're getting out of this Hell hole?" I shrugged my shoulders and moved so he kissed my cheek, rather than my mouth. "I hope it's soon, I don't know how much longer I can handle being around all these redneck ass wipes." He raised his voice loud enough for the people on the other side of the curtain to hear. I shot him a dirty look, but he paid me no attention. I'd noticed that he was rude to everyone, but me and my father. Actually, rude is putting it nicely. He was a straight up asshole to everyone that wasn't me or my dad. I called him on it one day; he just laughed and told me that I was normally worse than him.

Could I really be that horrible to people? I couldn't see myself ever being so rude and heartless, but Keller was my boyfriend. He would know right?

After thirty minutes of Keller's bragging, I grew weary and pretended to fall asleep. I'd look over and could see that he'd spend every second texting away on his phone, or checking his expensive watch for the time. One hour on the dot and he was gone, just like every day since I'd woke up. He'd kiss me quickly, say he'd call or be back in the morning and he was gone. Not that I was disappointed.

"Hey girlie." Maddie, my brother's fiancé, greeted me sweetly as she walked into the room with a smile plastered on her face. "I thought you'd like some girl time." I looked back at her skeptically. "Alicia will be in here in a sec, too. We thought you might want to take a shower, change your clothes or something."

"That'd be great." I sighed. "I feel disgusting. And this drab green gown doesn't do much for me."

"You're right. It doesn't." She chuckled as she swung a duffel bag onto the foot of my bed. "I brought your cheerleading sweats; I thought you'd be most comfortable in those."

"Cheerleading?" I gasped. "I'm..."

"Oh shit." She breathed, hitting herself upside the head with her palm. "I wasn't thinking. God, I'm so sorry."

"I can't learn everything on my own, Maddie." I sighed. "I'm surprised Keller hasn't told me that yet. He's told me about Callatin and my friends, how I was Homecoming attendant this past year. How he will be voted prom king and MVP of the baseball team. And how he and I are the most popular couple at Callatin, that we're going to Harvard together. He'll go nearby this year and then we'll both start in the fall after I graduate."

"Excuse me?" Alicia asked bitterly when she walked into the room. "He told you that you were planning on going to college together?" I nodded and Alicia shook her head in disbelief. I'd have to be blind to not have seen the warning glare Maddie shot her way.

"Am I not smart enough to go to Harvard?" I asked incredulously. Both girls burst out laughing.

"Jordan, you're borderline genius. Seriously, you have a 4.0 GPA. You're already taking college classes for credit." Alicia said.

"Caleb said you've been getting invites to visit Harvard, Yale and a hundred other colleges for the last five months. You're the total package, girl; brains, talent and a killer body."

"I'm really a cheerleader? For some reason, I feel like I'm not much of a girlie girl."

"You're not." Maddie laughed. "You play softball, too. Your brothers made you a tomboy and I guess there's no way to change that." She giggled. "You are remembering some things then, huh?"

"Not really. I just get feelings, I guess, that something doesn't feel right. As far as recognition of names, places or people, not at all."

"That's okay. It'll come in time." Alicia said. "My dad's a surgeon and he said he's talked to other doctors who have amnesia patients, and they all told him it was usually a slow, tedious process but it would eventually return, in time. And your doctor said the scans showed nothing physically hindering your recovery."

"So, it's just me." I mumbled, looking down quickly.

"No." Maddie gasped as she hurried to my side. "You were in a horrific accident Jo. You're lucky. A trauma like that would definitely make you want to forget everything."

"Even my family?"

"You were put on the spot, honey." Maddie said as she patted my hand. "It can't be easy."

"Do you think I'll remember why I was with *him*?" I asked quietly as I let my eyes dart to the other side of the room where Lance lay in the bed, unconscious. Both of the girls looked at each other sadly and shrugged.

"Who knows?" Maddie sighed. "But I do know that you are in serious need of a shower." She admitted hurriedly as she plastered on a million dollar grin. "So hop up girlie."

"Easy for you to say." I grumbled. Maddie just laughed and nodded before she and Alicia helped me up.

An hour later, I felt a hundred times better. Who knew a shower could be so therapeutic? Once I slipped into my Callatin cheerleading sweats I felt some familiarity, but each time I'd think I'd remember, it would dash out of my grasp. It was so frustrating.

Chapter 73

Maddie

"Jordan can go home today." Caleb said excitedly into the receiver, two weeks after the horrific accident had changed our lives.

"Oh Cale, that's amazing!!" I squealed. "I'll let Zack and Alicia know. Maybe I'll go get a cake and…"

"Maddie, baby, calm down." He laughed. "I don't know that she'll be ready for one of your shindigs."

"Just us Cale. Just the important people."

"Not all the important ones." Caleb said sadly. "She still doesn't remember Lance, or really anyone in his family."

"Subconsciously, she does." I replied quickly. "Alicia said every night Mrs. Bowman will leave for a little bit in the middle of the night and when she comes back, Jordan's curled up next to Lance. But she never remembers doing it."

"What?" Caleb gasped. "I didn't…"

"Mrs. Bowman didn't want to make a big deal of it. The last two nights she's gone to get the on call doctor to check Lance's responses when Jordan's with him and it's like, miraculous. If she's not touching him, he doesn't respond to anything. If she's touching him, he moves his leg or foot when touched, his fingers twitch. She said they were holding hands last night."

"But if Joey goes home…" Caleb began.

"Lance might not get better? Alicia said the same thing. Jordan's curious enough about her pull to him that she might go back willingly, just to see him."

"Obviously Keller doesn't know."

"Definitely not. He'd flip out."

"He's telling her stuff." Caleb started.

"I know. He's telling her lies. It's like he's trying to mold her into what he wants her to be."

"A Stepford."

"Yup. If we tell her it's all lies, if we tell her the truth, even though it's to save her, are we hurting her recovery too?" I asked with an exaggerated sigh. "I don't know what to do, Caleb. I can't sit back and let him…let him manipulate her."

"Things will be different when she's home. I can monitor him better; I can keep him away from her."

"But that could be detrimental."

"And if I don't, it'll be disastrous."

"What do we do Cales?"

"I don't know, Maddie. I was hoping you had the answer."

"Me too." I sniffled. "This is all Keller's fault anyway." I said turning angry in a second. "If he hadn't been lying to her in the first place, then she wouldn't have went to that party to confront Lance. They wouldn't have been fighting and they…"

"We can't change what happened, sweetie."

"I know." I murmured as tears rolled down my cheeks. "But Keller could have. I just want to punch him in the face."

"Take a number babe." Caleb responded with a sad chuckle. "There's a long line for that. I imagine Lance Bowman will be number one in line when he wakes up."

"What if he doesn't? What if he doesn't ever wake up and Jordan remembers? That'll devastate her more than anything. Especially if it takes a long time for her memory to come back. I mean, she'd never forgive herself for not being at Lance's side 24/7."

"I'm hoping the familiarity of home will help."

Caleb said. "But her memory is the least of our worries Maddie.

They weren't able to remove the entire tumor from her stomach.

She's taking the trial meds, but if they don't work then she'll

have to undergo radiation or chemo. We haven't even told her

yet. She doesn't even know they found a large tumor in her

stomach or how much damage it had done before they removed

it."

"I just don't understand how one girl, one amazing

girl like Joey could have such rotten luck."

"She doesn't get the easy way off, that's for sure."

Caleb muttered sadly. "It'd be really easy for her to fall into

mom's…"

"Caleb Donaldson," I hissed. "Don't you dare

finish that sentence. Jordan will get help before it ever gets to

that point."

"I wish…"

"I know." I interjected softly. "I'll call Lish and Zack, we'll be waiting at the house when you guys get there."

"Thanks Maddie. I love you."

"Love you too Cales." I whispered before I hung up the phone. I fell onto my bed, looked over at Jordan's empty one and had myself a good cry. Ten minutes later, I composed myself enough to call and tell Zack and Alicia the exciting news. I wouldn't tell anyone else though. I didn't want Keller to know, I wanted him as far away from my best friend as possible until Jordan learned the truth about him, or we figured out a way to dispose of him quickly.

THE END

About the author

Melissa Logan is a single mother of five; three boys and two angel babies. She is a Veteran of the U.S. Coast Guard, an author, a part time employee of the U.S. Postal Service and an online fitness coach. In her spare time she loves to workout, read, write, photography and spending time with her family. Melissa was raised in a small southern Illinois town and currently resides there today with her children.

Other books by this author

Callatin Academy #1 New Beginnings

Callatin Academy #2 Trust Me

Callatin Academy #3 Crazy Girl

The Brittany Files: Crossroads

The Brittany Files: Hostile

Available in print at Amazon.com

Connect with this author

You can friend her on Facebook at the following:

www.facebook.com/melissa.logansanders

www.facebook.com/authormelissalogan

www.facebook.com/melissasandersfitness

You can find her on Twitter @melissalogan79

Made in the USA
Columbia, SC
05 November 2022

70508101R00304